VOODOO, LTD.

Novels by Ross Thomas

VOODOO, LTD.
TWILIGHT AT MAC'S PLACE
THE FOURTH DURANGO
OUT ON THE RIM
BRIARPATCH
MISSIONARY STEW
THE MORDIDA MAN
THE EIGHTH DWARF
CHINAMAN'S CHANCE
YELLOW-DOG CONTRACT
THE MONEY HARVEST
IF YOU CAN'T BE GOOD
THE PORKCHOPPERS
THE BACKUP MEN
THE FOOLS IN TOWN ARE ON OUR SIDE
THE SINGAPORE WINK
CAST A YELLOW SHADOW
THE SEERSUCKER WHIPSAW
THE COLD WAR SWAP

Under the Pseudonym Oliver Bleeck

NO QUESTIONS ASKED
THE HIGHBINDERS
THE PROCANE CHRONICLE
PROTOCOL FOR A KIDNAPPING
THE BRASS GO-BETWEEN

ROSS THOMAS

VOODOO, LTD.

THE MYSTERIOUS PRESS
New York • Tokyo • Sweden
Published by Warner Books

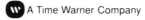 A Time Warner Company

Mysterious Press books are published by
Warner Books, Inc., 1271 Avenue of the Americas,
New York, NY 10020.

 A Time Warner Company

The Mysterious Press name and logo are trademarks of
Warner Books, Inc.
Printed in the United States of America

First printing: October 1992

10 9 8 7 6 5 4 3 2 1

Library of Congress Cataloging-in-Publication Data

Thomas, Ross, 1926–
    Voodoo, Ltd. / Ross Thomas.
        p.   cm.
    ISBN 0-89296-451-0
    I. Title.
PS3570.H58V66   1992
813'.54—dc20   91-51185
                                              CIP

VOODOO, LTD.

One

The two-passenger car that raced through Malibu shortly after 5 A.M. on New Year's Day at speeds exceeding 82 miles per hour was an almost new Mercedes-Benz 500SL with an out-the-door price of $101,414.28. It was driven with one hand, the left, by the not quite beautiful hyphenate, Ione Gamble, whose blood alcohol level would later be measured at 0.16, proving her to be quite drunk, legally and otherwise, for the second time in her life.

The actress-director, whose two crafts or professions made her a hyphenate in Hollywood parlance, still drove with her left hand as she used the right one to hold a telephone to her ear and listen to its thirty-fifth and final ring. She then traded the telephone for the pint of Smirnoff 80-proof vodka that lay on the passenger seat. After swallowing the last one and a half ounces, she lowered the right door's window with the touch of a button and tossed out the empty bottle, which smashed against somebody's 1986 Honda Civic.

Gamble was tempted to stop and leave a note offering to pay for any damage. But by the time the mental note was composed, revised and re-revised, she was already a mile past the Honda and nearing her Carbon Beach destination. When

1

she reached it seconds later, the note, the smashed bottle and the Honda had vanished from her memory.

By then she had slowed to the legal speed limit of 45 miles per hour and was almost coasting along the Pacific Coast Highway's center turn lane. She was also trying to find the misplaced electronic gadget that would open the steel gates guarding the $13-million house whose owner irritated nearly everyone by calling it his beach shack.

Gamble never found the electronic gate opener. But as she turned left across the highway's two east-bound lanes, her headlights revealed the gates to be already open. She drove through and parked in front of the three-car garage whose doors, almost seven days after Christmas, still offered a fanciful triptych of Santa Claus, his reindeer and the elves.

Gamble switched off engine and lights and again picked up the car phone. She called the number she had called before and let it ring fifteen times. She then gave up on the phone and started honking the Mercedes horn in a series of three-short-and-one-long tattoos, which were a rough approximation of Morse code for the letter V—the only Morse code she knew.

Gamble stopped the noise three minutes later, lowered the car's left window and waited for something to happen. She would have settled for an irate neighbor yelling at her to shut the fuck up. Or for Billy Rice to hurry out of his house and implore her, for God's sake, to come in and have a drink—or even for a suddenly lighted window somewhere to prove that life still existed in Malibu at 5:11 A.M. on Tuesday, January 1, 1991.

But when there were no rude shouts or drink offers or suddenly lighted windows, Gamble got out of the car, slamming its door as hard as she could and hoping something would break, but relieved when nothing did. She went around the car's rear, backed up three overly cautious steps, sucked in as much air as her lungs would hold and yelled, "BILLY RICE FUCKS MICE!"

She waited, listening, but when there was neither denial nor rebuttal she turned and headed for the front entrance.

VOODOO, LTD.

As she did, a light came on in the second floor of a yellow house across the highway. But it came from a small high window, the kind that bathrooms have, and Gamble decided it was probably some poor old guy rousted out of bed by a troublesome prostate.

A short stretch of seven-foot-high wall, built of glazed brick, shielded the entrance to the house from the curious and served as a baffle against the highway traffic noise. The wall and the house itself formed a short ceilingless passageway that Gamble slowly walked along as she searched all three pockets of her cream suede jacket for the key to Billy Rice's front door.

It was only after searching each pocket four times that she remembered, if dimly, tearing out of her house in Santa Monica and pausing just long enough to grab the car keys and the pint of vodka, but not the brown leather clutch purse. And that's where the Rice front door key was, of course, in the purse's zippered coin pocket.

Gamble still believed there was a way to wake up Billy Rice. She could pound on his door and ring his bell and even howl and yap like a coyote until something happened. She had almost decided on the coyote imitation when she noticed the door was already ajar. She gave it a tentative push and then a hard shove that opened it all the way.

Once inside the dark house, Gamble fumbled for the switch she knew to be on the left, found it and turned on lights illuminating the marble foyer that led to the immense living room and, beyond that, to the equally immense deck.

The foyer's indirect lighting was designed to enhance two paintings that faced each other from opposite walls. On the left was the Chagall; on the right, the Hockney. Beneath the Hockney was a small square table of burled elm, just large enough to hold the day's mail, three sets of car keys and also, in this instance, a 9mm semiautomatic Beretta.

Gamble picked up the gun, examined it, then called, "Hey, Billy, wanta come watch me blow off my big toe?"

She waited, head bowed, pistol down at her right side, as if hoping for some kind of protest. But when none came, she lifted the Beretta, aimed carefully, squeezed the trigger, just as she had been taught at the Beverly Hills pistol range, and blew a small neat hole through the lower left quadrant of the Chagall.

When the gunshot produced neither outcry nor whimper, Gamble moved slowly along the rest of the marble foyer and into the living room. Through its far all-glass wall she could see the lights of Santa Monica and, much farther on, the dimmer lights of Palos Verdes, where, she knew for a fact, lived the dullest people in California and maybe even the world.

Turning from the view, she noticed a big pale lump in the room's southwest corner. The lump for some reason looked as if it had been lost, abandoned or maybe just forgotten. Ever curious, Gamble crossed the living room, shifting the pistol to her left hand. With her right hand she switched on a table lamp and discovered the lump to be William A. C. Rice IV.

He lay on his back, blue eyes open and aimed at the beamed cathedral ceiling. The long right leg was slightly bent at the knee. The long left leg was straight. His arms and hands were haphazardly arranged with the right hand pointing due north and the left hand south by southwest. There were two dark holes in his bare hairless chest just to the left of the right nipple. His feet were also bare and his white tennis shorts were stained.

Ione Gamble stared down at the dead man for at least thirty seconds, breathing through her mouth in short gasps until she stopped gasping and said, "Aw, hell, Billy, I wish I were sorry."

She turned then, swaying a little, and made it to the small wet bar where she poured two unmeasured ounces of whisky into a glass and gulped them down. The whisky caused a coughing fit. When it ended two minutes later, she stumbled across the room to a console telephone, collapsed into what she knew to be Billy Rice's favorite chair, placed the Beretta in her lap, picked up the phone and tapped out 911.

The police emergency number began to ring. On the

eighth ring she yawned. On the tenth ring she put the still-ringing phone on the table, wrapped both hands around the butt of the Beretta in her lap, closed her eyes and passed out.

She was still passed out and still clutching the Beretta when two deputy sheriffs entered the living room at 6:27 A.M., snatched away the pistol, shook Ione Gamble awake, read her her rights and arrested her on suspicion of murdering William A. C. Rice IV, who, ever since 1950 when he enrolled in Kansas City's first private kindergarten, was called Billy the Fourth by all who disliked or despised him, which, someone later said, "was almost everyone who'd known him for more than three minutes."

Two

By the third week in January of 1991, Ione Gamble had been indicted for the murder of William A. C. Rice IV and released on bond. An assistant Los Angeles County attorney had argued for a bail bond of at least $2 million but the county Superior Court judge in Santa Monica had instead set it at $200,000 and defended his decision with a rhetorical question: "With a face known throughout the world, where can she possibly skip to and where can she possibly hide?"

Gamble was now concealed, if not hidden, in her 35-year-old, thirteen-room mission-style house on Adelaide Drive in Santa Monica. She lived there alone, except for the Salvadoran couple in the garage apartment and her six cats, three dogs and a housebroken flop-eared rabbit who spent most of his waking hours hopping up and down the staircase.

Gamble was up in the second-floor study she called her office, discussing criminal defense lawyers with Jack Broach, her combination business manager, agent and personal attorney. Broach was a product of UCLA ('68), Boalt Hall ('71) and the William Morris Agency ('73–'79). Like many entertainment industry agents in their mid-forties, he resembled a meticulously groomed character actor who would be perfect to play either a young lean-jawed President or an aging lean-jawed fighter pilot.

The office-study had three walls of bookshelves, filled mostly with novels and biographies, and one wall of glass that offered a view of Santa Monica Canyon, some mountains and also the Pacific Ocean. Gamble was seated behind her 1857 Memphis cotton broker's desk and Broach was in a nearby businesslike armchair.

After sipping some bottled diet Dr Pepper through two paper straws, Gamble said, "So far I've talked to the Massachusetts Unitarian, the Wyoming Jew, the Texas Episcopalian and the New York Baptist. Comes now the Washington what?"

"I'm quite sure he's not a Muslim," Broach said.

"Tell me about him—the guy from Washington."

"I called him," Broach said, "just as I called all the others and said, in effect, 'Hi, there, I'm the best friend and personal attorney of Ione Gamble and she needs the best damn criminal lawyer alive. You interested?' The other four said, Gosh, yes, but the guy in Washington said, 'Not especially.' As usual, I was impressed by the unimpressed."

"He's good though—the one from Washington?"

"He's not as well known as the others, but the legal minds I revere most say he's top gun."

Gamble frowned. "Is 'top gun' your cliché or theirs?"

"Mine. I use clichés because everybody understands them. That's why they're clichés."

Gamble sipped more diet Dr Pepper and said, "You think I should pick him, don't you—the guy from Washington?"

Broach shook his head. "I think you should pick the one you trust and respect most."

"What about like?"

"Like's got nothing to do with it."

"Will he ask me if I killed Billy?"

"I don't know."

Ione Gamble looked at the ceiling, as if notes for her next remarks were written there. She was still looking at it when she said, "I liked the Jew and respected the Baptist and

7

trusted the Episcopalian—despite his shit-kicking Texas ways—but the Unitarian seemed consumed by the notion that he and I'd finally wind up in bed."

"Is there something wrong with optimism?"

Her gaze came down.

"Help me, damnit."

Broach shook his head. "You'll know—or your instinct will."

"You're sure?"

"Positive."

They heard the two-note front door chimes. Broach rose and said, "He's here. I'll go down, bring him up, introduce you and be on my way."

"Do I look all right?"

Jack Broach didn't bother to reply.

*　　*　　*

Ione Gamble, wearing jeans, a checked shirt and scuffed Timberlands over bare feet, was standing at the glass wall, staring out at ocean and canyon, when Broach came back with the Washington lawyer. She turned and found him to be a medium-tall man in his forties who wore a very expensive but ill-fitting dark blue suit along with plain black shoes, a white shirt and a muted tie. He had extraordinarily long arms, a face that seemed to have been put together from odds and ends, and the wisest black eyes she had ever seen. As Gamble looked into them she found herself engulfed by an intense feeling of relief.

Jack Broach said, "Ione Gamble, Howard Mott."

Gamble smiled and walked toward Mott, her right hand outstretched. "I very much hope you'll be my lawyer, Mr. Mott."

Howard Mott took the cool dry hand, smiled back and said, "Let's see whether you still feel that way after we talk."

*　　*　　*

Mott had arrived at 11 A.M. and at 12:45 P.M. they sent out for a giant cheese and pepperoni pizza. The Salvadoran housekeeper-cook served it in the office-study along with a bottle of beer for Mott and another diet Dr Pepper for Gamble.

Mott took a polite bite of the pizza, chewed, swallowed, drank some beer and said, "Tell me how you met him."

"Billy Rice?"

Mott nodded and had another bite of pizza.

"You know who he was, don't you? I mean, before?"

"Before Hollywood? Yes, but tell me who you think he was."

"He was the *Kansas City Post*," she said.

"The paper Hemingway didn't work for."

"It was also one of the first newspapers to go into radio in the twenties and TV in the late forties. It wound up owning three TV and four radio stations around the country, six small dailies, a farm magazine, a block-long printing plant and a big chunk of downtown Kansas City. Ninety percent of the stock in all this was owned outright by William A. C. Rice the third, who was the grandson of William A. C. Rice the first, the one who'd started it all. When Billy the third died, everything went to Billy the fourth."

"When did the third die?" Mott asked. "Ten years ago?"

"Twelve," she said. "Billy the fourth hung onto everything for eight years, then sold out in early eighty-six at the top of the market. He walked away with at least a billion, maybe more. Then he moved out here and announced he was an independent motion picture producer and, with a billion or so in the bank, everybody said, 'That's right, you are.'"

"Is that when you met him?"

She nodded. "He had an office in Century City—just him, a secretary and a story editor."

"That was when—eighty-six, eighty-seven?"

"Late eighty-six—a month after my thirtieth birthday, which makes me thirty-four, going on thirty-five, if you don't want to bother with the math."

Mott only smiled and drank more beer.

"I also got drunk and blacked out on my thirtieth birthday,"

9

she said, making it a statement of fact rather than a confession.

"Why?"

"For an actress, thirty means you're no longer on the ascent but've reached the plateau where you'll stay, if lucky, till you hit forty and start the descent, which is sometimes slow and sometimes fast, very fast."

"Thirty's awfully young," Mott said. "But so is forty, for that matter."

"But forty-five isn't and that's why I used every trick I knew to get directing jobs. That meant guesting on TV sitcoms and episodic action-adventure stuff—but only if they'd let me direct. And that's how I served my apprenticeship."

"I get the impression that directing to you is something like an annuity."

"Look. I still intend to act when I'm forty-five and fifty-five and sixty-five, if I live that long, although the roles will get fewer and fewer. But a good director can get work at almost any age."

"You decided all this at thirty?"

"Sure," she said. "For an actor, thirty's still young. He's just getting rid of the last of his baby fat and for the next twenty-five or thirty-five years he can go on playing leads opposite actresses who're twenty-five and thirty and forty. But do you know any fifty-five-year-old actresses who're doing love scenes with thirty-year-old actors—unless it's some kinky incest story? I'll give you an hour to name one."

"Is Ann-Margret fifty-five yet?" Mott said, picking up the last slice of pizza.

Gamble began a smile that turned into a grin. "You a fan of hers?"

"Merely a preservationist," Mott said and bit into his pizza.

"Well, anyway, that's why I got drunk on my thirtieth birthday and why I haven't had more than three beers and eight glasses of wine since—until the thirty-first of December."

"Let's go back to your first meeting with Mr. Rice."

"Okay. He had this office, as I said, in Century City. He'd

10

called Jack Broach and Jack'd called me and suggested I give it a go. So I ride the elevator up to the what—the thirty-fifth floor?—where I'm ushered into this okay-but-nothing-special office, where Billy turns on the charm and hands me a screenplay based on Lorna Wiley's novel, *The Milner Sisters*."

She looked at Mott apprehensively until he said he'd read it. After a small relieved sigh, she said, "So after somebody brings in the coffee, Billy says, 'I want you for this.' Well, both sisters are great parts, but Louise is the plum, so I ask, 'Which do I play—Louise or Rose?' And guess what he says?"

"I can't."

"He says, 'I think the director should make that decision and since you'll be directing, the decision is yours.' And right about then I thought I ought to fall in love with Billy Rice, the prick."

"So far, he sounds fine."

"So far. Well, we make *The Milner Sisters* and it gets great reviews and doesn't make a dime. But Billy doesn't seem to care and plunks down a one-hundred-thousand-dollar option on some god-awful techno-thriller, then pays another million for a screenplay, exercises his option on the novel— another one point four million—and hires himself a twenty-four-year-old British MTV director. I'm to play Mavis, the gutsy heroine who walks and talks like a fella, opposite dumb old Niles Brand, who's getting five million plus points. Well, the whole thing costs thirty-eight million and it's a hit and a half. I win the L.A. film critics award and get nominated by the Academy and don't win, but who the hell cares except me?"

"Then what?"

"Then Billy asks me to marry him. This is around the first of last year. And I, the eternal klutz, say sure, Billy, love to, and we set the wedding date for December thirtieth. In the meantime, Billy buys *The Bad Dead Indian*, which has been on the *NYT* bestseller list for thirteen months. It cost him two million. Cash. No options. He spends another million or so on writers and announces that his bride-to-be will not only star in this sixty-five-million-plus epic of the Old West with dumb old Niles Brand, but she'll also direct it. Still with me, Mr. Mott?"

"You make it exceedingly clear."

"Then it's Christmas Eve, a little more than a month ago. Billy issues what the newsies call a 'terse' three-line press release that says he's not going to marry Ione Gamble after all and she's not going to direct or star in his wonderful picture about native Americans either. And this is all one big goddamn surprise to me."

"Had you signed either a contract for the picture or a prenuptial agreement of any kind?"

"Jack Broach was still negotiating the movie deal. And when Billy'd hinted at a prenuptial agreement, I told him I wanted a marriage, not a merger, which wasn't original, but he didn't seem to've heard it before."

"Why do you think Rice changed his mind?"

"I don't know. I never spoke to him again. At least, I don't think I did."

"But you tried."

"I must've called him a couple of hundred times but never got through. Then on New Year's Eve, the day after our cancelled wedding day, I started drinking. I drank all day, slept a little, woke up and drank some more. Then I remember getting into my car with a pint of vodka and heading for a showdown with Billy at his place in Malibu. But I don't remember anything else until the deputies woke me up at the beach house with Billy lying there dead on the floor."

"You blacked out?"

"Yes."

Mott leaned back on the couch with the chintz slipcover and studied Gamble, who was now across the coffee table from him, perched on the edge of the businesslike armchair. "Then this was your second blackout," he said. "What do you know about them?"

"Until I saw a doctor, I only knew they were plot twists for soap operas. Need a conflict? Give her a blackout. Or amnesia. The doctor told me blackouts are a form of alcohol-produced amnesia common to alcoholics and some binge drinkers. He said that hypnotism's been used to regain memory lost by blackouts. Sometimes it works; sometimes it doesn't. But if I wanted to try it, he could recommend several very well qualified hypnotherapists. I told him I'd think about it."

"Did you?"

"Sure. I thought about it. I also thought about what would happen if I confessed to something embarrassing or incriminating—maybe even to Billy's murder. If the hypnotist had it down on audiotape, he could sell it for a whole lot of money. If he'd videotaped it, he could sell it for God knows how much."

"He'd also go to jail."

"Not if he claimed somebody broke in and stole it from him. I remember Watergate—well, part of it. They did something like that then, didn't they?"

"Not quite."

"But there's one more thing he could do with the tape that nobody'd ever have to know about," she said. "He could sell it to me, which, I believe, is called blackmail."

She gave Mott the small cool smile that debaters use after making a telling point. Mott scratched the back of his left hand and said, "What if I could find you a hypnotherapist whose discretion is guaranteed? Would you be interested in trying to regain your memory of that night?"

Gamble frowned. "It's important, isn't it? My memory?"

"Extremely so."

"You know any hypnotists?"

"I know of somebody who does."

"You mean that's his business—supplying hypnotists for wives and girlfriends who get drunk, black out, do in their husbands or boyfriends, but remember fuck-all about it?"

Mott smiled. "He supplies extremely well-qualified, extremely discreet professionals to perform any number of extremely delicate tasks."

She stared at him, frowned again and said, "Do all those extremelys mean you're going to be my lawyer?"

13

"If you like."

"Okay. As my lawyer, what d'you recommend?"

"A discreet and well-qualified hypnotist."

"Then you'd better go ahead and call your jobber—whoever he is."

"His name is Glimm," Howard Mott said. "Enno Glimm."

Three

The left cheek of Enno Glimm, the walk-in, was flawed by a puckered scar that would almost pass for a dimple—just as his English could almost pass for American were it not for those Rhine-flavored *w*'s that turned Wudu, Ltd., into Voodoo, Ltd.

Quincy Durant, sensing profit, made no effort to correct the prospective client. As for the scar, Durant guessed it could have been made by a small-caliber round—either a .22 or a .25—or by some 9-year-old bully jabbing a pencil through Glimm's left cheek thirty-five years ago during a schoolyard scuffle.

It was Arctic cold in England and throughout most of Europe that February. Eight inches of snow fell on London and a few flakes had even dusted the French Riviera. The cold and damp penetrated everywhere, including the panelled conference room/office of Wudu, Ltd., where Durant had hauled a three-bar electric fire out of a closet and stuck it in the false fireplace to supplement the building's inadequate central heating.

Enno Glimm sat in one of the twin wingback chairs that flanked the fireplace. Above its mantel hung a large oil portrait of Mrs. Arthur Case Wu (the former Agnes Goriach) and the two sets of Wu twins.

The seated 14-year-old twin girls looked both worldly and a trifle mischievous. Their standing 17-year-old brothers, Arthur and Angus, wore identical half-smiles that made them look faintly sinister. The artist had brilliantly caught the mother's handsome features, regal bearing and even the sparkle in her huge gray eyes that suggested she was thinking of something bawdy.

Enno Glimm ignored the portrait and remained hunched-over in the wingback chair, toasting his palms before the electric fire and frowning, as if sorry that he had let Durant relieve him of the black double-breasted cashmere overcoat.

Durant guessed the coat had cost at least a thousand pounds or, more likely, three thousand deutsche marks. After hanging it on the overly elaborate coatrack that had been carved out of black walnut, supposedly in 1903, Durant went over to the other wingback chair, sat down, crossed his legs and waited for Glimm to say whatever he had come to say.

Glimm was still toasting his palms when, without looking at Durant, he said, "Mr. Wu won't be joining us?" This time he made Artie Wu's surname sound like the *vieux* in Vieux Carré and even gave it a passable French pronunciation.

"He's away," Durant said. "A family matter."

Glimm looked up at the portrait with pale gray eyes that Durant thought weren't much darker or warmer than sleet. "Someone is ill?" Glimm asked, coating the question with just the right amount of concern.

"His sons are having a problem at school," Durant said.

"Neglecting their studies?"

"Something like that."

"Their school is here—in London?"

"Why?" Durant asked, turning the one-word question into a warning and possibly a threat.

It made Glimm smile. "You think I'm a kidnapper—a terrorist maybe?"

VOODOO, LTD.

"I don't know what you are," Durant said. "Maybe we should get to that."

"Listen. When I deal with a business, any business, I like to deal with its principals, its top guys, the yes-or-no people. In this case, you and Voo. So after I fly into Heathrow last night in the snowstorm—"

"From where?"

Glimm ignored the question. "—and check into the Connaught, where they've got rooms going begging, I decide to take a little walk, snow or no snow, and have a look at Eight Bruton Street, Berkeley Square, London Doubleyou One, heart of Mayfair and all that. I wanta make sure Voodoo, Limited's a real business and not just some combination Xerox copy shop and accommodation address—know what I mean? And if it is real, then I'll walk in the next morning unannounced and unexpected."

"And possibly unwelcome."

"We'll see," Glimm said. "Anyhow, when I walk into your pretty little reception room out there, the first thing I notice is there's no pretty little receptionist to go with it. Then I notice some dust on her desk—not much, but enough to tell me she hasn't been to work in a week or ten days. But so what? Maybe she's out sick in bed with a doctor."

Durant smiled faintly. "A temporary indisposition."

"Just like I thought. And since there's nobody to receive me, I knock on the door that says Private and wait while all those locks and dead bolts and chains are shot back and undone. Finally, the door opens and I see some guy wearing way too much tan for February—a guy who's six-three or -four and carries maybe one-seventy-five or -eighty pounds, if that. This is a guy who'll never see forty again and probably not even forty-five, but who's got the moves of somebody in their twenties. Okay. Their late, late twenties. And right away I know I'm in the presence of none other than that fucking Durant, which is what everybody I talked to calls you."

"My references," Durant said. "And bona fides."

Glimm nodded.

"Name two," Durant said.

"Ever know a Manila police captain called Cruz?"

"I knew a police lieutenant called Hermenegildo Cruz."

"He got promoted," Glimm said. "What about a Maurice Overby in Amman?"

Something changed in Durant's expression—a certain tightening around the mouth. But then it went away and he said, "What's Overby doing in Jordan?"

"He claims he's there to analyze the BYK's personal security system."

"All by himself?"

"He says his principal resource asset, whatever that means, is Dr. Booth Stallings, the world-famous expert on terrorism that I never heard of. You ever hear of him?"

Durant only nodded.

Glimm permitted himself another small smile. "I notice you don't ask what BYK stands for. I don't know and have to ask Overby. He's down there in Amman, Jordan, and I'm calling from—well, it doesn't matter where—and Overby goes all snotty over the phone and tells me BYK stands for Brave Young King, which is what he and all the other old Middle East hands call King Hussein." Glimm paused. "Even though the King's not all that young anymore, is he?"

"Overby told you he's an old Middle East hand?" Durant said.

"You saying he's not?"

"I'm saying it's just another fascinating and heretofore undisclosed chapter in Mr. Overby's life."

"Okay. So he's a liar. Who the hell cares about Overby? What about you? You ever been there—the Middle East? I mean on business?"

"Beirut," Durant said.

"When?"

"A few years ago."

"A few years ago was when it was still kinda hairy, right?"

Durant only shrugged and waited for what came next, which he assumed would be the sell. Instead, it turned out to be a silence that went on and on until it had Glimm crossing

and uncrossing his legs and even shifting a little in the wing-
back chair. Because silences had never bothered Durant, he
waited it out with a small polite smile, and Glimm finally
ended it with yet another question. "What were you doing
there—in Beirut?"

"Looking for something," Durant said.

"Find him?"

"I don't think I said 'him.' "

"Okay. Him? Her? It?"

"We found what we were looking for."

" 'We' meaning you and Mr. Voo, right?" Glimm said and,
not waiting for confirmation, hurried on, his manner and
tone brusque and just shy of rude. "What you guys went
looking for in Beirut was somebody fairly important's dead
body. I hear this somebody fairly important's widow wants to
collect on her missing-and-presumed-dead husband's mil-
lion-dollar life policy, but doesn't want to wait around seven
years—or whatever it is—till he's declared legally dead. And
her dead husband—or whoever he's working for—must've
been paying one hell of a premium if the insurance company
agreed to waive its act-of-war and insurrection rider, which
it sure as hell did or the widow wouldn't've hired you and
Voo to go find proof he was dead—or maybe buy it from
somebody."

"Tell me something," Durant said. "Since you don't really
have any trouble with your w's, why mess up Mr. Wu's name?
Is it a test? A sales gimmick? Or just your notion of cute and
clever?"

A grin made a quick white slash across Glimm's bony face.
His pale eyes crinkled with pleasure or perhaps even delight
and Durant prepared himself for a chuckle that never came.
But Glimm still wore the pleased look when he said, "It's a
test."

"How'd I do?"

Glimm glanced at his fat gold wristwatch. "Not bad. You
lasted twelve minutes. That means you're hungry all right,
but not exactly starving."

Although Durant made no response, Glimm didn't really

seem to expect one and went on talking with the glib confidence of a veteran salesman who's decided it's time to close the deal.

"Here's how it works: whenever I negotiate anything, I always mispronounce either the name of the guy I'm negotiating with or the name of his company."

"Or both," Durant said.

"Yeah. Right. In this case, both."

"Why?"

"Because if the guy corrects me right off, I know he's not hungry. If it takes him ten or fifteen minutes, he's just medium hungry. But if he never does correct me, I know he's practically starving to death and I can negotiate my own deal."

"We're not negotiating anything," Durant said.

"The hell we're not," said Enno Glimm.

Four

Artie Wu sat in front of the headmaster's desk in the massive armless 121-year-old wooden punishment chair where countless small boys had perched, awaiting their fates with tears and dangling feet.

At a little less than six-foot-three, and with his weight back down to just under 250 pounds, Wu was much too large to perch anywhere. But he did manage to relax, if not quite loll, in the big chair—even tipping its front legs up a few inches as he leaned back and listened to Perkin Ramsay, the headmaster, deliver a bill of indictment against the Wu twins, Arthur and Angus.

The charges were made in a tenor drone that Wu feared might never end. As it went on and on, he looked up to admire the enormous room's vaulted stone ceiling, then over to his left at the fireless fireplace that was so vast you could walk right into it, providing you were no more than five-foot-two or -three.

The public school that had undertaken the education of the twin Wu males was seventeen miles north of Edinburgh. Much of the school was contained within a small castle, thought to have been completed around 1179 and still in remarkably good repair. It was here that the Reverend Rob-

21

ert Cameron had founded his school in 1821 after persuading the prosperous parents of his first pupils that he could indeed transform their wee monsters into wee gentlemen scholars. Since then, all Goriach males had attended Cameron and Agnes Goriach Wu saw no reason why her twin sons shouldn't carry on the tradition.

His indictment delivered, the headmaster drew a large handkerchief from a pocket and delicately blew his nose, one nostril at a time. It was a bright pink nose, thin and sharply pointed, that went nicely with his gaunt cheeks and the deep sockets that sheltered eyes of a startling blue. A high forehead soared up and back from the blue eyes until it finally caught up with the retreating thicket of coarse red hair.

After Perkin Ramsay put away his handkerchief, Wu spoke for the first time in nearly fifteen minutes. "You say the twins sent five of them to your infirmary?"

Ramsay's answering sigh was melancholy. "Please listen carefully this time, Mr. Wu. *Five* boys went to hospital in Edinburgh—not to our infirmary. Angus and Arthur were attacked by *eight* boys of their own approximate age and size. *Three* of these *eight* boys escaped to tell the tale. It was not a fair fight."

"Eight against two? I think not."

"I mean your sons did not fight fairly."

Artie Wu looked relieved. "Used whatever was lying around, did they? A rock or two? A bit of stick? A nice length of pipe?"

"They used their hands, feet, knees and elbows."

"How long did it last?"

"Three or four minutes. Not more."

Wu took a long fat cigar from an inside coat pocket, studied it with evident longing, then put it away again. "You say the name-calling started it?"

"Yes."

Wu nodded thoughtfully as if all at last had been revealed. "So this gang of eight called the twins names, then jumped them and got knocked about a bit for their trouble. Still, the gang did have the satisfaction of using all those grand old names such as chink and wog and slope and dink and—"

Ramsay's right hand shot up, palm out. A traffic cop's warning. Wu stopped talking and the headmaster said, "Do I have your full attention, Mr. Wu?"

Wu nodded.

"Splendid," Ramsay said. "I've been trying to gain it by telephone and post without success these past two months."

Wu's expression shifted into one of mild polite interest. His tone grew bland. "Oh. That."

"Yes, Mr. Wu. *That.* Or more precisely, *those.* The fees. They still haven't been paid."

Artie Wu took the cigar from his pocket again, stuck it in his mouth, clamped down hard, then eased the clamp just enough to growl, "Was there a fight?"

"Exactly as described," Ramsay said. "The twins, by all accounts, were formidable."

Wu beamed around the cigar, removed it and said, "I seem to recall Mrs. Wu taking care of the fees with a check some time ago."

The dam containing Ramsay's exasperation broke. He almost sprang from his chair, but caught himself, rose more slowly and, with palms planted flat on the desktop, leaned toward Artie Wu. "The reason I wanted you here in this very room, seated in that very chair, was to inform you, sir— no, guarantee you—that unless the fees are paid today, not tomorrow, but today, the twins will accompany you back to London this after—"

The telephone rang. Ramsay snatched it up, snapped out an irritated hello, listened, frowned, said, "One moment," and offered the instrument to Wu.

After Wu rose, accepted the phone and said hello, he heard Durant's voice: "I hold here in my hand a certified check drawn on Barclays for twenty-five thousand pounds from our new client, Herr Enno Glimm. The check will be deposited in approximately six minutes and you'll again be solvent."

"And what exactly is required of us?"

"We have to find a pair of hypnotists, a brother-and-sister act, who've gone missing."

"Where?"

"Who cares?"

"A most sensible attitude," Wu said. "I'll be back tomorrow morning."

"We meet Glimm here at two."

"I'll be there," Wu said, turned and handed back the telephone.

"Good news?" Ramsay asked.

"So-so," said Wu as he took a checkbook from a suit pocket, placed it on the desk, absently patted his other pockets for something, then smiled at Perkin Ramsay and said, "Do you have a pen?"

*　　*　　*

In Carriages Bar of the Caledonian Hotel in Princes Street in Edinburgh, the sons of Artie Wu sat in a booth across from their father and watched him sign his name to a check for the second time that day. Arthur and Angus had half-pints of lager in front of them. In front of their father was a large and yet-to-be tasted whisky.

Wu tore out the check and handed it to Arthur, the older son by nine minutes. He glanced at the amount, raised an eyebrow and passed the check to his brother.

Angus studied it and said, "Four hundred quid," letting a dubious inflection raise the specter of insufficient funds.

"It won't bounce," Wu said. "And it should get you through to the end of next month when I'll send more. Now all you guys have to do is finish the term, bum around the Continent this summer and head for Princeton in August."

Angus gave the check back to his brother and carefully examined his father before asking, "Have you really thought about what it'll cost to send us through four years at Princeton?"

Wu sipped his whisky and ran some figures through his mind. "About a hundred and sixty grand," he said.

"That's for four years without frills. If you want frills, try poker."

"Like you and Durant did?" Angus said.

"We played a few hands."

"Durant says you two averaged six hundred a month from stud and draw," Arthur said. "And that was back when the dollar was worth three or four times what it is now."

"We got by," Wu said.

"He also claims there were a lot of rich fish around Princeton then who were more than willing to sit down to an evening of cards with the pretender to the Chinese Emperor's throne and his silent, ever-present bodyguard."

Wu smiled and nodded, as if remembering. He was instead studying his sons and discovering yet again, with almost embarrassing satisfaction, that they looked as much like him as they did their mother.

They had his height but their mother's rangy build. His slow smile and her lithe walk. His black hair and her gray eyes, which, along with Wu's epicanthic folds, gave the twins what they called their all-Amerasian preppy look.

"Did you like it—Princeton?" Arthur asked.

Wu stared suspiciously at Arthur—then Angus. "Whenever you two want something, you always take me by the hand and try to lead me back down Reminiscent Row. So let's hear it. What's up?"

The twins traded quick looks and Angus won the invisible coin toss. "We know where we can make a lot of money this summer."

Wu stuck a fresh cigar in his mouth and, just before lighting it, asked, "Doing what?"

"It's sort of a summer intern program," Arthur said.

Once the cigar was lit, Wu said, "Summer intern jobs never pay a lot of money."

"These will," Angus said.

"Where is it and what is it?" Wu said. "Be specific."

"Kuwait," Angus said. "Or it will be when the war's over next week, next month—whenever. There'll be a ton of money floating around during reconstruction and this consulting firm we heard from already has a lock on a lot of it. But the firm needs bodies, American bodies, and it's willing to pay for them."

"What's the firm?" Wu asked.

"Overby, Stallings Associates."

Artie Wu's eyes narrowed and his face grew still. Nothing moved. Then his lips moved just enough to say, "Overby as in Maurice Overby?"

Arthur grinned. "As in Uncle Otherguy, Pop."

*   *   *

Agnes Wu sat before the dressing table in the Caledonian Hotel room, brushing her hair and listening to her husband's word-for-word account of his telephone call from Quincy Durant.

Wu packed while he talked. He packed automatically, almost without thinking, folding whatever needed to be folded and wadding up whatever needed to be washed. It all went into an abused leather satchel with brass fittings that she called the Gladstone and he called the bag.

The hair that Agnes Wu brushed was still the palest of pale gold, which she kept that way with only minimal assistance from her hairdresser. She now gave it what she hoped was its one-hundredth brush stroke, turned from the mirror, looked at Wu with her large clever gray eyes and said, "That was a hell of a coincidence—Quincy calling at that precise moment."

After removing his partially smoked cigar from an ashtray, Wu said, "Coincidences are seldom more than good or bad minor accidents that happen all the time. Quincy's call was neither. He got the check from Glimm, knew we were broke and picked up the phone."

Agnes Wu rose from the dressing table's padded bench, went to a window, stared down at Princes Street with its handful of half-frozen pedestrians and asked, "Can we really afford it—Princeton?"

"That's an August-September problem. This is February.

But you can't very well send two kids to Princeton at the same time unless you're in the top two or three percent income bracket—which I trust we'll have reentered by September."

"Then you're counting on Herr Glimm?"

"Somewhat."

"Perhaps you'd best find out whether you should."

Wu blew a fat smoke ring. "You can do it faster."

Agnes Wu turned with an answering grin that transformed her face. The cool, even remote look changed into something reckless, merry and even a trifle sly. "Cousin Duncan?" she said.

"Money knows money," Wu said. "If Glimm has it, Duncan will know."

"I really should see him now that I'm up here," she said. "I could brag about the kids, slip Duncan some London gossip and find out whether he's still cross with you and Quincy for not letting him invest in Wudu."

"Since we kept him from investing in a damn near bankrupt outfit, he's got nothing to be cross about."

The first cousin with nothing to be cross about was Sir Duncan Goriach, the 62-year-old titular chief of the Goriach clan, who had been knighted in 1984 for services to the Crown—services that consisted largely of making enormous profits for himself and a few carefully selected others during the North Sea oil boom.

Agnes Wu said, "Duncan wouldn't've cared about the money. He thinks you and Quincy lead spicy, eventful lives and merely wanted to buy himself a vicarious slice. So I'll call him and invite myself up to Aberdeen for a long weekend."

"There's something we need to talk about first."

Agnes left the window to sit on the edge of the bed next to the leather satchel. She clasped her hands in her lap and settled a carefully neutral look on her face. It was the look she assumed when anticipating terrible news. She had worn the same look during her marriage more times than she thought really necessary.

After Wu remained silent for a number of seconds, his wife said, "Well?"

He blew another smoke ring, this time at the ceiling. "The boys've been offered summer jobs."

"Where?"

"Kuwait."

"By whom?"

"Otherguy Overby."

Agnes Wu's neutral look vanished. Her eyes lost their cool remoteness and seemed to turn a hot smoky gray. Her voice dropped into a lower register, which transformed it into an urgent warning when she said, "Don't tell them no. If you do, they'll be off like a shot."

"They'll go no matter what I say. To them, Otherguy's the crown prince of fun."

There was another brief silence as Agnes Wu considered what must be done. After reaching her decision, she issued a command—although it sounded as if she were merely asking her husband to please pass the salt. But Wu knew better and it gave him a small erotic thrill when she said, "Stop him, Artie."

Artie Wu blew a final smoke ring at the ceiling and smiled up at it. "I'm not going to stop Otherguy," he said. "I'm going to hire him."

Five

The only coats and ties in the bar of the Inter-Continental Hotel in Amman were worn by two men who sat at a table drinking Scotch and water. Most of the other drinkers were European and American correspondents who were either bunched up together at one end of the long bar or scattered about at tables in reclusive twos and threes. Nearly all of them wore quasimilitary desert gear, much of it obviously ordered by mail from either Banana Republic or Eddie Bauer. Safari jackets, or their first cousins, seemed to be the universal favorite.

Along with his coat and tie, the older of the two men also wore a thick cap of short-cropped pewter-gray hair and a well-seamed face that easily could have belonged to the board chairman of some small hungry international firm that dealt in esoteric and even suspect services. The younger coat and tie had dark brown hair shot with gray; bleak eyes; a guarded expression, and might well have been the older man's chief executive officer, who hired, fired and looked after the bribes.

The older man swallowed the last of his drink, rattled his ice cubes, looked at the younger man and said, "Tell me about the rabbits again."

29

The man who wanted to hear about the rabbits was Booth Stallings, expert on terrorism, doctor of philosophy, author of *Anatomy of Terror*, onetime White House consultant and recognized adept at grantsmanship, who, five years before at age 60, had abandoned it all to go adventuring.

"What rabbits?" asked Maurice Overby, also known to a number of law enforcement agencies as Otherguy Overby. Over the years, Overby had protested—with notable success—that it was never he, but some other guy, who had done all that stuff the cops wanted to question him about. Usually involved in a variety of enterprises, some of them legitimate, Overby was by trade a journeyman confidence man and much admired by his peers.

After Overby denied any knowledge of the rabbits, Stallings shook his head sadly and said, "If you don't know about Steinbeck's rabbits, then tell me again about those wonderful job offers from Artie Wu that'll materialize any second now."

"Why d'you want to hear it again?"

"Reassurance."

Adopting a weary tone, Overby said, "Okay. Remember when we bumped into Count von Lahusen here in the bar last week?"

"An evening with the Graf von Lahusen is not easily forgotten."

"So he'd had a few. What if you'd just spent two months in the GDR, or what used to be the GDR, trying to reclaim your ancestral estates only to be told, 'Go fuck yourself, Count'?"

"At the sad tale's third telling, I took to my bed."

"And missed the best part," Overby said. "Look. Me and the Count and Artie and Durant've known each other for years and even went in on some things together a time or two, know what I mean?"

"Where?"

Overby nodded in the general direction of the South China Sea. "Mostly out there," he said. "On the rim. Where else? Anyway, the Count tells me he's in Berlin about a week or ten days ago, staying at the Am Zoo, when he gets a call from some guy called Enno Glimm."

"German?"

"What else would he be with a name like that?"

"Austrian. Possibly Swiss."

Overby ignored the suggestions. "What Glimm wants from the Count is a rundown on Voodoo, Limited. At first, the Count thinks he knows jack shit about Voodoo, Limited, until it hits him that what Glimm means is Wudu, Limited, the outfit Artie and Durant set up in London just before they took their big bath in the eighty-seven market."

"They should've invested their funds more prudently—as did you and I."

"Don't start," Overby said. "It took you less'n twenty days to make that million you flew out of Hong Kong with and about eighteen months to lose it. Or most of it. For a while there, on paper, you were worth two, almost three million."

"Cold comfort, Otherguy," Stallings said. "Very cold. How much did Wu and Durant lose?"

"I hear half a million apiece."

"I feel better. Now you can continue with what the Count told Herr Glimm."

"Well, von Lahusen's not about to bad-mouth Artie or that fucking Durant either so he gives them a big buildup. But Glimm's not satisfied and wants to know who else he can check with. The Count tells him to call me here at the hotel and that's what he did."

"Then what?"

"Glimm asks me about Artie and Durant and I ask him why he wants to know. He's not about to tell me, of course, but I can guess it's something pretty fat. So I tell him that Wu and Durant are top of the line—although Durant can be a mean bastard. Glimm says that's exactly what he's looking for, thanks me and hangs up. So I think for a couple of minutes, then call Artie's twin boys, Arthur and Angus, at their school just outside Edinburgh. That's in Scotland."

"Thank you," Stallings said. "And now you're going to tell me why you called them, aren't you?"

"To offer them summer jobs in Kuwait City after the war's

over—jobs that'll pay them three thousand U.S. a month each."

"Sweet Jesus," said Stallings.

The smile that Overby gave Stallings should have been, by rights, hard, calculating and even cruel. Instead it was benign, almost gentle, and strangely contented. Stallings had seen it before and always thought of it as The Smile of the Christian About to Devour the Lion.

Much of it was still in place when Overby said, "I offered them jobs on the condition that they'd check it out with their folks, especially their mother, Agnes, and that's why Artie'll be calling any minute now with the job offer."

Stallings shook his head slowly. "For once, Otherguy, I fail to follow."

"It's simple. The twins are seventeen or eighteen. They'll tell their folks about Kuwait and Agnes'll go ape and tell Artie, very quiet-like, the way she does, that her sons will not, by God, spend a summer in the clutches of Otherguy Overby." He paused, as if to check his logic, nodded comfortably and continued. "Of course, none of this'd play if I didn't know how Artie's mind works."

"And how is that?" Stallings asked, resigned to his role of interlocutor.

"Artie'll never tell his kids not to do something he'd've done at their age. But he also has to keep Agnes happy. So what he'll do is move the pieces around till they form a new pattern."

"You being one of the pieces?"

Overby nodded. "And you, too. Artie'll decide to hire me and that's when I'll tell him you're part of the deal. He'll agree and I'll call the twins and tell them the Kuwait jobs fell through but maybe we can aim for something next summer. That way the kids don't get their feelings hurt, Agnes is happy and Artie gets himself a couple of guys he can trust on the Glimm deal, whatever it is."

Booth Stallings rose slowly and stared down at Overby with awe. He was still standing and still staring when he said, "Minds like yours really do exist, don't they?"

32

After giving it some thought, Overby said, "Yeah, I guess there still must be a few around."

*   *   *

At 1:08 A.M. the next day, Booth Stallings was awakened by the pounding on his hotel room door. After he opened it, Overby strolled in, exuding even more confidence than usual.

"I just talked to Artie," he said as he crossed to the room's desk and poured himself a measure of Stalling's whisky.

"And?"

"I go to London day after tomorrow and you, well, you've gotta be on the next flight to Manila."

Something exploded in Stalling's chest. He knew it wasn't a heart attack because there wasn't any pain. And he knew it wasn't fear or its evil twin, terror, because he had known both and neither felt like this. But the unfamiliar sensation, whatever it was, made his heart rate jump to around 130 beats a minute and produced a strange coppery taste, which, while not unpleasant, couldn't be swallowed away. Then suddenly he knew what it was and gave it the only name it deserved—wild anticipation.

After realizing that Overby was staring at him curiously, Stallings breathed in deeply through his nose and coughed to make sure his voice wouldn't crack when he spoke. "What's in Manila?"

"A coming-out party."

"Whose?"

Overby again produced his smile of benign calculation. "Georgia Blue's. She's getting herself sprung and Artie says he and Durant can use me, you and her."

"All right," Stallings said, not trusting himself to say more.

"Artie was wondering if you're still kind of stuck on Georgia," Overby said. "Not that it'd make any difference, but he was just curious. I told him I'd ask."

Overby waited. When Stallings made no reply, he said, "So what do I tell him?"

"Tell Artie it's none of his fucking business," Booth Stallings said.

Six

After British Rail made its run from Edinburgh to London in seven hours rather than its much touted five, Artie Wu came out of Victoria Station at 7:04 A.M., carrying his leather satchel. But instead of going home to the rented house in St. John's Wood or to the Wudu, Ltd., office in Mayfair, he took a taxi to Durant's small flat in Maida Vale.

In the mid-seventies a cautious speculator had bought and gutted a large aging two-story house in Ashworth Road, dividing it into what he called four luxury flats—two up and two down. The upstairs flats shared a common interior staircase but the downstairs flats had separate entrances. Durant's was the one on the left.

He had lived there for nearly three years, but knew little about the other tenants and had yet to say much more than "Good morning" or "Nice day" to the cats-and-small-dogs-only veterinarian, a 42-year-old bachelor, who lived in the other ground-floor flat. The fiftyish married couple who lived just above Durant were so anonymous that he recognized them on the street only because the wife was six inches taller than her diminutive husband. A pretty blond woman lived alone, most of the time, in the flat above the veterinarian, but all Durant knew about her was that she left each weekday morning at 8:25 sharp and hurried down the street and around the corner toward the Maida Vale underground station in Elgin Avenue.

Artie Wu, satchel in hand, paid off the taxi, went through the small decorative iron gate and up the short flagstone walk to Durant's door. He rang the bell twice and counted to 41 before the door was opened by a woman in her thirties who wore one of Durant's blue oxford cloth shirts and little else. She gave Wu a long cool stare and said, "You're a bit large to be out so early."

"I'm 'ere for what's owed me, miss," Wu growled in his best East End accent.

"I suspect you're the Wu in Wudu," she said. "So do come in before we both freeze."

"Who is it?" Durant called in a voice muffled by walls and distance.

"A Chinese gent," she called back, leading Wu from the small entranceway into the sitting room. "Wants to do your kneecaps."

"Give him a cup of tea," Durant said from the bedroom.

The woman stood, fists on hips and feet apart, challenging Wu with her still-cool stare. He now noticed that she wore not only Durant's shirt but also his thick white athletic socks.

"I'm Jenny Arliss, overnight guest," she said. "Tea?"

"Artie Wu. Milk, please. No sugar."

"Put your bag and coat anywhere," she said, disappearing through a swinging door into the kitchen.

Because Durant had lived much of his life in hotels, Wu always felt that the Ashworth Road flat should have resembled a comfortably furnished small suite on the ninth floor of some elderly hotel that had sprung for a new Pullman kitchen. Instead, the flat resembled a contemporary museum's near-miss exhibit of "How We Lived in the Thirties and Forties."

Ninety percent of the sitting room's contents had been created or manufactured before Durant was born. One hundred percent of them had been chosen by his landlord, the cautious speculator, who swore the old stuff's value doubled every three or four years and even claimed to know "certain chaps who'd kill for a nice fresh bit of nineteen fifty-four lino."

The grate in the sitting room was filled with plastic lumps of coal that glowed bright red at the flick of a switch. Placed nearby was a matching pair of boxlike easy chairs upholstered in zebra hide—or something supposed to resemble it. Within easy reach of the chairs was a sleek chrome, glass and ebony liquor cabinet that, when opened, played the first few bars of Duke-Gershwin's "I Can't Get Started With You."

On the walls were poster-size black-and-white art photographs of Paris, New York, London and Rome in the 1920s and '30s. The wallpaper offered gray vertical stripes of varying widths and shades. Close to a long, long pink couch was a 1938 radio that a wartime family could gather round to learn how the campaign against Rommel was going in the Western Desert.

Wu found the sitting room faintly depressing, like twice-told knock-knock jokes. Durant said he no longer noticed it.

*　*　*

The two now sat facing each other in the matching easy chairs and waiting for the unseen Jenny Arliss to leave through the flat's front door. After they heard the door's soft click and slam, Artie Wu asked, "Where'd you find her?"

Durant looked at the grate's false glow, as if the exact time and place lay there. "Two Sundays ago at the Tate in front of a Turner," he said, now looking at Wu. "Although I'm not sure which Turner."

Wu finished his tea, put the cup down, clasped his hands across his belly and smiled, which made him look even more benign than usual. Like Buddha on the perfect day, Durant thought.

"It was nasty out two Sundays ago," Wu said. "Rain followed by sleet, as I recall."

"I go to galleries when the weather's nasty because they're less crowded," Durant said. "And because the women there on such days are more approachable."

36

"Lonely, you mean."

"Do I?"

"What's Jenny Arliss do?"

"She says she's a researcher for BBC," Durant said. "But the BBC's never heard of her. A dozen calls later, I found out she's with *Help!*—that's *h-e-l-p* followed by an exclamation point, mark, whichever. Its specialty is supplying highly qualified experts on extremely short notice to fill technical but temporary jobs all over the world. Very high pay and hard work for a month or two—often less. You call *Help!* if you need a microbiologist in Madagascar, an artist in Anarctica or other alliterative examples."

"A urologist in Uruguay," Wu said.

"Exactly. This is no small outfit either. It's *Help!* in English, but *Hilfe!* in German, *Au Secours!* in French and *¡Socorro!* in Spanish—except in Spanish it has two exclamation points, the first one upside down."

"I assume it's also in the States," Wu said.

Durant nodded. "And in Canada, Singapore, Hong Kong, Japan and Australia."

"What does our Jenny do at *Help!*?" Wu asked.

"She's managing director."

"For London?"

"For Britain."

"Well," Wu said.

"Exactly my reaction," said Durant.

Wu removed a cigar from an inside pocket, held it up for close inspection, then gave Durant a long sly look and said, "I was told only yesterday that *Help!*'s international headquarters is in Frankfurt and that its president, chairman and principal stockholder, all rolled into one, is none other than our new best friend, Enno Glimm, who only yesterday rescued us from ruin."

Durant smiled appreciatively. "You've been talking to Sir Duncan, right?"

"Agnes has."

"What's Duncan say?"

"That Glimm's big money," Wu said. "Maybe even great

big money. Duncan says Glimm founded *Help!* after he'd founded another equally profitable company called *Camaraderie!*—which also has an exclamation mark tacked on at the end. *Camaraderie!*, in fact, gave Glimm the idea for *Help!*"

"*Camaraderie!* is what?"

"A packaged tour business catering to xenophobes. Glimm's premise was—and is—that nearly everybody'd rather go on a foreign holiday with either family or friends or, failing that, with people as much like themselves as possible. In nineteen seventy-four Glimm leased a 727, or maybe it was a 707, filled it with happy chemical workers from Hoechst just outside Frankfurt and flew them to the Costa del Sol for a two-week vacation that cost half of what it would've cost on the Italian Adriatic. And it was there on the beaches of Franco's Spain that *Camaraderie!* was born."

"Then what?" Durant said.

"Then *Camaraderie!* went upscale. While not forgetting its working-stiff customers, it also began catering to professionals who might enjoy three weeks in, say, Borneo, providing they were accompanied by their own kind and given all the comforts of home plus a possible tax write-off. So Glimm segregated them by profession into groups of chartered accountants, doctors, lawyers, stockbrokers, engineers and what have you."

"You still haven't told me where Glimm got his idea for *Help!*"

"While recruiting the straitlaced professionals, Glimm discovered quite a few others of a different sort—loners and malcontents mostly—who'd rather die than go on a packaged tour. A lot of these oddballs told Glimm they wouldn't mind hiring out for several weeks or even a month or two or three in some exotic distant land, providing the money was right. And that's when Glimm set up *Help!*"

Wu stopped talking when he noticed his cigar had gone out. He relit it, blew smoke to his right and away from Durant, then said, "*Help!* can, if but asked, supply Tibet with choreographers and Malaysia with lieder singers—all of them temps. Cousin Duncan says he's been told that Glimm has the names of some fifteen thousand experts in his Rolodex and fat retainers from at least three dozen international firms."

"If he has all those experts on tap, why come to us?" Durant asked.

"Maybe he heard we're the best."

"At finding lost hypnotists?"

Wu shrugged. "Did you get around to asking him why he wanted them found—or how they got lost?"

"He said we'd go into that at the two o'clock meeting."

"He say anything else?"

"Not much," Durant said. "Only that the twenty-five thousand quid is ours to keep whether we take the job or not."

Durant liked to watch Artie Wu trying not to look surprised. The opportunities were few and Durant found himself grinning at Wu's small judicious nods that were accompanied by a slight wise smile. Finally, Wu said, "What else should I know?"

"That Glimm's thorough. It's obvious that when he walked in yesterday, Jenny Arliss had been feeding him reports on you and me for at least a week or two. He himself's been checking us out with people like Hermenegildo Cruz in Manila, who's a captain now, and Overby in Amman. When I asked him what the hell Otherguy's doing in Amman, Glimm said he and Booth Stallings were overhauling King Hussein's personal security system."

"Glimm also checked on us with the Count in Berlin," Wu said.

"With von Lahusen?"

"How many counts do we know? That's how Glimm got onto Otherguy."

Durant raised an eyebrow, his left one, giving himself a dubious look, which perfectly matched his tone. "You talked to Otherguy?"

Artie Wu blew a faltering smoke ring off to the left. "I didn't just talk to Otherguy. I hired him."

Because they had been partners ever since they had run away together at 14 from a Methodist orphanage in San Francisco, Wu could easily read the signs that forecast Durant's anger. First, Durant grew very still. Then his mouth flattened itself into an unforgiving line. By then his eyes had narrowed and, on close inspection, a slight pallor could be found beneath his wear-ever tan. But the true betrayal was Durant's voice. It turned soft, gentle and almost coaxing, which is the way it sounded when he said, "Tell me why you'd do a stupid fucking thing like that, Artie?"

Wu sighed first, then said, "To ensure domestic tranquillity. Otherguy'd called Angus and Arthur and offered them summer jobs in Kuwait at three thousand a month each. Agnes was—well, she'd rather have them rob banks than come under Otherguy's tutelage. I could've told them they couldn't go, but if I had, they'd've been out the door and halfway to Amman by now."

"I would've helped you lock them in the cellar."

"I thought it best to lure Otherguy here. And to do that I had to offer something that'd make him drop whatever he had going in Kuwait and Jordan."

Durant's voice grew even more gentle when he said, "He had fuck-all going and you know it."

"Perhaps," Wu said. "But I told him we'd just taken on a fat new project and needed not only him but also Booth Stallings and—bear with me on this, Quincy—Georgia Blue."

Durant knew when to give up. He leaned back in the zebra-striped chair, gazed at something just above Wu's head and let indifference creep into his voice when he said, "If I know Otherguy and, by God, I should—right after he talked to the Count, he called the twins and offered them imaginary jobs because he damn well knew what Agnes's reaction would be and exactly what you'd do. He cut himself in."

"True," Artie Wu said. "But I'm perfectly aware of how Otherguy's mind works."

"There's that," Durant admitted. "So what happens to Otherguy and Company if we don't take the Glimm job?"

"We have to take it," Wu said, paused, then added, "You do realize that?"

After a moment or two, Durant nodded and said, "Okay.

I can work with Otherguy and watch him at the same time. And Booth always lends a bit of tone. But you have to sell me on Georgia."

"I'm not sure I can," Wu said. "I received a letter from her a few weeks ago. She's being released from that women's prison on Luzon."

"The one in Mandaluyong," Durant said, then asked, "When?"

Wu looked at the ceiling, as if trying to remember. "Either tomorrow or the day after. Her letter was apparently smuggled out and mailed from San Francisco. Georgia says she's cut a deal with Aquino's opposition. They've agreed to finagle her release, providing she gives them everything we did in eighty-six that can still embarrass Aquino and friends in the ninety-two elections."

"Political ammunition," Durant said.

Wu nodded. "I assume Georgia made up a lot of stuff— enough to secure her release anyway. Her letter asked about jobs, contacts—anything to help her get reestablished." He paused. "I didn't answer the letter."

"You just hired her instead and sent Booth to Manila with the glad tidings."

Wu studied his cigar and said, "Maybe I believe in redemption after all. Or want to."

"Know how I remember Georgia?" Durant asked, his voice again soft and gentle and altogether sinister. "We're back on that Hong Kong ferry. She's in her Secret Service half-squat with her piece in that two-handed service grip and aimed right at me. In less than a second she'll pull the trigger and blow me away. That's how I remember her—when I remember her at all."

Wu nodded and blew another smoke ring, but said nothing.

Durant's voice was back to normal when he said, "Okay. She's hired. But don't ask me to count on her. Ever."

After two more glum nods, Wu brightened. "What if we teamed her with Booth Stallings?"

"He still stuck on her?"

"I asked Otherguy that," Wu said. "And just before I caught the train last night, he called back from Amman to give me a message from Booth. The message was, 'Tell Artie it's none of his fucking business.'"

"He's still stuck on her," Durant said.

Seven

Neither Wu nor Durant displayed any surprise when Enno Glimm arrived for the 2 P.M. meeting accompanied by Jenny Arliss.

Durant merely told Wu, "You've already met Jenny," then introduced him to Glimm. They were all standing in what Glimm had called the pretty little reception room. After the introduction was made, Wu took over and ushered everyone into the office and over to the seven-foot-long oval walnut slab that served as both desk and occasional conference table.

Four small place cards, standing like tents, had been nicely hand-lettered by Miss Belle Hazlitt, Wudu's office manager, receptionist, secretary, bookkeeper and chief of protocol. Miss Hazlitt, who had insisted on being called that when hired three years before, was neither pretty nor little, as Enno Glimm had guessed, but a handsome, smartly dressed 66 who had spent thirty-five years doing something either vague or secretive for the Foreign Office until retiring at 62. She soon grew bored, answered a blind ad in *The Times* of London for a "flexible perfectionist"—Artie Wu's phrase—and was hired five minutes into her interview.

Miss Hazlitt cheerfully worked twelve-hour days when necessary or, with equal cheerfulness, did nothing at all for days

43

or even weeks when Wu and Durant were away on business. She passed the idle hours by reading American novels and was particularly fond of those with steamy Deep South backgrounds. Whenever Wudu, Ltd., ran short of funds and couldn't pay her salary, Miss Hazlitt stayed home, returning to work only after Wu or Durant proved that fresh funds had indeed been banked.

Satisfied that everything in the large office was as it should be, Miss Hazlitt softly closed the door, went to her desk, sat down and picked up a novel about a brokenhearted middle-aged lawyer in Savannah in the 1930s.

* * *

Behind each of the place cards were bottles of Evian water and Dortmunder beer with separate glasses for each. Teacups were provided for later, if needed, and ashtrays were placed to the right of each place card, except Durant's because he no longer smoked. The oval table was covered with a rarely used green baize cloth, one of Miss Hazlitt's first purchases. Two just-sharpened pencils rested on each of the four unlined notepads.

Jenny Arliss seemed more amused than surprised when she found her name on a place card. She looked up at Durant, smiled and said, "How long've you known I was with *Help!*?"

"Since the day after you picked me up at the Tate. If you play mystery lady again, don't use your real name."

"I've always thought I lie rather well."

"You do all right," Durant said.

After half listening to Arliss and Durant, an obviously impatient Enno Glimm turned to Wu and said, "Can we for Christ sake sit down and get started?"

"Of course," Wu said, pulled out his own chair and waited for the others to sit. After all were seated, Glimm was on Wu's right, Jenny Arliss on his left. Wu smiled at Arliss, turned to Glimm and said, "Suppose you tell us your problem and we'll tell you what, if anything, we can do about it."

"I wouldn't be here if you couldn't do something."

"Don't overestimate us," Durant said.

"Look," Glimm said. "My business is never overestimating anybody. But before we get to me and my problem, I need to ask you guys something."

"Please," Artie Wu said.

"What d'you call yourselves? I mean, if somebody says, 'I take from Voodoo, Limited, the whatchamacallit people,' that's not much of a description, especially if you two're depending on word of mouth."

"Not much," Durant agreed.

Glimm frowned at Durant, then turned again to Wu. "And don't get pissed off at the way I pronounce your company name. That's what I started calling it and now it just pops out. But let's get back to what you guys are. I know you're not private enquiry agents. And your overhead's too big to be con men. You might be into industrial espionage, but everybody tells me that's kind of boring. So what do you think you are? High-priced gofers? Noncombatant mercenaries? I classify everybody I meet by occupation and not being able to pigeonhole you two's giving me the jimjams."

"The jimjams?" Durant said.

"They're sort of like the willies."

"Would you be offended," Wu said, "if I were to ask where you learned your English?"

"In a minute. I want a job description first."

"Wudu, Limited," Wu said slowly, "is a closely held limited liability company that does for others what they cannot do for themselves."

"For a price," Glimm said.

"Certainly for a price."

"Then if it wasn't for the fucking price," Glimm said, "you guys could call yourselves saints."

"But since we do charge," Wu said, beaming, "why not just think of us as professional altruists?"

"I'll try," Glimm said, paused, then asked, "So you wanta know where I learned my American? In Frankfurt, that's where. Not far from a big PX and within spitting distance of the I. G. Farben building and its funny nonstop elevators that your Air Corps forgot to bomb for reasons there's no need to go into because it's all ancient history."

"Very ancient," Durant said.

Glimm poured himself a glass of beer, tasted it and said, "My mother was a maid after the war, a live-in *Putzfrau* for American army officers and later for army civilian personnel. I grew up surrounded by GIs and bilingual. My old man was either an American army captain, a lieutenant or maybe even a certain staff sergeant. Mom could never quite pin it down. I was born in late forty-six when she was twenty and after all my possible daddies had gone back to the States."

"You ever try to locate him?" Wu asked.

"What for?"

"Curiosity."

"I'm not that curious," Glimm said. "Nineteen forty-six, in case you don't know, was a tough year for us Krauts and Mom did whatever she had to do to keep us from starving. And if that 'whatever' hadn't included a certain amount of fraternization with the Amis, we could've starved. She's sixty-five now and lives in Hamburg but spends her winters in Spain or Florida. A couple of years ago she tried Hawaii and liked that okay, too. So that's me, Enno Glimm, rich bastard." He turned quickly to Wu again and said, "What's all this crap I hear about you being a pretender to the Chinese Emperor's throne?"

Before Wu could reply, Jenny Arliss said, "Mr. Wu does have a well-documented, if tenuous, claim to the Chinese throne."

Glimm, still staring at Wu, said, "China's never gonna have another Emperor."

"One can but hope," Wu said.

Durant leaned forward, elbows on the table, his eyes on Glimm. "Okay. Tell us what you want done and we'll tell you if we can do it. If not, we'll all have a goodbye drink."

Glimm turned to Jenny Arliss and said, "You tell it."

She thought for a moment or two, frowned, as if having

trouble with her phrasing, then said, "We want you to find two British hypnotists who've gone missing in California."

There was a brief silence. During it Wu and Durant refrained from looking at each other. Then Wu nodded, smiled and said, "I believe we can handle that nicely."

Eight

Jenny Arliss said the two missing hypnotists, Hughes Goodison, 32, and his sister, Pauline, 27, had wandered into the hypnotist's trade by accident.

"Their fascination with it began at a drinks party," she said. "Hughes was twenty-five then, a bookkeeper, and Pauline was five years younger and a clerk-typist. They shared a flat in Hammersmith left to them by their parents who'd died the year before of food poisoning while on holiday in Malta."

"Botulism," Glimm said. "Somebody forgot to boil the milk." Artie Wu made a careful note on his pad that read, "Cigars."

"It was at this party," Arliss said, "that an amateur hypnotist was putting people into trances and suggesting they do silly things such as barking like a dog, crowing like a rooster or meowing like a cat. Silly harmless nonsense."

"That fascinated them?" Durant said.

"Of course not. What did fascinate them was that they themselves were such easy subjects. The amateur hypnotist told them he'd never worked with anyone more susceptible."

"You can't hypnotize anyone who doesn't wanta be," said Glimm, looking at Wu, as if expecting him to make another note. Wu obliged by writing another reminder, "Call Booth in Manila."

Jenny Arliss said that brother and sister were so intrigued by their brush with hypnotism that Hughes Goodison bought a book on the subject. "It was one of those oversimplified popularizations, something like, 'How to Hypnotize and Amaze Your Friends.' They practiced on each other first, then on their chums, and discovered they were really quite good at it. They even laid on a study course and began reading books by recognized authorities such as, well, Estabrook was one, then there were Moodie and Gilla and Fromm and, let me think, Shor."

"Some memory, huh?" Glimm asked.

"Remarkable," Durant said.

It was just after the Goodisons began their course of study, Arliss said, that Hughes began looking into ways he and his sister could become certified hypnotists and discovered the requirements were surprisingly lax. He also learned of schools of hypnotism where the course lasted only forty hours—followed by sixteen hours of supervised practice. He and his sister could even attend classes at night and, once all courses were completed, hang out their shingle as certified hypnotists.

"And that's exactly what they did," Arliss said.

"Tell 'em about their gimmick," Glimm said.

She nodded. "Right. Their gimmick, as Mr. Glimm calls it, was to open a lose-weight, stop-smoking clinic—except they didn't call it a clinic. They called it a workshop and their success rate was about what it is for most such places—anywhere from fifteen to twenty percent, if that. But one boasts about successes, not failures, and Hughes and Pauline were quite good at self-promotion. They worked up a fairly witty lecture-cum-demonstration, wisely keeping it to fifteen minutes, and offered it free to civic and professional groups that met weekly or monthly. They sprinkled their act—I suppose I should call it that—with generous dollops of psychobabble and lots of audience participation. Pauline was especially clever at choosing those in the audience who were most easily hypnotized."

"Real operators, huh?" Glimm said.

"But so far very small-time," Durant said.

"Just wait."

"Opportunity knocked or banged on their door," Arliss said, "when a woman detective, who happened to be a heavy smoker, attended one of the professional women's meetings, although I don't remember which one."

"Doesn't matter," Glimm said.

"The detective signed up for the Goodison's stop-smoking program and even joked that if they didn't make her stop smoking, she'd arrest them for fraud. But after only two sessions she did stop smoking, apparently forever."

"Why apparently?" Wu asked.

"Because I haven't seen her in several months. The detective was working on a rape case when she met the Goodisons. The victim was a seven-year-old girl who suffered traumatic memory loss and couldn't or wouldn't say who'd attacked her, although the detective had begun to suspect Uncle Ned."

Arliss poured herself some Evian water, sipped it and said, "The detective and the Goodisons were chums by then and she asked them if they'd done much work with children. They said children were often the most receptive subjects— which obviously didn't answer the question. The detective then asked if they'd be willing to hypnotize a seven-year-old rape victim suffering from traumatic memory loss. This time Pauline admitted they'd never done anything quite like that but very much wanted to cooperate with the police in any way they could."

"You're putting in too much detail," Glimm said.

"I like detail," Wu said, smiling encouragingly at Arliss.

She had another sip of Evian water. "The detective had by now struck up a kind of silent rapport with the seven-year-old girl, who hadn't said a word since her rape. But sometimes she'd nod or shake her head to the detective's questions, which is more than she'd do for her parents or anyone else. So after getting the parents' permission the detective explained everything to the child, then went to her masters and told them what she had in mind. After a certain amount of bureaucratic bump and shuffle, it was decided to give the Goodisons a try, providing a doctor was present."

"I thought the Metro cops had their own hypnotists," Durant said.

"They do," Arliss said. "But they're all male coppers. In any event, Pauline—with brother Hughes as backup—hypnotized the child, who regained both speech and memory and promptly named her dad as the rapist."

"Well, now," said Wu because Jenny Arliss had paused, as if expecting comment or exclamation.

"Then what?" Durant said.

"Then the story was leaked by someone," she said. "The police still don't know who, but I always suspected Hughes. The tabloids had a perfectly marvelous time. Hypnotized Tot Says Daddy Raped Me. Stuff like that. The tot's name was never mentioned, nor were the names of her parents—until much later. But the names of Hughes and Pauline were all over the papers and that's when I swooped in and gathered them up."

"When did all this happen?" Wu said. "A couple of years ago?"

"Just about. Since then, the Goodisons have opened four more lose-weight, stop-smoking workshops, the police've consulted them repeatedly and they've given ever so many interviews and made any number of television appearances."

"You're what—their agent?" Durant asked.

"No. *Help!* signed them solely for foreign representation on a just-in-case basis. That's how we sign all our clients. We neither charge them a fee nor take a percentage of their gross because the employer always pays our fee."

"Which is how much?" Wu asked.

"Twenty-five percent on top of what our client gets," Glimm said.

"Sounds profitable," Wu said, opened a beer, poured himself a glass, had two swallows and said, "I'd like to hear about California now—and how the Goodisons went missing."

"Okay," Glimm said. "But first I wanta mention a couple of names because, if you recognize them, it'll save a hell of a lot of time and explanation. The names are Ione Gamble and William A. C. Rice the Fourth. Ring any bells?"

Durant said, "Jilted Actress Slays Billionaire, Cops Claim."

"What about you?" Glimm said to Wu. "You up on it?"

"I've kept abreast," Wu said. "It would've been difficult not to."

"Then you know she claims she got drunk and blacked out and can't remember anything. You know about that, right?"

"We know," Durant said.

"You know about her auditions?"

"For what?" Wu said.

"For criminal defense lawyers," Glimm said. "She flew 'em in from all over, guys with big reputations. Then she picks one from Washington, D.C., who she says is the smartest man she ever met and I've gotta agree with her there. She picked Howard Mott. Know him?"

Wu looked at Durant, then said, "I don't think we've ever actually met, have we?"

"No," Durant said. "We haven't."

"But you know who he is?" Glimm said.

Wu nodded.

"Well, Mott and I've done business before so I wasn't all that surprised when I got a call from him. I was in Frankfurt and he was in L.A. Santa Monica, anyway. He tells me he's representing Ione Gamble and wants me to tell him about Hughes and Pauline Goodison. So I tell him to call Jenny here in London—or I'll have her call him. Mott says he's in a hurry, so I give him her number and he calls her. She'll tell you what happened then."

Durant and Wu looked at Jenny Arliss. She stared at Wu first, then shifted her gaze to Durant and said, "Mr. Mott rang and grilled me for thirty minutes or more about the Goodisons. I gave him some telephone numbers to call, including several at the Metropolitan Police. Two hours later he rang back and said he'd like to employ or retain the Goodisons to help Ione Gamble recover her memory. I was curious as to why he'd pick them when southern California is brimming over with all sorts of hypnotherapists, reputable and otherwise. So I asked him."

"What did he say?" Durant asked.

She looked away for a moment to stare at the portrait of Agnes Wu and the two sets of twins. She then looked back at Durant and said, "Mr. Mott wanted to engage a hypnotist— in this case, a pair of them—whose discretion would be guaranteed. He then asked if *Help!* would guarantee the Goodisons' silence or discretion, whatever. I told him of course— that we guarantee the discretion of all our specialists. We then settled on a fee and—"

Durant interrupted. "What do you mean 'guarantee'?"

"She means we'll indemnify any loss Ione Gamble takes because of the Goodisons," Glimm said. "Which could be a great big bundle." He paused to stare at Wu. "That's why I want 'em found."

After nodding pleasantly, Wu looked at Jenny Arliss and said, "You were talking about their fee."

She said, "I rang Hughes and asked whether he and Pauline would fly to Los Angeles and hypnotize Ione Gamble for one hundred thousand dollars plus expenses. He almost went into a fit but accepted, of course, and they left the next day."

"Then what?" Wu asked.

"A week later I had a call from Mr. Mott, who said the Goodisons had had three sessions with Ione Gamble. After the third session, they rang Mr. Mott at two in the morning to report a serious problem, but refused to discuss it over the phone. Mott told them not to stir, that he was coming right over. He was in a Santa Monica hotel and they were in the Bel-Air Hotel. I understand it usually takes twenty or twenty-five minutes to get from one to the other. Mr. Mott made it in less than twenty. But the Goodisons had already vanished."

"Have they been heard from since?" Wu asked.

"Mott got a call from the brother," Glimm said. "He said it was nothing but gibberish."

"So what's worrying you—blackmail?" Durant said.

"Exactly," Glimm said.

"There's no proof of it," Wu said.

"Yet," said Glimm. "Look," he continued. "Maybe they're blackmailers or maybe they aren't. Or maybe they've been kidnapped and somebody else is the blackmailer. I could maybe this and maybe that the rest of the afternoon. But maybes aren't answers, are they?"

"If it is blackmail," Wu said, "who pays—you or Gamble?"

"I do."

"You could wiggle out of it," Durant said.

"Sure," said Glimm, "but the word'd get around, wouldn't it? I'd lose all my clients and spend the rest of my life kicking myself because I didn't fork over a lousy million bucks. And when I wasn't kicking myself, I'd be talking to lawyers about how to wiggle out of the ten or fifteen million Ione Gamble's suing me for. But I don't wanta do any of that, which is why I'm hiring you guys."

"To find the Goodisons," Wu said.

Glimm nodded vigorously. "Dead, alive or in between."

"What's Howard Mott think?" Durant said.

"It doesn't matter what he thinks," Glimm said. "What matters is what I think. Mott's her defense lawyer. He's paid to think she's innocent. I don't care if she is or isn't. What I care about is finding the Goodisons. And as far as I'm concerned, guessing time's over. I want you guys out in California and I want you to either find them or find out what happened to them. You do that and maybe I can salvage something."

"Then I suggest we talk money," Wu said.

"Go ahead. Talk."

"You pay all expenses."

"If itemized."

"Some will be. Some won't be."

Glimm thought about Wu's assertion, then nodded and said, "So far, so good."

"Our fee is seven hundred and fifty thousand, regardless of outcome," Durant said. "We want two hundred and fifty thousand now, the same amount two weeks from today and the balance when it's over. If your outfit emerges from this without stain, we want a guaranteed bonus of another two hundred and fifty thousand."

"Dollars or pounds?" Glimm asked.

"Dollars."

"The bonus would jack it up to an even million. But I never paid a bonus in my life and I'm not gonna start with you two. I pay my help well, but if they don't deliver, they're out. The same goes for you. I'll pay you two hundred and fifty thousand now, two hundred and fifty thousand two weeks from now and, if I get out stain-free, you get the other two hundred and fifty thousand. If I come out dirty, you're cut off at five hundred thousand—plus that twenty-five-thousand-quid advance. That's the end of the dickering. Yes or no?"

"I think yes," Wu said. Durant only nodded.

Glimm looked at Jenny Arliss. "Cut 'em a check for the two-fifty."

"We're leaving for California tomorrow, so we'd like it this afternoon," Wu said.

Arliss glanced at her watch. "Then you and I had best share a cab to my office." She pushed back her chair and rose.

Artie Wu, again beaming, also rose and walked swiftly around the table to help Arliss into her coat.

"That woman detective," Durant said to Arliss. "How do I get in touch with her?"

She finished buttoning the coat before she replied. "Why would you want to do that?"

"She might know something useful about the Goodisons."

"She won't talk to you."

"Why not?"

Jenny Arliss started to reply, changed her mind, picked up a yellow pencil from the table, wrote something on one of the pads, ripped off the sheet, handed it to Durant and said, "Find out for yourself."

Nine

The address turned out to be a flat over a chemist's shop in Shirland Road on the northern edge of Paddington and, weather permitting, within walking distance of where Durant himself lived. After paying off the taxi, he read the names that had been printed with different ballpoint pens on two cards thumbtacked above a pair of doorbells. The name on the left was Joy Tomerlin. The name on the right was Mary Ticker. Durant rang the bell on the right.

Moments later it was answered by a woman's voice, made tinny by the intercom. "Yes?"

"It's about the Goodisons, Hughes and Pauline."

"Not interested."

"My name's Durant. I'm a friend of Jenny Arliss. She gave me your name and address."

"American, are you?"

"Right."

"Sure you're not some bloody reporter?"

"Positive."

"Well, come up, then."

The unlocking buzzer rang and Durant went through a thick glass door and up a flight of stairs to a small landing where a pair of doors gave entry to the front and rear flats.

The front flat was Mary Ticker's. Durant knocked and the door was quickly opened by a lean, not quite gaunt woman in her late thirties who wore a thick wool pullover, gray pants and a melancholy expression. A cigarette burned in her left hand.

She had very dark blue and possibly bitter eyes that had developed what Durant guessed to be a nearsighted squint. Her hair was light brown and thick and cropped short to the point of indifference. She also had a red nose, pale wide lips and prominent cheekbones, which saved the face from plainness. She had to look up at Durant, but not as much as most women, and he guessed her height at five-foot-nine or -ten.

"Detective Ticker?" Durant said.

She examined him carefully, head to foot and back up again, then shook her head and said, "No."

"But you *were* Detective Mary Ticker?"

She nodded.

"I'd like to talk to you about the Goodisons."

"Why?"

"They've disappeared."

Her instant smile was happy, even delighted, and displayed a lot of well-cared-for teeth. Then it vanished, as quickly as it came, but not before it had softened her face and erased some of the bitterness from her eyes. After the smile was gone and the bitterness back, she said, "Perhaps you'd best come in and tell me the juicy bits."

The sitting room was small and cramped and focused on a large television set with an attached VCR. Opposite the set was a kitchen alcove and just beyond it was a closed door that Durant guessed led to the bedroom and bath. Three easy chairs were drawn up to the TV set. In front of the center chair was a low table just the right size and height to hold tea and supper trays, which Durant suspected it did. The walls, he noticed, were papered with climbing pink roses interrupted here and there by inexpensive prints of rural scenes that Durant thought looked like Devon. A mirrored armoire served as a closet, and four pine shelves attached to a wall held a collection of china cats. A real cat, a fat calico, slept in one of the easy chairs.

"Do sit down," Mary Ticker said as she lowered herself into the chair by the small table. Durant thanked her and sat down in the chair not occupied by the cat. Mary Ticker lit a cigarette from the butt of the one she was smoking. Durant counted seven ashtrays scattered about the room.

"I thought the Goodisons cured you of that," he said.

"The cure didn't take, did it?" She made a small gesture with the cigarette. "Mind?"

"No."

"Tell me about their vanishing act."

"I don't know much," Durant said. "All I know is that they flew to Los Angeles to hypnotize Ione Gamble—then vanished."

"Must of been a bit of money in that."

"Quite a bit."

"Where do you fit in?"

"My firm's been hired to find them."

"What's your firm?"

"Wudu, Limited."

"Never heard of it."

"It's a small firm."

"That what it does mostly, go look for people gone missing?"

"Sometimes."

"What's it do the rest of the time?"

Durant only smiled.

"Jenny hire you?"

"Her boss did."

"The German bloke?"

Durant nodded and, after a long silence that was accompanied by a frown and three drags on her cigarette, Mary Ticker said, "They're bent, you know."

"The Goodisons?"

"Mmm."

"How bent?"

"They killed their mum and dad, they did. In Malta. Poisoned them for a flat in Hammersmith and a few thousand quid insurance money."

"But you can't prove it."

"They'd be locked away if I could."

"I thought you and the Goodisons were friends."

"That what Jenny said?"

Durant nodded.

Mary Ticker inhaled more smoke, blew it out and said, "That was before."

"Before what?"

"Before they made a fool of me." She ground out her cigarette in an ashtray, taking her time, mashing it down hard, enjoying its destruction. "You care for a drink—whisky?"

"Thanks."

"Water do? There's no ice."

"Water's fine."

She went to the kitchen alcove, poured the drinks and served them. Durant noticed that his was paler than hers. She took a swallow, lit yet another cigarette with a disposable lighter and said, "It didn't happen all at once."

Not sure what she was talking about, Durant raised an eyebrow and said, "No?"

"They played me along. Very clever they were. Know how I really quit smoking?"

"Hypnotism?"

"That was all pretend on my part. I never went into a trance. Afraid to. But after the second session I stopped smoking just to please dear Hughes and sweet Pauline. I fancied them, the pair of them."

"Anything come of it?"

"At first it was just a bit of kiss and cuddle, the three of us, with them pretending shock and shame, then leading me on and on 'til I did it."

"What?"

"Got 'em some police work."

"The rape case?" Durant said.

She nodded. "Jenny told you about that, did she?"

59

"A little."

Mary Ticker finished her drink in two swallows, then said, "Let's call her Alice."

"The little girl—the one who was raped."

"Sodomized. Made her bleed something dreadful. Parents horrified and panicky, not knowing what to do. They finally rang Paddington P.S. and I caught it."

"That's where you worked—Paddington Police Station?"

She nodded. "I got Alice to hospital and didn't let her out of my sight. Stayed right with her while the doctor made his repairs, her lying there, facedown, not making a sound, half in shock, not even crying. The doctor let me hold her hand. She was seven then, going on eight."

"Jenny Arliss said she couldn't or wouldn't talk."

"Not a word, not a sound. Didn't even shed one tear. But when the doctor was all done, she gave me a weak little smile that broke my heart."

"When did you tell the Goodisons about Alice?"

"That same night—after I got her home and tucked up in bed and made sure her mum and dad were half-sober and her uncle was there to pitch in if mum and dad passed out."

"That was Ned, wasn't it? The uncle."

The stare she gave him was cold, level and unforgiving. A true cop stare, Durant thought. "Jenny tell you Ned's name?" she asked.

Durant nodded.

"Sometimes she speaks out of turn."

"Let's get back to the Goodisons," he said.

"I needed to tell someone about Alice so Hughes and Pauline and me had supper at this Indian cafe where they do a nice curry. When I told them about Alice, they were proper shocked or acted like they were. And then, I don't know, I suppose I brought it up about them hypnotizing Alice to see if she'd say who did it."

"How'd they react—the Goodisons?"

"They were always a foxy pair. They'd been hammering

me to get 'em some police business and now, when I offer it, they go all modest and say they're not sure and perhaps they need more experience and silly things like that 'til I find myself almost begging them to do it. First they say no; then, well, perhaps, and finally they say yes. To celebrate we all go to their flat in Hammersmith and do a lot of kinky sex stuff."

"Then what?"

"Next day I talk to my governor at Paddington P.S. He's cool to the idea, but I keep after him and finally he warms up enough to say maybe—providing a doctor's present. It takes near a week to bring him around and every evening I'm spending as much time as I can with Alice, who'd started humming."

"Humming what?"

"Songs. She'd lie there and hum one song right after another. But she wouldn't say anything. Not a word. Her mum and dad're still into the gin and her Uncle Ned's flitting about, oh-dear-me-ing it all and trying to keep things tidy."

"How old were the parents and Uncle Ned?"

"All in their early thirties. Why?"

"No reason," Durant said. "Just curious."

"Well, we set a date for the session, but the Goodisons want to talk to Alice's mum and dad first. So we all meet at a cafe where Pauline and Hughes explain what they hope to do, keeping it nice and simple. But mum and dad start fretting about how much it'll cost and I keep telling them not to worry, that Paddington P.S. is paying the bill. After I finally drill that into them, they cheer up and are off to the nearest boozer. And that's when I take the Goodisons over to meet Alice and Uncle Ned. That's also where I leave 'em because I have to get back to the station."

Mary Ticker held up her empty glass and asked, "Care for another?"

Durant said, "Yes, thanks, I would."

After she came back from the kitchen alcove and handed him his drink, she swallowed some of her own, sat back down and said, "Where'd I leave off?"

"The Goodisons were with Uncle Ned."

"And Alice," she added. "It was two or three days later when they did the hypnotizing in mum and dad's sitting room. Present are me and another PC, the medic, mum and dad, Uncle Ned and the Goodisons, of course. Pauline puts Alice into a trance in less than a minute and a minute later Alice is saying it's her dad who buggered her."

"You believed her?"

"Course I did," she said. "Well, you never saw such a commotion. Dad goes for Alice and I have to knock him down. Mum's screaming bloody murder or whatever silly women scream. Uncle Ned is mincing around, wringing his hands and saying, poor little thing, poor little thing over and over 'til I tell him to put a cork in it. The other PC and the medic are trying to shut mum up and Alice just keeps babbling about all the times dad did it to her. So I collar dad and he eventually goes to trial and gets five years. Mum just disappears and Alice goes to live with her Uncle Ned and by then the Goodisons are halfway to being famous from all the publicity."

"How were you getting along with them by then?" Durant asked.

"Not at all. They dropped me."

"You ever see Alice after she'd gone to live with Uncle Ned?"

"I'd stop by sometimes when I had a moment. And I had a moment one Sunday morning. It was her birthday, her ninth, and I went by with a present. I knocked because the bell'd never worked. When no one came I tried the door and it was off the latch and I went in. I thought I'd leave my present and go. Then I heard it. A kind of moaning. It wasn't a big flat, about like this, but on the ground floor."

She paused to swallow more whisky and light another cigarette. She then sighed the smoke out and said, "There they were, starkers and having at it, sweet Alice and nice Uncle Ned. I went quite mad."

"How?"

"I grabbed Alice and locked her in the bath. Then I went for Uncle Ned and broke his fucking arm, the left one. Then I swore I'd break his right one if he didn't tell me the truth. Well, he told me the truth and I broke his fucking right arm anyway."

"It was Uncle Ned and Alice all along, not dad and Alice, right?" Durant said.

She gave him a weary nod. "They'd been going at it since she was five. Uncle Ned'd paid Hughes and Pauline three thousand quid to make it look real. Hughes and Pauline'd coached Alice how to act hypnotized, what to say about her dad and how to say it. Hughes got a friend to tip off the press. It was a right mess."

She finished her second drink, which seemed to have had no effect. There was a cigarette burning in an ashtray that she must have forgotten because she lit a fresh one with the lighter. She blew out the smoke and said, "Nobody believed me. Uncle Ned claimed I'd broken in and assaulted him. Alice backed him up and said I'd tried to fondle her more than once. When the Goodisons were questioned they said I'd made advances to Pauline. I was allowed to resign without any fuss. It was all kept very, very quiet—especially since it was about then that poor old dad killed himself."

She looked at Durant with her cold hard cop's stare. "You know what happens to kiddy freaks in the nick?"

Durant nodded.

"Well, they did old dad over and over. When he couldn't stand any more, he went to bed one night with a plastic sack over his head and never woke up."

"You making it all right now?" Durant said.

"I work in the shop downstairs. He deals uppers and downers to a select clientele and likes having an ex-copper around in case a customer drops in and gets nasty when he can't buy on credit. I'm paid off the books and, well, it's enough."

"What happened to Alice?"

"I never asked," Mary Ticker said, frowned as if she'd just thought of something and said, "Any chance they're dead?"

"The Goodisons?"

She nodded.

"It's possible."

"That's nice," she said with a small smile that almost made her look content, if far from happy.

Ten

Because of the international date line, Artie Wu's 12:04 A.M. long-distance call on Tuesday from London was answered by Booth Stallings at 8:04 A.M. on Wednesday in his three-room suite at Manila's Peninsula Hotel.

Wu and Stallings had not spoken to each other in five years and, consequently, there was a minute or so of what Stallings regarded as expensive pro forma greetings and salutations before Wu got to the business at hand.

"Let's talk money, Booth, because if we can't agree on that, there's no point in talking about the rest."

"Suits me."

"The initial fee is five hundred thousand. If we do what we've been hired to do, there'll be another two hundred and fifty thousand, making a total of seven hundred and fifty thousand. Out of the total, Quincy and I, as principals, will draw two hundred thousand each. You, Otherguy and Georgia, one hundred thousand each."

"Sounds plump, if not fat," Stallings said.

"The client retained our firm's services for a nonrefundable twenty-five thousand pounds. But that money's earmarked for back salaries, debts and overhead."

"You must've passed through a dry spell, Artie."

"Bone dry."

"If my addition's right," Stallings said, "the figures you mentioned, not counting the retainer, add up to seven hundred thousand, not seven hundred and fifty thousand."

"That remaining fifty thousand will be held in reserve for contingencies until the job's done. If there aren't any contingencies, it'll be split into five equal shares as either a bonus or getaway money."

"Or both," Stallings said.

"Or both."

"You're beginning to make it sound kind of interesting. What do we have to do to earn it?"

"Find two missing hypnotists."

"What else?"

"That's the goal, but to reach it we'll probably have to travel the usual twisty byways."

"Where're these byways located?"

"Los Angeles and environs."

"Well, shit, I was kind of hoping for London and environs."

"The weather's better in L.A."

"There's that," Stallings agreed.

After the briefest of pauses, Wu said, "Can you talk?"

"Georgia's not up yet."

"When did she get out?"

"Yesterday afternoon. I picked her up at the Women's Correctional Institution in Mandaluyong in a Mercedes I rented from the Peninsula. Even brought along flowers and a bottle of champagne. She drank some champagne but left the flowers in the car when we got back to the hotel."

"How is she?"

"Doesn't look much different."

"Mentally?"

"Quick as ever. Maybe even quicker. But I suppose there're some emotional dents that need smoothing out."

"What've you told her?"

"Just that you and Durant have something going and want her, Otherguy and me to help out."

"What'd she say?"

"She said it sounded like more nursery games."

"That all?"

"That's all so far."

"She may need a large helping of reassurance."

"Tell me something, Artie. How d'you reassure someone with a rock-solid ego?"

"You'll find a way," Wu said and paused. During the pause Stallings heard a faint click from twelve thousand miles away, which he assumed was Wu's lighter. The click was followed by either a sigh or the sound of exhaled cigar smoke. Then Wu was saying, "I have a little news and a little clarification. The hypnotists are a rather bent British brother-and-sister team who've been involved with Ione Gamble."

"America's heartthrob," Stallings said.

"She really called that?"

"Mostly by old crocks like me who find comfort in the clichés of their youth. Truth is, Artie, I haven't kept up with Hollywood much since Sheilah Graham died."

"Then you may not've heard that Ms. Gamble has been indicted for the murder of William A. C. Rice the Fourth."

"They deliver *USA Today* right to your hotel room door all over the world. I saw the headlines, but can't say I've followed it closely."

"Then you may want to do some research on it."

"Okay."

"My news is that Ms. Gamble has retained your son-in-law to defend her."

"I've got two sons-in-law," Stallings said. "One of 'em's too dumb to pour piss out of a rubber boot and isn't a lawyer anyway, so you must be talking about Howie Mott, right?"

"Yes."

"You know Howie? I guess you do since he's the one who recommended you guys to me back in eighty-six."

"We've never met," Wu said. "But we seem to have a number of mutual friends."

Stallings only grunted and said, "When d'you want us in L.A.?"

"Can you leave tomorrow?"

"First-class?"

"I think Georgia deserves some first-class."

"So does she," Stallings said. "Anything I can do in L.A.?"

"Yes. Rent us a furnished house, something ostentatious in the Palisades or Malibu. One that's large enough to accommodate the five of us. Rent it for a month with the understanding that we can extend for another month. I'll wire-transfer fifty thousand in your name to the Bank of America—the branch on the old Malibu Road. Establish a regular checking account with you, Quincy and me as signatories, draw what cash you need and ask the bank manager to recommend a real estate agent."

"Who am I?" Stallings said.

"You're the permanent representative of Wudu, Limited, Eight Bruton Street, Berkeley Square, London west one. You were formerly our permanent representative in the Middle East, headquartered in Amman, where you conducted research, surveys ad nauseam."

"Speaking of ad nauseam," Stallings said, "has Otherguy shown up?"

"Quincy's giving him dinner—or supper—and telling him pretty much what I've told you."

"I bet Otherguy tells Quincy he knows Ione Gamble personally."

In London, there was either a sigh or more cigar smoke being exhaled before Artie Wu said, "The wonderful thing is, he just might."

*   *   *

After the room service waiter had rolled in the breakfast cart and left, Booth Stallings crossed the suite's living room, heading for Georgia Blue's closed bedroom door. Before he reached it, the door opened and she came out, walking on bare feet and wearing one of the hotel's white terry-cloth robes.

Stallings noticed for what must have been the seventh time in less than twenty-four hours that she still moved with the same graceful stride on those long, long legs that made her stand five-ten in her bare feet and at least six-even in heels. Her light green eyes skipped over Stallings to the breakfast cart. When she reached it, she lifted up lids and sniffed hungrily at each dish. Just before reaching for a serving spoon, she ran her hand through her short reddish-brown hair that now boasted a short streak of white less than an inch wide. It had turned white in prison shortly after her thirty-fifth birthday not quite two years ago. The streak was centered above her high broad forehead, behind which, Stallings had long thought, lurked far too many brains.

As Georgia Blue stood there, heaping scrambled eggs, sausage and tropical fruit onto her plate—wearing no makeup, her hair brushed and combed by that one swipe of her hand—Stallings tried to decide whether his infatuation with her had finally turned into an obsession. He had just decided he didn't really give a damn what it was when she added two soft rolls to her plate and said, "Christ, Booth, you ordered enough for six."

"Breakfast is the most important meal of the day if you listen to the hog growers, cereal manufacturers and the butter and egg folks."

"Milk," she said, pouring herself a glass. "I never thought I'd dream about milk."

She carried the plate and glass over to a small dining table, set them down and returned to the cart for a fork and spoon, ignoring the knives. Once seated, she attacked the food, sending an occasional wary glance at Stallings, who was filling his own plate with bacon and eggs.

He looked at her, noticed one of the wary glances and said, "Slow down, Georgia. Nobody's going to snatch it away from you."

She ignored him and went on with her rapid eating.

Stallings sat down opposite her, buttered a roll and asked, "Why didn't you lose any weight?"

"Because I took food away from the smaller and weaker women."

"Wonder they didn't get together and beat up on you."

"By then I was the mean gang's number one ass-kicker."

Although her plate was still half-full, she put her fork and spoon down, leaned back in the chair, stared at Stallings and said, "If we're going to leave tomorrow for Los Angeles, I have to buy some stuff."

"Don't think I said anything about leaving tomorrow."

"Artie did. I picked up his call between rings, just like the Secret Service taught me, and listened to you two fretting over me like a couple of old-maid aunts. Whatever shall we do about Georgia, poor thing? Well, the first thing you can do is get me some stuff."

"What kind of stuff?" Stallings asked.

She smiled at him. "You think I mean dope, don't you?"

"Whatever you want."

"Look, I'm a convicted felon with a commuted sentence, not a pardon. If I'd been convicted in the States, I couldn't vote or serve on a jury or be elected President unless one of the states restored my civil rights—although the only civil right most felons in California want restored is their right to own a gun. But I was convicted in another country and I'm not sure what the law is, although I'm damn sure the American embassy isn't going to bust its collective gut to supply me with a fresh passport or the piece of paper it gives felons who want to go home."

"How come you weren't deported?"

"That was part of the deal I cut—no deportation."

"Okay. You need a passport. What else?"

"Clothes."

"Get dressed and we'll go across the street and take care of the passport photos. Then I'll give you some money and you can buy what clothes you need while I go find you a passport."

"You know how?"

"I know how."

"Must've been quite a learning experience—hanging out with Otherguy for what—five years now?"

"About that."

"How is he? Not that I give a damn."

"As ever."

70

"Why'd Artie and Durant send you to fetch me and not Otherguy?"

"Because Artie thinks I'm still stuck on you."

"Are you?"

"What d'you think?"

"I hope not because I can't give you anything but sex," she said and then tacked on a perfectly neutral, "baby."

"Maybe that's all I want," Stallings said.

Eleven

After his third taxi ride, Booth Stallings made his fourth telephone call, this time from the lobby of the Manila Hotel. It was answered on the first ring by yet another Filipino-accented voice, a woman's, who told him the pickup would take place in exactly six minutes, one hundred meters south of the hotel on Roxas Boulevard. Stallings was there at 12:08 P.M. and a minute later was climbing into the rear seat of a 1974 Toyota sedan that had a young Filipino driver and failed air-conditioning.

Next to the driver was his equally young wife, girlfriend or even, Stallings suspected, the other half of a New Peoples Army hit squad, which the Filipinos, with their love of nick-names, had dubbed sparrow teams. The pair gave Stallings a sweltering, aimless and mostly silent tour of Manila that lasted exactly fifty-nine minutes.

Stallings was surprised, if not shocked, by how much the sprawling city had decayed since he was last there in early 1988 with Otherguy Overby during their attempt to make a financial comeback after their losses in the stock market crash of 1987.

It was only after Overby explained his scheme again and again, step by step, that Stallings had agreed to buy into the syndicate then being formed to search for the five or fifty or even one hundred tons of gold bullion that, according to legend, had been buried, booby-trapped and abandoned by General Yamashita Tomoyuki, the Tiger of Malaya, as his Japanese army retreated from Manila in the early months of 1945.

Stallings, who considered himself something of an authority on the Philippines, argued that Yamashita's Gold, as it was called, hadn't been buried by Yamashita at all, but by Iwabuchi Sanji, the tough and ruthless Japanese rear admiral who reoccupied Manila after Yamashita fled.

It was the admiral who had waged the bitter house-to-house battle for Manila, destroying the city in the process. And it was this last utterly senseless battle that had given Admiral Iwabuchi the time he needed to bury the gold bullion.

Otherguy Overby had listened patiently to Stallings's lengthy recitation. When it was over, he asked, "You really believe the gold's there, don't you?"

"You don't?"

"I believe other people believe it's there," Overby said, "just like I believe other people believe in immaculate conception. And that's what we're buying into, Booth—pure blind faith."

After three gold bars with Japanese stampings were discovered a month later at the site of the digging just north of Manila, the syndicate shares soared and Overby and Stallings promptly dumped theirs, realizing an 800 percent profit even after taking into account the cost of the three gold bars Overby had bought, doctored and with which he had salted the digging.

*   *   *

The young woman in the front seat who, Stallings guessed, couldn't have been more than 20 or 21, finally turned around and asked, "How do you like our deterioration?"

"Seems to be coming along nicely."

"You have been to Manila before?"

Stallings said he had been there in 1945, 1986 and 1988.

She turned back to the driver and said, "He was here with MacArthur!" The driver shrugged, muttered something that sounded like "Who cares?" and honked at an errant motor scooter.

The aimless tour ended at a large one-story house on the very edge of a vast dismal slum. Built of concrete blocks, the house boasted a sharply pitched roof of corrugated iron that was half-covered by a magnificent bougainvillea. A crude stake-and-chickenwire fence surrounded the hard-packed dirt in front of the house and served as a pen for two goats, three ducks, six hens and a rooster.

After the Toyota came to a stop, the young woman again turned to say, "She's waiting for you."

Stallings said, "Thanks for the ride," left the car, finally figured out how to open the gate, went through it, carefully fastened it behind him, walked to the open front door and knocked.

A muscular Filipino of 35 or so, wearing a faded Batman T-shirt, appeared and greeted Stallings with a scowl and a long hard stare that was finally ended by an abrupt nod, which Stallings interpreted to mean, "Well, now that you're here, come on in."

Inside, the man vanished through another door and Stallings found himself in a square room with two dozen folding metal chairs arranged in three rows in front of an old flattop wooden desk. In the center of the desk was a telephone. Around the four edges of the desktop were scores of closely spaced cigarette burns. Against a wall to the left of the desk stood a padlocked steel cabinet, the kind that holds office supplies, and just to its left was an aging Toshiba copier.

A round-faced woman in her mid-forties with graying hair sat behind the desk. She wore a large, loose-fitting cotton dress patterned with giant sunflowers. Despite the tentlike dress, Stallings decided she wasn't nearly as heavy as she was when he had last seen her in Hong Kong five years ago.

"How are you, Minnie?"

Minnie Espiritu leaned back in her chair, studied him gravely, then smiled and said, "Sit down, Booth."

Stallings chose one of the folding chairs in the front row. "You've taken some weight off," he said. "Looks good."

"The cancer took it off and I look like hell."

"Sorry. I didn't know."

"Why would you? They went in and cut and claim they got it all, but . . ." She shrugged.

"Anything I can—"

"Nothing," she said, not allowing him to finish.

There was a short silence until Stallings said, "Those two kids gave me a tour. Everything's falling apart, isn't it?"

She sighed first, then nodded and said, "They traded Marcos-style graft for the Aquino brand and now everybody's shocked that there's not a damn bit of difference. Our economy's a basket case but all we do is squabble with Washington over those lousy military bases. You know something, Booth? We slid from a third world country into a fourth world catastrophe, right down there with Bangladesh, and nobody's noticed and nobody's cared."

"How goes the revolution, Minnie?"

"The Berlin Wall almost squashed it. But we're still struggling. Somebody has to—although I sometimes think if it was really up to me, I'd sell it all to the Japanese and let 'em turn it into golf courses and whorehouses."

She sighed again and lit a cigarette after first offering the pack to Stallings, who declined with a headshake. When the cigarette was lit, she blew smoke at the ceiling and said, "What d'you want, Booth?"

"A passport."

"What kind?"

"U.S."

"Who for?"

Stallings reached into the side pocket of his tan poplin jacket, brought out a passport-size color photograph, rose and placed it on the desk. "Remember her?" he asked as he sat back down.

Minnie Espiritu leaned forward to peer at the photograph of Georgia Blue. "Sure. Miss Hardcase of 1986. The ex-Secret Service lady. She crossed you guys and did five years here in

Welfareville. Then she cut herself a deal with Cory's opposition and they got her sentence commuted."

Minnie Espiritu looked up at Stallings, gave him a smile that was almost a grin and asked, "Is this business, romance or a little of both?"

"I'm of an extremely forgiving nature."

"You're also a damned old fool," she said, glared at her cigarette, dropped it on the concrete floor and ground it out with a shoe. She was still grinding at it when she said, "It'll cost you five thousand U.S."

"Jesus."

"That's my last price."

"What's the quality?"

"Perfect. We found ourselves a degenerate gambler in your embassy, bought up his markers and sold 'em back to him for ten virgin passport blanks. We can offer you something that looks like it just came out of Washington."

"Sold."

"Then I need Blue's full name and a date and place of birth."

Stallings's right hand dipped back into the jacket pocket and came out with a slip of paper. He rose, handed it to Minnie Espiritu, sat back down and asked, "When can I pick it up?"

"If you brought the money, you can wait for it."

"I'll wait," Stallings said, unbuttoned the three middle buttons of his shirt and zipped open the nylon money belt.

*　　*　　*

At 11:25 A.M. the following day, Stallings and Georgia Blue sat in the departure lounge of China Airlines at Benigno Aquino International Airport, waiting for their flight to Taipei, when a medium-size Filipino in his late thirties or early forties came up to them, smiled and said, "You two make a cute couple."

Georgia Blue looked up from her copy of *Time* to examine the faultless ice-cream suit, shiny black pompadour, pale beige complexion, inquisitive nose, perfect, if meaningless, smile and the big dark brown eyes that advertised just how smart he really was.

She smiled back, nudged Stallings and said, "You remember Lieutenant Cruz, sweetie—the nice policeman?"

"*Captain* Cruz," the man said.

"Of course," she said. "It would be by now, wouldn't it? Congratulations."

Cruz gave her a brief smile of thanks, turned to Stallings and said, "You and I met five years ago."

"So we did."

"I'm here for two reasons. The first is to wave goodbye and the second is to ask you about a funny-strange phone call I got a week or ten days ago. But before we go into that, I need to see your passports and tickets."

"Why?" Stallings said.

"Why not?"

Stallings shrugged and handed over his passport and the tickets. Georgia Blue's passport followed a moment later.

Captain Cruz examined the tickets first. "China Airlines to Taipei, then a connection with Singapore Airlines for a first-class, one-stop flight to Los Angeles. Should be fairly pleasant."

After handing back the tickets, he studied Stallings's passport. "How was Jordan?"

"Raining when I left," Stallings said.

"Really," Cruz said, returned the passport and began a careful examination of Georgia Blue's. Finally, he looked at her and asked, "Enjoy your extended stay in the Philippines, Miss Blue?"

"Not really."

"Planning a return trip?"

"No."

"Remarkable document," he said, tapping her passport against his left thumbnail. He went on with the tapping as if it might help him decide whether to confiscate or return it. Beneath Cruz's creamy jacket there was a slight movement of the shoulders, which Stallings interpreted as a shrug. He discovered he was right seconds later when Cruz handed Blue her passport and said, "Have a safe flight."

Before she could say thank you or anything else, Stallings asked, "What about that funny-strange phone call?"

"Right," Cruz said. "The phone call. Well, it came from Germany—Frankfurt—and the caller said his name was Glimm. Enno Glimm. Know him?"

Stallings shook his head.

"He wanted to know if I'd recommend, or maybe just vouch for, Artie Wu and Quincy Durant, your ex-what? Partners?"

"Recommend them for what?"

"Some sort of vague and strictly temporary deal. Glimm wasn't specific. In fact, the only thing he was specific about was that it's not going to happen here, whatever it is. But I had to work to even get that much out of him. Then after I heard you were passing through town, it hit me that maybe you'd know what Wu and Durant are up to."

"Haven't seen either of them in at least five years."

"Too bad."

"Did you?" Stallings said. "Recommend them?"

"I told Glimm that, as a policeman, I couldn't possibly recommend them to anybody. But if I weren't a policeman and needed somebody to, say, see me safely to the gates of hell and back, I'd certainly call on Wu and that—uh—Quincy Durant."

Georgia Blue rose and said, "They're calling our flight."

Captain Hermenegildo Cruz cocked his head to the right and smiled up at Georgia Blue, who, in her heels, topped him by four inches. He said, "Don't come back. Don't even think about it."

She gave him her nicest smile. "What a sensible suggestion."

Twelve

Seated once again behind the Memphis cotton broker's desk, Ione Gamble used only silence and a pencil to create a tension so palpable that Howard Mott thought he could almost taste and feel it. If she were to increase the tension only slightly, he suspected it would taste like electricity must taste and feel like a death threat must feel.

He judged Gamble's performance to be superb and wondered which bits and pieces he would eventually steal or borrow for his own use in future courtroom appearances. Mott particularly admired the way she had helped set the scene by skinning her thick light brown hair back into a spinster's knot and scrubbing all makeup from her face to emphasize its remarkable character and minimize its essential prettiness. However, the prettiness quota was amply filled by her obviously bare breasts beneath a simple white polo shirt.

And finally there was the pencil—long, yellow and freshly sharpened—which she had studied for nearly three silent minutes, turning it this way and that, but making sure its point always swung back, compass-like, until it was aimed directly at Howard Mott's throat.

Mott was again sitting on the couch with the chintz slip-cover. Jack Broach, the elegant agent-lawyer-business manager, was back in the no-nonsense armchair and it was he who broke the tension with a question: "Ione, will you stop fucking with that pencil?"

Gamble looked up with a practice-perfect expression of surprised hurt, then looked down at the pencil, as if she had never seen it before. Slowly opening her hand, she let it roll from her fingers and fall to the desk with a small clatter and bounce. "I'm sorry," she said. "I—I didn't realize."

Jack Broach praised the performance with three weary handclaps.

Ignoring Broach, she gave Mott a too-sweet smile and said, "I was wondering, Howie, if you'd mind explaining just one more time—and do try to make it simple—why you ever hired those two shit-for-brains hypnotists."

"Of course," Mott said. "As I mentioned before, I first learned of them from a favorable account in a British law journal. But I hired them only after talking to three reputable barristers in London, who recommended them highly, as did two ranking Metropolitan Police officers. Of equal importance, at least to me, was the fact that the Goodisons, brother Hughes and sister Pauline, were clients of Enno Glimm—"

"The hypnotist broker," she said.

"—which is in itself sufficient recommendation."

"You mean Glimm offers a money-back guarantee that his hypnotists won't turn out to be blackmailers or rip-off artists?"

"Exactly," said Mott. "In fact, he's already taken corrective measures, not the least of them being the return of the hundred-and-twenty-five-thousand-dollar fee you paid for the Goodisons' services." Mott turned to Broach. "You got the money, right?"

Broach nodded. "By wire transfer yesterday."

Gamble again picked up the yellow pencil and absently tested its point with a thumb. "You said Glimm's taken 'corrective measures.' What are they—other than sending back my money?"

"He's retained—at his own considerable expense—a London firm called Wudu, Limited. Its job is to track down the

Goodisons and provide any assistance you and I might require."

"Spell Wudu."

After Mott spelled it, she asked, "What's it mean?"

"Nothing. It's only a play on the two partners' surnames, Arthur Wu and Quincy Durant."

"Wu'd be what—Chinese?"

"Yes."

"So now I have to depend on a couple of English twits to save me from the gallows."

"Gas chamber," Broach said.

Before Gamble could snarl or swear at Broach, Mott said, "Both Wu and Durant are American and I assure you they're not twits."

"What are they, then—confidential inquiry agents to the gentry?"

Mott was about to reply when Broach snapped his fingers and said, "Christ, yes! Ivory, Lace and Silk, right?"

The question went to Mott, who, after a moment's hesitation, agreed with a slight nod.

Obviously irritated, Ione Gamble asked, "The folksingers? The ones I used to listen to when I was a real little kid? What the hell've they got to do with me?"

"With you, nothing," Broach said. "But with Wu and Durant, a hell of a lot. Remember when Silk disappeared back in the seventies?"

Gamble shook her head.

"It was these same two guys, Wu and Durant, who found her and turned Pelican Bay inside out doing it." He again looked at Mott for confirmation. "Right, Howie?"

"That's a fair summary."

"What happened to them?" Gamble asked.

"Wu and Durant?"

"No, goddamnit. Ivory, Lace and Silk."

Broach studied the back of his hand for a moment, then turned it over and studied his palm. One side or the other apparently jogged his memory. "Ivory died of an overdose in Miami, I think. Lace'd married a semi-billionaire and got

81

out of the business. The last I heard of Silk she was down in El Salvador doing the Lord's work."

Gamble turned to look through her floor-to-ceiling plate-glass window at canyon and ocean. She was still staring at her view when she said, "What brand are they, Howie?"

A puzzled Mott turned to Broach, who said, "She wants to know their religion—Wu and Durant's."

"May I ask why?" Mott said, putting an edge on his question.

Gamble turned from the window. "I don't care what they are. It just helps me crawl inside their heads."

"They're not characters in a play."

"Humor me."

Mott flicked an invisible something from the left sleeve of his dark blue suit and said, "I believe both Wu and Durant are nominal Methodists since, at age fourteen, they ran away together from a Methodist orphanage in San Francisco. By now, of course, they may've switched brands—or abstained altogether."

"When do I meet them?"

"Late this afternoon or early evening?"

"Anytime," she said, paused, then asked, "If you had to pick one word to describe them what would it be?"

"Resourceful," Mott said without hesitation. "Extremely resourceful—although that's two words."

"Resourceful enough to find the Goodison creeps?"

"Definitely."

"Resourceful enough to find out who killed Billy Rice?"

Mott looked at her steadily before asking, "If you're really sure you want to know that."

Ione Gamble frowned and bit her lower lip. Then the biting stopped and the frown went away and she said, "I'm sure."

*　　*　　*

The manager of the Bank of America branch on the old Malibu Road wasn't particularly impressed by the $50,000 Artie Wu had wired Booth Stallings. She routinely opened a regular joint checking account for him, provided two signature cards for Wu and Durant to fill out and handed over $5,000 in cash without caution or comment. When Stallings asked for the name of a real estate agent who handled "the larger beachfront rental properties," she promptly recommended Phil Quill.

"He's also an actor," she said. "You probably saw him in either *Miami Vice* or an episode or two of *Jake and the Fatman*."

Quill's name was somehow familiar to Stallings, but not from any television series. He admitted as much to the bank manager, excusing his ignorance by again mentioning that he had spent much of the past five years abroad, most recently in Amman as the permanent representative of Wudu, Ltd.

She said, "I was almost sure they'd dubbed *Miami Vice* into Arabic."

* * *

After they arrived at Los Angeles International Airport the previous evening, Stallings had rented a Lincoln Town Car from the Budget people. He and Georgia Blue then headed for the 405 freeway and switched from it to the 10 that ended at the Pacific Ocean. Fifteen miles farther north on the Pacific Coast Highway, they found themselves in Malibu, looking for a motel.

Georgia Blue was the first to notice the Malibu Beach Inn, a large three-story affair of an artful Spanish Colonial design that almost made it look old. From a brief visit to Malibu in 1986, Stallings thought he remembered another motel that had once stood on the same site. The vanished motel had had a vaguely Polynesian name—something like the Manakura or the Tonga Lei or maybe even the Tondaleya.

The Malibu Beach Inn rented them two adjoining rooms for $180 a night each. They were large nicely furnished rooms that featured an ocean view and the sound of pounding surf. The man who helped with the bags looked like a retired lifeguard or maybe a superannuated surfer who, without the hint of a leer, informed Stallings that X-rated videotapes were available from the motel's library. Stallings said he was too sleepy, tipped the bellhop, or whatever he was, five dollars and, when he was gone, knocked on Georgia Blue's connecting door.

She said through the door that she'd see him in the morning. Stallings found some miniatures of Scotch in the mini-refrigerator, mixed a drink, opened a can of cashew nuts and went out on the balcony. He sat there, drinking the Scotch, eating the nuts and wondering why he hadn't moved to Malibu in 1949 and gone into real estate.

*   *   *

The next morning Stallings and Georgia Blue went down to the lobby for the inn's complimentary buffet breakfast. Stallings's breakfast was two cups of coffee. Georgia Blue had just finished two glasses of milk, whole-wheat toast and a mound of fruit when a tanned stocky man entered the lobby, looked around, saw Stallings and Blue, gave them a dazzling smile and walked toward them with quick small steps that scarcely seemed to touch the Mexican tiles. Those quick light steps nudged Stallings's memory and he finally remembered who Phil Quill had once been.

The real estate man was wearing double-pleated gabardine slacks that were several shades paler than daisy yellow; sockless thin-soled loafers, which Georgia Blue, if not Stallings, knew to be Ferragamos; a dark blue polo shirt, probably from the Gap, and five or six hundred dollars' worth of light blue cashmere sweater that hung down his broad back, its sleeves crossed over his breastbone in the loosest of knots. Quill had just shoved a pair of sunglasses up into thick, still-blond hair, revealing a pair of blue eyes that nearly matched his sweater and the ocean.

When he reached their table, he used a soft southern voice to say, "I'm Phil Quill, the real estate man. Betty at the bank said you all'd like to rent a beach place for a month or so." He smiled again. "Providing, of course, that you, ma'am, are Miss Blue and you, sir, are Mr. Stallings."

Stallings rose, said, "We are indeed," then shook the offered hand and invited him to join them for coffee or even breakfast.

"A cup of coffee would be nice and I'll fetch it myself."

As Quill quickstepped away, Georgia Blue watched him go and said, "I wonder why he walks like that?"

"At one time he could do it backwards or sideways almost as fast."

"When?"

"When he was quarterback for Arkansas in the early sixties. He even made UPI All-American his senior year."

"You saw him play?"

"On TV."

Quill returned, sat down, sipped his coffee, then asked a question. The first half of it was directed to Georgia Blue, the second half to Stallings. "I wonder if you folks could give me some idea? Of just what kind of place you're looking for?"

"We'd like something right on the beach with at least five bedrooms," Stallings said.

"For how long?"

"One month—with an option to extend for another month."

"You all want it close in, far out or sorta in between? Reason I ask is because Malibu's about twenty-five miles long and a mile thick."

"What about around in here?" Blue said.

"Well, around in here, Miss Blue, is practically Carbon Beach and that gets expensive now that it's February and the snowbirds are flying down from Canada and the Europeans are swarming in to take advantage of the two-dollar pound, the sixty-nine-cent mark and the damn near twenty-cent franc."

"What do you call expensive?" Stallings asked.

"Ten, fifteen, twenty thousand a month."

"You have anything with five bedrooms in that price range?"

Quill gave his magnificent chin a quick brush with his left thumb, as if it helped him think. Stallings touched his own chin, almost by reflex, and said, "You used to do that just before you passed, didn't you?"

It had been a long time since Stallings had seen a grown

man blush, but Quill turned quite pink. He then tried a grin that was almost a grimace. "I keep hoping folks'll say, 'Hey, didn't I see you in *Bloody Valentine* and also in that MOW turkey, *Pickled Noon?*' But none of 'em ever remember the fourteen features and fifty-one series episodes I've been in. All they remember is football."

"Sorry I mentioned it," Stallings said.

"Well, it's just that I'd rather be known for what I've done these last twenty-five years instead of for what I did between the ages of eighteen and twenty-one. I could've turned pro but didn't. Instead, I came out here right after college and thought of myself as an actor ever since—even though there was one month in nineteen eighty-eight when I made more in real estate commissions than I ever made acting—and that includes all my TV residuals."

"I'll always think of you as an actor, Mr. Quill," Blue said.

"Appreciate that, Miss Blue, but right now I gotta change back to Phil Quill, real estate man."

He looked at Stallings again, then back at Georgia Blue, frowned a little, gave the great chin another quick thumb brush and said, "You all seem like sensible, sophisticated folks, and I'm not using 'sophisticated' in any pejorative sense. So that's why I'm gonna ask you this question." After an actor's short beat, Quill said, "Would you consider renting a mighty fine six-bedroom house smack-dab on Carbon Beach for fifteen thousand a month even if its former owner got shot dead in it last New Year's Eve or thereabouts?"

"Who got shot dead?" Stallings said.

"William A. C. Rice the Rich. The cops say Ione Gamble shot him."

"It's right on the beach?" Georgia Blue said.

"With your own one hundred feet of sand."

"Fifteen thousand?" Stallings said.

"Yes, sir."

"Take twelve-five?"

"Take thirteen-five."

"With an option to extend?"

"Yes, sir, I can do that."

"We'll take it."

"Don't you all wanta go look at it first?"

"You said it was nice, Mr. Quill," Georgia Blue said. "Just how nice will be our surprise."

Thirteen

Artie Wu, pushing a loaded baggage cart, was in the lead at 1:37 that same afternoon when he, Otherguy Overby and Quincy Durant came up the long ramp that led from customs and immigration to the airport's international reception area where Booth Stallings waited with Georgia Blue.

Durant watched as Wu gave Georgia Blue a smile, a hug, a kiss and some words of warm greeting before turning to shake hands with Stallings. Overby was next. He patted her on the cheek, which almost made her flinch, then said something that almost made her smile.

An unsmiling Durant went up to her and held out his hand. She took it and said, "Let's hear it, Quincy."

He let her hand go and said, "Don't try to fuck me over again, Georgia."

They stared at each other for several seconds before she replied with two thoughtful nods, which Durant interpreted as, "Maybe I will" and "Maybe I won't." What she actually said was, "You look about the same."

"So do you."

"No, I don't."

Durant studied her streak of white hair. "You going to keep it?"

"As a reminder."

"I like it," he said and turned away to greet Booth Stallings.

*　　*　　*

With his coat and tie off and the sleeves of his custom-made white shirt folded back two careful turns, Otherguy Overby headed the rented Lincoln Town Car into the Airport Return shortcut that led back to the international terminal where Artie Wu by now should have completed his phone call.

Next to Overby in the front seat was Georgia Blue. In the rear were Durant and Stallings. After the four of them had reached the third floor of the parking lot and loaded the luggage into the Lincoln's trunk, Overby offered to drive. Stallings tossed him the keys and said, "It's all yours."

"Which way?" Overby said.

"Malibu," said Stallings, who thought of himself as one of those rare Americans who regarded automobiles as more nuisance than necessity. There had been times in his life, especially when abroad and poking around in terrorism, that he had gone for as long as eighteen months without ever riding in a private automobile. He had instead walked, bicycled or taken taxis and public transport. He was now almost sure he would never buy another car—unless, of course, he stumbled across an incredibly cheap Morgan or maybe a Jowett-Jupiter.

Overby spotted Wu waiting at the curb. After the Lincoln pulled over and stopped, Wu got into the rear seat next to Stallings and said, "Quincy and I're—" He broke off as Overby expertly cut off a hotel shuttle van, then bullied his way to the airport road's far left lane. Wu realized he had been holding his breath until assured of safe passage. He used the withheld breath to complete his announcement. "Quincy and I're to meet Ione Gamble at five this afternoon."

"You talked to her?" Durant asked.

"No. To Howard Mott." He looked at Stallings. "Your son-in-law asked me to tell you your grandson and namesake is thriving."

The new grandfather smiled slightly. "They named the kid Booth Stallings Mott. It didn't occur to either of them that by the time he's in the second grade, or maybe even the first, the other kids'll be calling him B.S."

Georgia Blue asked, "Have you seen him yet?"

"Not yet. But I haven't been back to Washington in five years. Anyway, the kid's still in the gurgle-and-coo stage so maybe I'll wait till he's three or four and has something to say."

Overby had turned north on Sepulveda, heading for Lincoln Boulevard. Wu leaned forward and asked, "Where to, Otherguy?"

"Booth says Malibu."

Wu leaned back and asked Stallings, "Any problem with the checking account?"

"None. I have blank checks and signature cards for you and Quincy in my pocket."

"Any leads on a house yet?"

"Remember Phil Quill?"

Wu frowned, then brightened. "The Razorback quarterback."

"He rented us a house."

"His?"

"No, he's a Malibu real estate agent now—when he's not acting, which seems to be most of the time."

"Nice place?" Durant asked.

"Right on the beach."

"How many bedrooms?"

"Six bedrooms, seven baths."

"How much?"

"Quill was asking fifteen but came down to thirteen-five."

"Whose house is it?" Wu said.

To make sure he didn't miss Wu's reaction, Stallings turned to look at him. He noticed Georgia Blue had also turned around in the front seat. "The house is in a kind of legal

90

limbo right now," Stallings said. "But it belonged to William A. C. Rice the Fourth."

Artie Wu expressed surprise in his usual manner with a series of small judicious nods and a slight wise smile.

"Well?" Stallings said, ready for either praise or condemnation.

"I think Rice's house could prove useful," Wu said. "I also think you and Georgia have done remarkably well."

"I can't think of any use we can make of it—except to draw attention," Durant said.

"Exactly," said Wu.

From the driver's seat, Otherguy Overby said, "Christ, I can think of half a dozen ways we can use it."

Wu settled back into the seat, clasped his hands across his belly, closed his eyes and said, "Let's hear two of them, Otherguy."

*   *   *

By 3:15 P.M. the travelers had unpacked, toured Billy Rice's $15-million beach shack, taken a short stroll along the beach itself and were now gathered in the enormous living room, where Artie Wu had been drawn, as if by a chain, to the dead man's favorite chair—an elaborate leather recliner the color of port wine.

There were no unsightly levers to even hint it was a recliner. It looked instead like an ordinary brass-studded wing-back chair—providing three or four thousand dollars was what one ordinarily paid for a chair. A cleverly concealed button made it recline and adjust to any number of positions. Another button switched on the electric vibrating mechanism. Still another one controlled the room's sound system.

Next to the chair was the six-line telephone console Ione Gamble had used to dial 911. There was also a swing-away reading table. On the chair's lower left side was a deep leather pocket still stuffed with screenplays. Light came from a floor lamp whose chrome stand and flat-black metal shade were still positioned just so.

Booth Stallings and Georgia Blue shared one of the room's

three couches, as if to imply, if not announce, some kind of loose alliance. Overby had chosen an Eames chair, the genuine article, and had his feet up on its stool. Durant stood at the wide expanse of glass, his back to the room, inspecting the ocean.

After asking if anyone would care for a drink and getting no takers, Artie Wu said, "Booth has given each of us a thousand in cash for walking-around money. He's to be our exchequer, logistician and householder. Should anyone ask, you're colleagues of Dr. Stallings and his charming research associate, Ms. Blue. Any comment?"

Stallings had one. "I think during the next day or so I'll work the neighborhood, Artie. Introduce myself as old Doc Stallings, the motormouth academic, who'll talk your arm off if you give him half a chance. I've found that people will tell you all sorts of interesting stuff just to make you shut up and go away."

"Try to find out what Billy Rice did for fun and who he did it with," Wu said.

"Plan to."

Wu looked around the room. "Any other questions?"

Durant had one. Without turning, he said, "What'll you tell the neighbors you're working on, Booth?"

"Nothing. By that I mean I'll tell them I'm resting from my labors in Amman while my associates at Wudu, Limited, negotiate a confidential research project in L.A."

"Good," Durant said and continued his inspection of the ocean.

"As I mentioned earlier," Wu said, "Quincy and I are meeting with Ione Gamble at five. Howard Mott'll also be present. I should add he's associated himself with one of the old downtown law firms, which enables him to represent Gamble in California. Her personal attorney, Jack Broach—who's also her business manager and agent—may be at the five o'clock meeting. I'll spell Broach for you."

After spelling it, Wu looked at Georgia Blue and said, "Check him out, Georgia."

"Something specific or all the way?"

"All the way."

Wu next turned to Overby. "Otherguy, I want you to begin the hunt for the missing hypnotists. Quincy managed to locate one of the Goodisons' promotional leaflets that has photos of them. He also talked to an ex-Paddington Police Station detective, a woman, who gave him a rundown on their habits and peculiarities. It's all in a memo he wrote."

"He already gave me a copy," Overby said.

"Good. After Georgia does Jack Broach, she'll join you in the hunt for the Goodisons."

"How much time've we got?" Overby said.

"Not much. Mott says the trial date is set for March twenty-third in Santa Monica Superior Court. He hopes he can get a continuance, but he's worried that if it does come to trial, she'll lose."

"Does anybody know of any connection between this dead guy Rice and the Goodisons?" Overby said.

"None that I know of," Wu said. "But it won't hurt to look for one."

"What if we find the Goodisons dead?" Georgia Blue asked.

Wu thought for a moment. "Then our job's done—unless Enno Glimm says otherwise."

"And what if," Durant said, still staring at the ocean, "we stumble across something that indicates Ione Gamble killed Rice and had something to do with the Goodisons' disappearance?"

Before Wu could reply, Overby said, "We could sell it and retire—all of us."

Wu sighed. "That's a bit raw—even for you, Otherguy."

"Don't tell me it didn't cross your mind, Artie."

Wu sighed again and said, "I think we should proceed from two assumptions, the first being that the Goodisons are alive, but in hiding, maybe of their own volition, maybe not. Our second assumption is that Ione Gamble didn't kill William Rice. Since the cops have gone at her from the opposite direction, there's a slight possibility that our approach will turn up something new and even exculpatory—although I really don't have much hope."

There was a brief silence as he looked at each of them, taking his time, especially when his gaze reached Durant's back. Wu was still staring at it when he said, "Anything else?"

"We need more cars," said Overby.

"There's a Budget place just down the highway," Stallings said. "We can rent what we need there."

"Anything else?" Wu said.

After a somewhat longer silence, Georgia Blue said, "One thing bothers me. It's about the two hypnotists—the Goodisons. Under California law, the testimony of any witness who's been hypnotized is considered tainted. So why did Mott send all the way to London for a pair of hypnotists if he knew that Ione Gamble, once hypnotized, couldn't testify in her own defense?"

Durant, still staring at the ocean, said, "That's the second question I'll ask Mott."

"What's the first?" she said.

"Why he imported two bent hypnotists."

"Maybe he didn't know they were bent."

"That's my third question," Durant said. "Why didn't he?"

Fourteen

Artie Wu brought the Lincoln Town Car to an abrupt nose-bobbing stop in front of Ione Gamble's house on Adelaide Drive at 4:56 P.M. Durant made no move to get out and instead stared at the house as if it sheltered six of his worst enemies.

"Don't much care for Spanish Colonial?" Wu said.

"It's your rotten driving I don't care for. Question: why is a ride with you like an IRS audit? Answer: because I know it'll end in disaster."

"We arrived safely."

"By God's grace."

"What's really bugging you?"

"Probably the Goodisons," Durant said and opened the curbside door.

*   *   *

Shortly after Wu rang the two-note chimes, the front door was opened not by the Salvadoran housekeeper, but by Howard Mott in his dark blue suit, white shirt and quiet tie. He looked up at the visitors, studied them briefly, nodded twice and said, "If you're Mr. Wu, then he's Mr. Durant and I'm Howard Mott. Come on in."

Once they were inside and the handshakes were over, Wu said, "First of all, we thank you for the business you've sent our way over the years—especially that Beirut deal."

"The widow was both pleased and enriched, as well you know," Mott said. "I also appreciate the clients you've referred to me. Some have been a bit odd, of course. A few were fascinating. All of them, thank God, were solvent and every last one of them was guilty as hell."

"If they weren't," Durant said, "why would they need a thousand-dollar-an-hour lawyer?"

"I don't charge quite that much. Yet."

"How's your batting average?" Wu said.

"Eight of the ten you sent me were acquitted. The other two are improving their Ping-Pong skills at various minimum security joints in Pennsylvania and Florida." Mott again stared, first at Durant, then at Wu, shook his head slightly and said, "I was just thinking it's strange we haven't met until now."

"We try to avoid the need for legal counsel," Durant said.

"Very wise," Mott said, then asked, "Overby's not coming?"

"No."

"I hope to meet him while he's in town. We've talked over the phone so many times I've come to think of him as a prospective client."

"As well you might," Wu said.

"So how's my father-in-law?"

"In love," Durant said.

"Really? Who with?"

"An ex-Secret Service agent. Georgia Blue."

Mott frowned. "Wasn't she the one in Hong Kong who they extradited to the Philippines for murder and—"

Wu didn't let him finish. "The very same."

"Well. The five of you. Together again. Must seem like a reunion."

"Fortunately," Durant said, "like all reunions, it's only temporary."

Mott obviously wanted to say more and even ask a question or two. Instead, he moved something around inside his mouth. Bit his tongue, Wu thought. Mott then glanced at his watch and announced the meeting would be upstairs in Ione Gamble's office.

"Just the four of us?" Wu said as they started up the stairs.

"Is there supposed to be someone else?"

"You mentioned Jack Broach."

"Jack couldn't get away," Mott said.

*   *   *

Ione Gamble wore a dark blue cable-knit cotton sweater with a deep V-neck over what looked like a raw-silk T-shirt. She also wore gray flannel pants and white Reeboks. As Mott made the introductions, Gamble shook Durant's hand first and murmured something polite as she assessed the tweed jacket, custom-made chambray shirt, twill pants and the aged loafers that encased a pair of spirited argyle socks she wouldn't see until he sat down and crossed his legs.

She smiled at Artie Wu next, shook his hand and said something nice as she took in the tieless white shirt with the semi-Byronic collar, the faintly raffish double-breasted blue blazer, the putty-colored pants and the gleaming black pebble-grained wing tips that he wore like a badge of respectability. She also noticed that Wu wore a wedding ring but Durant didn't.

After the introductions, Gamble resumed her seat behind the Memphis cotton broker's desk. Mott took the businesslike armchair and Wu and Durant settled for the couch with the chintz slipcover.

It was then that Durant crossed his legs, revealing the argyle socks, smiled at Ione Gamble and said what he'd been planning to say. "We've rented William Rice's house in Malibu."

Her surprise came and went quickly, replaced by a bleak stare that was aimed at Durant while she asked a question of Howard Mott. "Am I paying for the house, Howie?"

"Enno Glimm is," Mott said.

The bleak stare gave way to a smile and she said, "Then I hope you guys enjoy it because it's a lovely place."

97

"Did you rent it just by happy chance?" Mott said.

Artie Wu nodded. "It's one of those fortuitous events that may or may not prove useful. But as Miss Gamble says, it's a hell of a house."

"You'd better call me Ione and I'll call you Artie and— Quincy, isn't it?"

"Quincy," Durant agreed. "Since we're here to ask questions, maybe we should establish the ground rules. Are there any areas you want declared out of bounds?"

"If there are, I'll tell you when to stay the fuck away."

"That ought to be warning enough."

"Okay," she said. "Where do we start?"

"With the Goodisons," Durant said. "Pauline and Hughes."

"Yes, the Goodisons. Well, they wanted me to call them Paulie and Hughsie two minutes after we met. I've lived in this town for thirty years—and by 'this town,' I mean L.A.— and I didn't have what you'd call a sheltered upbringing. By the time I was twenty I figured I'd met every kind of slime king and ooze queen known in Christendom—until I met the Goodisons."

"Tell us about them," Wu said.

"Okay. I met with them three times and it was after the last meeting that Howie got that phone call from Hughes Goodison who claimed he had all sorts of new information, important facts or something like that. Anyway, Hughes said he was calling from the Bel-Air but by the time Howie got there, the Goodisons'd disappeared."

"They check out?" Durant asked.

Mott said, "No, they simply vanished, leaving everything behind."

"Shall we go back to that first meeting with them?" Wu said.

"All right," she said. "Here we go. The Goodisons fly in from London and check into the Bel-Air. Then they call me—or Hughes does—and after the usual jabber-jabber, he gets to it—the hypnotism. Hughes thinks it'd be nice if I came to their Bel-Air suite that has an ever so quiet and relaxing atmosphere. I'm not going to bore you with an impression of his voice, but it's faux plummy, if you know what that sounds like and, being from London, I guess you do."

"Yes," Wu said. "We do."

"Well, I learned not to go to strange men's hotel rooms pretty early on—when I was around four or five. So I tell Hughes my house also has an atmosphere that's ever so quiet and relaxing and that's where the hypnotizing, if any, will take place. Then I give him the address and the directions and they show up in a limo, for God's sake."

"What time was this?" Durant asked.

"About four in the afternoon."

Durant looked at Mott. "Were you here?"

"No."

"Why not?"

"Because I wasn't told of either the Goodisons' arrival in L.A. or of their appointment with Ione."

Durant looked at Gamble. "Why not let him know?"

"I was going to call him, but then Jack Broach dropped by with some stuff I had to sign. He was still here when Hughes called and I asked him to stay. I also asked Jack if I should call Howie and he said it might be a good idea. But when I told him it was just going to be a let's-get-acquainted session, but no hypnotism, Jack said there probably wasn't any reason to bother Howie and I didn't."

Durant again looked at Mott. "You ever meet the Goodisons?"

"Just once. They came to the Santa Monica hotel where I'm staying, called me on the house phone and wanted to come up for a drink. I suggested the bar would be more comfortable. We had a drink there, some very idle talk of no consequence and they left."

"How did you read them?"

Mott smiled slightly. "Let's say I suspected that they lacked moral fiber."

"Bent?"

"I'm not a mind reader."

"Did Enno Glimm swear by them?"

"Nobody ever swore by them, Quincy. But a lot of people

in London, who should've known better, told me they were wonderful."

"They're bent," Durant said. "After I found out they'd gone missing, it took me less than twenty-four hours to learn just how bent. What bothers me is why Enno Glimm and company didn't do the same thing."

"I think we can get to the 'Who Struck John?' section of our agenda later," Wu said. "Right now I'd like to ask Ione a few questions. Any objections?"

Hearing none, Wu leaned forward on the couch, elbows on his big knees, hands clasped. He gave Gamble the kind of smile that made her smile back and said, "The Goodisons—your very first impression?"

"Star fuckers."

"I was thinking more of their act—the one they put on after the initial star fucking was over."

Gamble first looked suspicious—then interested. "You knew them in London?"

"Not them, but people like them. Everyone has a personal act of some kind—especially hypnotists."

"What's yours?" she said.

"We usually begin with terse questions and end up offering sympathetic understanding and a measure of hope."

She gave him a wry, even rueful smile and said, "You're right. They had an act. It was something like going to a doctor for the first time. Even before you tell him where it hurts, he's already into his act—shooting you those sharp little side glances while he jots down your vital statistics. Hughes and Pauline had that kind of patter. While Hughes said his lines, Pauline studied me for—well, for whatever they were looking for. Then it was Pauline's time to talk and Hughes's time to study."

"You're very observant."

"In Howie's trade and mine, we're always on the lookout for blinks, smirks and twitches to steal or borrow, right, Howie?"

Mott agreed with a small nod and a smaller smile.

"What happened when their act was over?" Durant said.

"They offered to hypnotize me—sort of a test run kind of thing. When I said I wasn't ready yet, they offered to put on a demonstration. So I said okay and Hughes put Pauline into a trance in about five seconds flat. I mean, zap—she was under. He then took her back to when she was six and asked her to show us what she'd learned that day at dancing school. She got up and did an awkward little time step and sat back down."

"Then what?" Wu asked.

"He brought her out of it looking relaxed, happy and not remembering anything—or saying she didn't. And that's when Hughes asked if he could test my receptiveness. I told him I still didn't want to be hypnotized yet. Well, he turns on all of his considerable smarm and says he can't hypnotize anyone who resists it and that he just wants to test my receptiveness, which was a word he really seemed to like. Then he starts talking about all the stars who're known for *their* receptiveness. About half of them are long dead but still it was kind of an impressive list. And since Jack was there, I said all right."

She paused then and asked, "Would you guys like coffee or something to drink?"

Wu shook his head. "I think we'd rather hear the end of the story."

"Okay. Well, we're all still here in the office—me, Jack, Hughes and Pauline. Then Hughes is telling me to relax, close my eyes and think of all the colors in the rainbow and name them one by one. So I do and feel myself sort of going—I don't know where—under, I guess. But I fight it and snap back. When I open my eyes, Hughes and Pauline are looking disappointed and Jack is looking half-amused, the way he always does. So I get rid of the Goodisons by agreeing to another session the next day."

She stopped talking and turned in her chair to stare again through the floor-to-ceiling window at ocean and canyon. She was still looking at the view when she said, "But by the next day I'd decided I wasn't going to be hypnotized by anybody—especially not by the Goodisons."

She turned back. "I let them try anyway and the same thing happens. I started to go under—then snapped myself back. Their third and last test of my so-called receptiveness ended the same way. And that's when I told them there weren't going to be any more sessions and it was the last time I ever saw them."

"What was their reaction?" Wu said.

"Nothing much. They apologized for not being more helpful and that was that. They left."

Durant looked at Howard Mott. "And this was the same day you got that panicky call from Hughes Goodison?"

"Yes," Mott said.

Artie Wu sighed and rose. He went slowly over to the Memphis cotton broker's desk, picked up the long yellow pencil and began rolling it with the thumbs and fingers of both hands. "When Hughes tested your receptiveness that first time, did he use any object such as this pencil?"

She stared at the pencil. "No."

"But he talked about the colors of the rainbow?"

"Yes."

"He asked you to concentrate on them, didn't he?"

"Yes."

"And say them aloud?"

"Yes."

"Yellow's a rainbow color, isn't it, Ione?"

"Yes."

"Like the yellow of this pencil."

"Yes."

"Close your eyes and tell me if you can still see the yellow."

"Yes."

"Doesn't it make you feel relaxed?"

"Yes."

"When you're fully relaxed, Ione, you'll go to sleep. To help you relax, think of the rainbow again. Start with red. When you get to the last color, yellow, you'll be fully, completely relaxed."

"All right."

"Have you reached yellow?"

102

"Yes."

"Do you want to remember something you tried to remember but couldn't?"

"Yes."

"Would you like to remember the night you drove to Billy's house?"

"Yes."

"Remember what happened that night, Ione. Remember it aloud—everything that happened from the time you left your house."

She began to speak in a soft voice and told all about her fast drive to the beach house of William A. C. Rice IV and what she found there and about the one phone call she made.

Fifteen

Ione Gamble still sat behind the Memphis cotton broker's desk with her eyes closed and her hands resting on the arms of the chair. Her lips had formed a faint smile and she looked rested, content—even happy.

After staring at her for almost a minute, Howard Mott turned to Wu and asked, "Can she hear me?"

Wu shook his head.

"She didn't kill him," Mott said, more to himself than to Wu and Durant.

"You thought she did?" Durant said.

"I try not to let hope interfere with logic," Mott said, turned to Wu and asked, "Where'd you learn that?"

"In a carnival when I was sixteen."

"Seventeen," Durant said. "It was Little Doc Mingo's Amazing Carnival and Traveling Panorama. Little Doc was a midget. Three feet tall. His regular hypnotist was Szabo, the Mystifying Mesmerist. Szabo's real name was Hank Steem and the only mystifying thing about him was how he could still drink a fifth of rotgut a day at sixty-eight."

"Hank was okay," Wu said.

"He was a happy drunk at least," Durant said. "And just

104

after we were hired as roustabouts, Hank decided to retire to his daughter's place in Corpus Christi. So Little Doc came up with a replacement—the Amazing Fu Chang Wu."

"Me," Wu said with a grin. "Quincy and I were hired in El Paso and the Mystifying Mesmerist was going to quit the carnival when it reached Longview—which is clear across Texas. In the four or five weeks it took to get there, Hank taught us everything he knew about hypnotism. After Hank finally left, Little Doc dressed me up in red and black silk pyjamas he'd found somewhere, stuck a funny hat on my head and turned Quincy into my roper."

"Your shill?" Mott said.

"Close," Durant said. "We had an outside act to draw the rubes into the tent, but it needed volunteers. Hank'd taught us how to pick the ones easiest to hypnotize—the loud-mouths, the gigglers, the extroverts and exhibitionists. While the talker gave his spiel about the Amazing Fu Chang Wu, I'd mingle with the rubes and tip Artie off to the three or four I wanted. Then after the talker asked for volunteers, I'd be the first to hop up on the stage and then Artie'd coax the three or four I'd picked out into joining me."

"To do what?"

"Perform the come-on," Durant said. "First, Artie'd hypno-tize me and I'd go stiff as a board. Then he'd pick me up and lay me on two chairs—my head on one chair, my heels on the other. Then he'd invite the three or four volunteer rubes to stand on me—which they were always happy to do. And that's what drew the rest of the crowd inside at four bits a head for the real show, which mostly involved letting the rubes we'd picked make idiots of themselves."

"How long did you guys . . . do this?"

Durant looked at Wu. "Five or six months, wasn't it?"

Wu nodded. "We played across Texas, north Louisiana and down into Cajun country—Crowley, Lafayette, New Iberia, Opelousas. We parted company with Little Doc just outside New Orleans, where we were going to ship out to either South America or the South Pacific."

"What happened?"

"We met a guy in New Orleans who thought we should go to Princeton instead."

Mott turned to examine Ione Gamble, who still wore her faint, contented smile. "The Goodisons hypnotized her, didn't they, and made her believe they hadn't?"

"It's not hard to do," Wu said. "And most actors are easy. They keep their emotions very near the surface, almost on tap, which makes them highly susceptible to suggestive hypnosis."

"When Ione wakes up, will she remember she didn't kill Billy Rice?"

Wu nodded. "This time she will."

"Aren't we forgetting Jack Broach?" Durant said. "If he was here for her first session, he must've heard her say she didn't shoot Rice. So why the hell didn't he say so?"

"What must've happened the first time," Wu said, "is that the Goodisons took her to the brink, saw how easily they could hypnotize her, then brought her back before she could say anything and claimed they'd failed. Broach may have assumed she couldn't be hypnotized—which is what Ione also believed—and didn't bother to show up for the second and third sessions when the Goodisons probably used a tape recorder."

Mott looked at Ione Gamble again and said, "They must've thought she'd confess to Rice's murder." He shook his head. "Which is exactly what she was afraid might happen."

"You could argue," Durant said, "that they did just what they were paid to do—help Ione regain her memory."

"The hell they did," Mott said. "They hypnotized her, all right, then pushed her erase button and made her believe, one, that she hadn't been hypnotized and, two, that she couldn't ever remember anything of what happened the night of Rice's murder." He looked at Wu. "You say that wasn't difficult to do?"

"Not at all," Wu said.

Howard Mott wasn't satisfied. He scratched his chin, then the back of his left hand, looked at Wu again and said, "When they called me late that night from the Bel-Air Hotel, they claimed they'd run into a problem. At least, Hughes said they had. He was the one I talked to. But he wouldn't say what kind of problem and by the time I got there, they'd gone— leaving all their personal stuff behind. It looked as if something had scared them away."

"Or that's the way they wanted it to look," Durant said.

"Perhaps. At any rate, it was a week or ten days later—I'll have to look up the exact date—when I got my other call from Hughes. He wanted to talk about the weather and how lovely it was for this time of year. I started asking questions, but he cut me off and told me not to worry about him or his sister, that they'd been under a strain and were trying to work out some personal problems that he'd rather not go into. It was a stall. An obvious one."

"What questions did you ask him?" Durant said.

"I asked why they had disappeared. Where were they? Was there anything I could do? How could I get in touch? He just kept telling me not to worry."

"You're sure it was Hughes's voice?" Durant said.

"Positive."

Mott turned to examine Ione Gamble, who still sat behind her desk, eyes closed, a faint smile on her lips. "Will she really remember what she said to us?"

"Every word," Wu said and used a soft, almost seductive voice to ask, "Remember the rainbow, Ione?"

"Yes, I remember," she said, her eyes still closed.

"Let's go through the colors again. When you come to the very last one—to yellow—you'll wake up and feel very relaxed, very rested and remember everything you said. Now start naming the rainbow's colors to yourself."

Six seconds later, Ione Gamble opened her eyes, smiled at Artie Wu, then frowned, exchanged the frown for a puzzled look and said, "I shot the Chagall, not Billy, didn't I?"

"That's right," Wu said. "You shot the Chagall."

Sixteen

Otherguy Overby had been sitting in the lobby of the Hotel Bridges for sixty-seven minutes before he finally saw someone who might prove useful. The hotel was less than thirteen years old but already had acquired a kind of genteel shabbiness that attracted those in need of an address just within the Beverly Hills zip code.

Although not cheap, the hotel was comparatively inexpensive and much favored by foreign and domestic journalists, promoters, actors and the occasional aging mercenary who thought his life story would make a wonderful movie.

The lobby, panelled in something that imitated oak, offered a variety of couches and easy chairs that were upholstered in a good grade of dark brown Naugahyde. On the walls were large prints of middle European landscapes and in the air was one of Los Angeles's classical FM stations with the volume turned down so low it sounded more like murmur than music.

The cashier's cage was protected by bulletproof plastic and behind the unbarred reception counter stood a melancholy-looking man in his forties. He wore a thick black mustache and the resigned air of someone who has learned nine languages and now wonders why he went to the bother.

VOODOO, LTD.

The house detective—renamed the security executive by the hotel—was a moonlighting Beverly Hills police sergeant who passed by Overby twice without giving him more than a glance. This may have been because Overby sat in one of the lobby's two armless straight chairs, feet and knees together, a dark gray fedora in his lap and the rest of him clothed in black shoes that had to be laced up, white shirt, dull gray tie and a double-breasted blue pinstripe suit he had bought off the rack in London. It was a carefully chosen costume that would stamp Overby as a foreigner, possibly a northern European, until he opened his mouth.

The someone who Overby thought might prove useful was a stout, medium tall man with three chins. He had just collected his mail and *Wall Street Journal* at the reception desk and was thumbing through four or five envelopes when Overby came up from behind and tapped him on the right shoulder.

The man froze—if only for an instant—then spun around on curiously small feet. He wore the same surprised jolly smile he would wear if encountering his oldest and dearest friend. Much of the smile stayed in place as he stuck out his right hand and said, "What the fuck d'you want?"

Overby returned the smile, shook the hand, let it go and said, "They send you *The Wall Street Journal* here, Dickie—and also your monthly Amex bill. That means you've been living here awhile. It also means you've been back in town long enough to maybe know something I need to know."

Richard Brackeen, 42, shoved his mail down into the right outside jacket pocket of his beautifully tailored black suit, secured *The Wall Street Journal* under his left armpit and clasped his hands across a wide expanse of belly. A dove-gray vest, decorated with a gold watch chain that featured a Phi Beta Kappa key, made the mound of belly look even larger than it was.

Hands still clasped, jolly smile still in place, Brackeen rocked back on his heels and inspected Overby with small eyes that had the color and sheen of quicksilver.

109

"Who the hell're you supposed to be, Otherguy? Somebody who barely caught the last flight out of Baghdad?"

Overby flashed his hard white smile in answer, then said, "Tell me what I want to know, Dickie, and you get three hundred. For telling me you know fuck-all, one hundred."

"I heard you were in Mesopotamia—or maybe it was Trans-Jordan."

"And here I am in L.A. Well?"

The jolly smile went away so the mouth could purse itself into something almost resembling a rosebud. The three chins bobbled up and down in a thoughtful nod and Richard Brackeen said, "Let's go get some refreshment."

*　　*　　*

The Hotel Bridges's bar was called The Toll Booth. It offered indifferent lighting, low tables and soft fat chairs. At 5:20 P.M. it was three-quarters full and the noise of the drinkers had already risen from a hum into something that approximated a chant.

Seated at a corner table, his back to the wall, Brackeen called the pretty young cocktail waitress "Love" as he ordered a martini, specifying not only the brand of gin but also the vermouth. Overby asked for a bottle of Mexican beer and said any brand would do.

When the waitress came back, she served the drinks, collected from Overby, grinned at her tip, turned to Brackeen and asked, "When d'you start shooting, Dickie?"

"Tuesday."

"You said you thought there might be a part for me."

Brackeen looked up at her and frowned, as if running past promises through his mind. The frown vanished when he said, "Only thing not cast is a small role in the third scene. You want it, it's yours."

"What do I play?"

Brackeen was losing interest. "Ever been in a real orgy?"

"I don't know. Maybe. I guess."

"Was it sometimes with guys and sometimes with girls and sometimes with both?"

She nodded.

"Well, the only difference'll be is that this is a period orgy and you have to wear a costume—for about ten seconds."

"What d'you mean 'period orgy'?"

"I mean historical. In this case, Roman." Brackeen had now lost all interest in the woman and was sipping his martini.

"But it could be a break, couldn't it?" she said with no trace of conviction.

"Of course," Brackeen said in exactly the same tone.

"Okay. I'll do it."

"Leave your right name, phone, address and Social Security number in my hotel box."

"Thanks, Dickie."

Brackeen nodded, the cocktail waitress left and Overby said, "I thought those guys from back east in Chicago had moved in and moved you out."

"I let them have the features, that's all. Who needs the overhead? Now I go right from videotape into cassettes and sell strictly mail-order. I run ads in the stroke books and I've also set up several nice little 900-number dial-a-porns." The discussion of business cheered Brackeen and his jolly smile reappeared. "And I've also become a devout follower of the cardinal business rule, Otherguy: lower the wages and raise the profits."

"Sounds good."

Brackeen shrugged. "Sufficient unto my needs."

"Suppose," Overby said, "you wanted to get lost for a few days or a week or maybe even a month or two?"

"Who from—the cops?"

"Or maybe from the back-east-in-Chicago guys."

"I'd go to Mexico—a little place just south of La Paz where nobody speaks anything but Spanish, including me."

"Suppose you didn't speak anything but English English?"

"Accent and all?"

Overby nodded.

"You're not talking about going to ground in some one-room studio in Palms with maybe a freezer full of frozen pizzas, a microwave and a TV set?"

Overby shook his head.

"Full service?"

Overby again nodded, then drank some of his beer.

"Well, the only place in the L.A. area I know of is Colleen Cullen's. Know her?"

"I think somebody told me her wrapping's come loose."

"She's a partisan, Otherguy, and all partisans are a bit touched."

"What's she offering these days—other than room and board?"

Brackeen looked up, as if to think about what his answer should be, then nodded to himself and said, "Say you need a fully automatic personal weapon to protect hearth and home? Or say you want to get into Canada rather quickly, but without troubling the bureaucracy? Or suppose you find something that fell off a truck—perhaps three dozen TV sets—but don't know what to do with them? For a fair price and minimum fuss, the person to see is Miss Colleen Cullen."

"She prejudiced?" Overby said.

"Who isn't? But prejudiced against whom?"

"The British."

"Hates the British."

"Think she'd do business with them anyway?"

"As always, Otherguy, prejudice exits when profit enters."

A thoughtful look settled on Overby's face. "Would she take their money and then maybe . . . you know?"

"Betray them?" Brackeen said.

Overby's reply was a slight shrug.

"She's a well-regarded businesswoman and to do what you *seem* to want her to do could put her reputation at risk."

"How much?"

"To do what you're hinting at? She'd want top dollar."

Overby reached into his shirt pocket, brought out three $100 bills that had been folded in half. He let Brackeen see them, then folded them again, covered the money with his

112

palm and slid it across the table. Overby's hand was still covering the money when he said, "Three hundred for Colleen Cullen's phone number and address."

"Like me to write them down?"

"Just tell me what they are," Overby said. "Twice."

Seventeen

The offices of Jack Broach & Co. were just south of Wilshire on the west side of Robertson Boulevard and a few blocks north of where Jane Fonda once had her aerobic studio. Broach's company occupied all three floors of a small U-shaped building that was covered by a veneer of carefully chosen used bricks that featured oozing mortar, long dried. A fine stand of jacarandas shaded a courtyard paved with slate and decorated with a gurgling three-tier Mexican tile fountain whose small carefully hand-lettered sign boasted, "I Use Only Recycled Water."

Whoever designed the Broach Building had been fond of small Roman arches, because Georgia Blue passed beneath three of them to reach the blond receptionist. After Blue gave her name and stated her business, the receptionist murmured into a telephone, then smiled at Blue and said Mr. Broach would see her presently. Georgia Blue tried but failed to recall the last time she had heard an American substitute "presently" for "soon."

After declining the receptionist's offer of coffee, tea or Perrier, Blue waited in a chrome and leather chair, unconsciously plucking at the hem of the dark gray Anne Klein dress she had bought at Neiman-Marcus earlier that day with much of the $1,000 in walking-around money Booth Stallings had given her. She then had spent most of what was left on a pair of Joan & David black pumps and was surprised to learn she now wore a 7-A shoe instead of a 7-AAA, which was her size when she had entered the Mandaluyong prison.

Blue wore the new shoes and dress out of Neiman's, using a shopping bag to carry away the outfit she had bought at Rustan's department store in Manila. Just before reaching the parking lot where she had left her rented Ford, she dropped the shopping bag into a trash bin.

After waiting sixteen minutes in the Jack Broach & Co. reception area, Georgia Blue got to watch a female motion picture star of the second or third magnitude make an unescorted exit. Two minutes later a young black kid of 22 or 23, wearing a T-shirt, raggedy jeans and $13,000 worth of Rolex on his left wrist, was ushered to the exit by two white males in their thirties who tried very hard not to look as if they were fawning over him.

And finally there was the face that made the nineteen-minute wait almost worthwhile. For it was a face from her childhood, but one now thickened and lined and crimsoned by age and sun and probably too much whisky. The golden hair had thinned and turned white, although the walk was still that same slithering lope and the back had stayed rake-handle straight. The old actor glanced at Georgia Blue, caught her staring at him, gave her his crooked, slightly mad grin—which he should have copyrighted—then winked at her and was gone.

*   *   *

Jack Broach rose, wearing a smile, and quickly came around the desk that could have taken some eighteenth-century French craftsman at least a year to build. But it was not until he was completely around the desk that Broach greeted her warmly by name and urged her to try the couch that was placed beneath what he called "the three little Daumiers."

Blue turned, gave the three pen-and-ink sketches a glance, turned again and sat down. Once they were seated, she on

115

the couch, he in a too-tall wingback chair, Broach said, "Instead of answering your questions, I've almost decided either to hire you or talk you into signing a representation contract."

"How sweet," Blue said, much as she might have said "bullshit."

Broach touched his forehead just where his widow's peak began and said, "That streak—it's real, isn't it?"

"Is it?"

"It must be, because you don't need it."

Georgia Blue smiled slightly, waiting for the next question.

Broach's right hand again strayed to his hairline. "How long did it take to turn? A year? A month? What?"

"Overnight," she said.

"Good God, what happened?"

"I was sent to prison. In the Philippines."

Broach seemed more fascinated than shocked. "For what?"

"For five years."

"I mean—"

She didn't let him finish. "They said I killed someone. I said I didn't. My sentence was commuted a few days ago."

"Not exactly a pardon, right?"

"Not exactly."

"And before all that?"

"I was a Secret Service agent."

"I didn't think they had woman agents."

"Neither did the Treasury most of the time."

"And now you're working for my client."

"I work for Wu and Durant."

"Wudu, Limited," he said. "Catchy."

"Easy to remember anyway."

"They must have hired you right out of jail."

"They had someone waiting for me as the prison gates swung wide."

"Then you must've known them before."

"Not necessarily—although I did. Know them before."

Broach leaned back in his chair, steepled his fingers under his nose and studied her for several seconds. Then he folded the steeple, put it away and said, "Know what I do for a living? I provide intensive care for ailing egos. And it's extremely rare to run across one that apparently doesn't need any."

"What about Ione Gamble's ego?"

"Remarkably sturdy."

"What do you do for her mostly?"

"I offer advice."

"Did you advise her to hire hypnotists?"

"That was her defense counsel's suggestion, although I went along with it."

"Did you meet them—the Goodisons?"

He nodded.

"And?"

Jack Broach leaned forward with a new and rather earnest expression that Georgia Blue decided was his standard you-can-trust-me-on-this look.

"I'm in the talent business," he said. "I find it. Nurture it. Package it. Sell it. And sometimes I have to decide when it's no longer marketable. That makes me an assessor of sorts. And my first assessment of Hughes and Pauline Goodison was that they were standard star fuckers with a short line of bullshit. By the end of my one and only hour with them and Ione, I'd reassessed them as two very sick fucks."

"You told Gamble that, of course?"

"I couldn't quite bring myself to second-guess her defense counsel."

"Howard Mott."

Broach nodded.

"He recommended the Goodisons?"

"More or less."

"Either he did or he didn't."

"Mott heard about them," Broach said, "then checked them out and hired them through a most reputable London agency. Everyone Mott talked to in London assured him the Goodisons were a blue ribbon pair."

"Who recommended Mott to Gamble?"

"She asked me to find her the best criminal defense lawyer in the country. I ran five of them past her and she chose Mott. I told her she'd made a wise choice."

"You still believe that?"

"Of course."

"Why?"

"I don't understand your question."

"Sure you do," she said. "You recommended Mott—among others. Ione Gamble retains him. He hired the Goodisons and suddenly everything goes to hell. My question is: do you still think she was smart to pick Mott?"

"Smart has nothing to do with it. Ione feels comfortable with Howie Mott. She trusts him. He's also a damn fine lawyer with impressive credentials."

"You're a lawyer, aren't you?"

"Why?"

"They usually stick up for each other." Blue paused, looked slowly around the large room, as if pricing its contents, then came back to Broach with another question. "What do you do for Ione Gamble besides give her advice?"

"I'm her best friend."

"What's it cost her to have you as best friend? I don't want the dollar amount, just the percentage."

"I'm her agent, business manager and personal attorney. For that she pays me twenty percent of her gross income. My friendship is free."

"You handle her investments?"

Broach nodded.

"Is she broke, comfortable, rich—what?"

"Her net worth today would have made her rich ten years ago. Now it just makes her extremely comfortable."

"What caused the breakup between her and William Rice the Fourth?"

"No idea."

"Guess."

"If Ione can't guess, I sure as hell can't."

"Anything wrong with her?" Georgia Blue asked. "By that I mean is she psychotic, HIV-positive, drug-addicted, sexually deviant, alcoholic or suffering from any mental or physical maladies that could affect her career?"

"What the hell're you talking about?"

"Blackmail," Georgia Blue said. "Well, is she?"

"No."

"Think she killed him—Rice?"

"No."

"Who do you think did?"

"No idea. None."

"Why do you think the Goodisons did a flit, bolted?"

"If they did, I again don't know why."

"If you were the Goodisons and wanted to vanish, where would you go?"

"To a very big city," Broach said, then smiled and added, "Los Angeles maybe."

"Thanks for your time, Mr. Broach," Georgia Blue said, rose and turned to give the Daumier drawings a closer examination. Then she turned back to Broach, smiled and said, "Those three Daumiers are fakes, just in case you didn't know."

Broach was also smiling as he rose from the too-tall wing-back chair. "But very good fakes, right?"

"Not bad."

"The Secret Service teach you to do that?"

"They taught me to spot counterfeit."

"Even counterfeit people?"

"My specialty."

"Sure you don't want a job?"

"Quite sure."

"One more question?"

She nodded.

"Have dinner with me tonight?"

"Sorry."

"Some other night?"

"Who knows?" Georgia Blue said, smiled her goodbye, crossed to the door, opened it and was gone. Jack Broach assessed it as an absolutely first-class exit.

Eighteen

ere it not for the Hollywood Freeway, the old Trussel mansion would never have made the forty-four-mile journey in 1947 from the fringe of what was then downtown Los Angeles to a five-acre lot near the top of Topanga Canyon.

Once a loosely knit community of assorted free spirits, dopers, mystics, working stiffs, 1960s holdouts, actors, writers, artists and other poor credit risks, Topanga in the late 1970s and '80s suffered a plague of gentrification that transformed it from a low-rent semi-rural hideout into what one critic called bosky dells with neon.

The fifteen-room mansion that would make the long trip to Topanga in 1947 had been built in 1910 just late enough to escape the Victorian gingerbread craze. The house, destined to be torn down in 1948 because it was in the path of the freeway, was saved only because its owner, Miss Martha Trussel, who had been born in the house in 1911 and fully intended to die there, called on the senior partner of her law firm, handed him a brown paper bag containing $10,000 in cash—a considerable sum in 1947—and told him to "go grease whoever has to be greased, Henry."

Permission was quickly granted and the mansion was eventually sliced into three sections and hauled at 3 to 4 miles per hour to the fairly flat five-acre lot in Topanga Canyon that had been left to Miss Trussel by her dead father, who had accepted the five acres in 1932 as repayment for a $300 debt.

Because of breakdowns, steep canyon grades and minor accidents, it took thirteen days to move the house to its new site. The *Los Angeles Times* thought the event newsworthy enough to run a three-column photograph on page seven of one of the twenty-one traffic jams it caused. The move was directed by Miss Trussel herself, who later supervised the mansion's reassembly and modernization. She lived in the huge old house alone, save for a series of Mexican housekeepers, until she died in bed of emphysema in 1981, an unlit Chesterfield in one hand, an unstruck kitchen match in the other.

By then the old Trussel mansion had deteriorated to the point where it brought only $165,000 at probate auction in 1982. Twenty-two-year-old Colleen Cullen purchased it with twenty certified checks, each drawn on a different bank or savings and loan, and each made out for less than $9,000. Miss Cullen made it a point to tell anyone who would listen how she planned to turn the old place into a bed-and-breakfast inn, which she boasted would be "the best in the West."

*   *   *

From the San Fernando Valley, State Highway 27 winds up through the Santa Monica Mountains to Topanga. It then winds back down the other side to the ocean and the Pacific Coast Highway. There, at the junction of Highway 27 and the ocean, knowledgeable drivers, heading for San Francisco or Santa Barbara or even Oxnard, slowed down lest they fall prey to the county deputy sheriffs who had been rented by the recently incorporated city of Malibu, which was suffering from a shortage of funds.

About halfway between the ocean and the Valley, at the very top of State Highway 27, is the Summit Bar & Grill. And it was there that Otherguy Overby sat behind the wheel of his rented Ford sedan, studying a Thomas Brothers map of

Los Angeles County. Minutes later, Georgia Blue pulled in beside him, got out of her own rented car and into his.

"You eat yet?" Overby said, not looking up from the map.

"No. Did you?"

"We can get something here."

Georgia Blue gave the Summit Bar & Grill a quick appraisal, shook her head and said she would eat later.

"You can have a grilled cheese sandwich and a bottle of beer," he said. "How can they fuck up a grilled cheese sandwich?"

"They'd find a way."

"Maybe you're right," Overby said, closing the map book.

"Know where we're going?" she asked.

Overby nodded and started the engine. "How was what's his name—Broach?"

"Slick."

"He say anything interesting about Ione Gamble?"

"Only that he's her very best friend and also her agent, business manager and personal attorney. He doesn't charge for being best friend but gets twenty percent of her gross for the rest."

"What'd he say about the Goodisons?"

"That he pegged them right off as two sick fucks."

Shrugging, as if at old news, Overby then asked, "You ever hear of Colleen Cullen?"

Georgia Blue frowned first, then looked at Overby and said, "There was a Cullen years back in Chicago who had ties to both the Black Panthers and the IRA, but her first name wasn't Colleen. Why?"

"This Cullen's supposed to run the best lie-low place in L.A."

"And you want to ask her about the Goodisons?"

He said he did.

"Think she passes out free information?"

"If she's got any, it'll cost us. You still have that thousand Booth gave you?"

"I spent it."

"On what?"

122

"Shoes and a dress."

Overby took his eyes off the road and inspected her new shoes and dress, as if for the first time. "Nice. How much?"

"Nine hundred and sixty-something with the shoes."

Nodding his approval, Overby said, "You and me, Georgia, we always did understand why the right clothes can give you an edge."

*   *   *

Overby turned his rented Ford off a narrow winding blacktop and onto a brick drive. The Ford's headlights illuminated a green sign with gold lettering that read, "Cousin Colleen's Bed & Breakfast Inn." Stuck up on top of the wooden sign, almost as an afterthought, was a row of small red neon letters that blinked "No Vacancy."

As the brick drive went on and on, Overby guessed that the inn had been set as far back from the narrow blacktop as possible—probably at the point where the flat land suddenly turned itself into the steep slope of a Santa Monica mountain. There were a great many trees, which, even at night, Georgia Blue identified by shape and size as pines, sycamores and the odd eucalyptus. The headlights revealed no lawn to speak of, but did give glimpses of neglected flower beds that featured freeway daisies, Mexican poppies and other drought-resistant strains whose names she didn't know or had forgotten.

The brick drive ended just past the old house and fanned out into a parking area large enough for a dozen cars. Yet it now held only two cars. One was a white Toyota pickup, fairly new, and the other was an elderly MG roadster with no top. Overby stopped the Ford, shifted into park, switched off the engine and lights, looked at Georgia Blue and said, "Well?"

"Nine steps up to a covered porch that wraps around the front and the west side," she said. "The front door's solid wood and lit by what're probably hundred-watt bulbs inside two frosted globes. There's a narrow stained-glass window just to the right of the door. Bunches of fruit, I think. It's a three-story house and big, probably fifteen, sixteen, even seventeen rooms, and there's a light on in one room on the

123

second floor, but it's dark on the first and third floors. No cars except for that Toyota pickup and the MG that looks like it hasn't been moved in six months, maybe a year."

"No cars and a 'no vacancy' sign don't match," Overby said.

"Maybe her lie-lows all come by limo."

"Maybe," Overby said and opened his door. She joined him at the steps and they mounted them together. It was Overby who found the doorbell and pressed it, causing a loud buzz instead of a ring. When no one answered the summons, he rang again—this time for at least twenty seconds. They waited another twenty seconds before Georgia Blue tried the door. It was locked. Overby shrugged and turned away, as if giving up. If she hadn't been watching for it, Georgia Blue wouldn't have seen the quick sudden move of his right elbow as it slammed back against the narrow stained-glass window, breaking a six-by-ten-inch panel of what had been a bowl of ripe cherries.

Overby spun around, reached through the broken panel and unlocked the front door from the inside. "I must've slipped," he said with his hard white grin just before he went inside.

It was Georgia Blue who found the light switch and turned on a pair of lamps that revealed a large foyer with a well-cared-for parquet floor. The two lamps were a pair of milky globes on fluted brass columns that grew out of the staircase's twin newel-posts. The staircase went halfway up to the four-teen-foot ceiling before turning back on itself for the rest of the rise. A hall on the left side of the staircase led back to what seemed to be a pantry and probably, farther on, to a kitchen. At the far left of the foyer were two panelled sliding doors. On the foyer's far right, the same thing.

Overby cleared his throat, then barked a question: "Any-body home?"

When there was no reply, Georgia Blue said, "The doors on the left probably lead to a dining room and the ones on the right to the living room."

"A house this old, it'd be the parlor."

"Okay. Parlor."

Overby went to the sliding doors on the right and knocked. When there was still no response, he shoved one of the doors back into its walled recess and again asked, "Anybody home?" He waited a moment or two, heard nothing, then looked back at Georgia Blue, who nodded.

Overby moved slowly into the room, followed by Blue. He fumbled for a switch, found it and turned on some lights that were at the room's far end. Before either he or Blue could turn toward them, a woman's voice snapped out a warning, "You move, I shoot."

Overby and Georgia Blue froze. Then Overby, moving only his lips, asked, "You Colleen Cullen?"

"Hands on your heads," the voice said. "Do it."

Overby and Blue did as instructed.

"Turn around slow, then go down on your knees, but keep your hands where they are."

"That's kinda hard to do," Overby said.

"Try one knee at a time, asshole."

"You want us to turn around first?" Overby said.

"You as dumb as you sound? Turn around, get down on your knees and lemme see if you look as dumb as you sound."

Overby and Georgia Blue, hands on their heads, turned around slowly and stared at the woman who held a sawed-off 12-gauge double-barrelled shotgun with a chopped stock.

"What's the matter?" she said. "You expecting something with blue eyes, blond hair and dimples?"

"Well, sepia's nice, too," Overby said.

Nineteen

Georgia Blue frowned at the woman with the shotgun for nearly ten seconds before the frown went away and she said, "Now I remember."

"Remember what, Slim?"

"Junior Gibbons. Before he joined the Panthers he lived with Mary Margaret Cullen, who used to raise money for the IRA in Chicago. You're their daughter, right?"

The twin barrels of the shotgun moved until both were aimed at Georgia Blue. "On your knees, sis. You, too, Ace."

Once Blue and Overby were on their knees with their hands on their heads, Cullen said, "Okay. You know my name and my mama's and daddy's names. Now let's hear yours. You first, Slim."

"Georgia Blue."

"And you?"

"Maurice Overby."

"*Maw-reese.* That sounds way uptown, don't it?"

Her skin had too much luster to be the sepia Overby had called it. It was more like coffee two-thirds diluted by rich cream. Although her eyes were too large and her nose a trifle thin, and her mouth a bit wide, the combination was so striking it would make her face stick in memory far longer than mere prettiness and almost as long as true beauty.

Below the face was a long neck, then a black tank top that revealed smooth shoulders, well-muscled arms and the outline of small taut breasts. A pair of tight black pants advertised a firm butt and exaggerated the length of the long legs. Her stance and the familiar, confident way she held the shotgun suggested good coordination and also a possible oversupply of self-assurance.

Colleen Cullen gave her head an almost reflexive shake that got the thick black hair out of her eyes. The hair had been cut in a virtual 1920s bob—short in back, parted in the middle and long enough at the sides to hang down just below her ears. With the hair out of her eyes, she stared at Overby and said, "I gotta hear why you broke into my house."

"Maybe we should talk about the money first," Overby said.

"Whose money?"

"Mine."

The shotgun barrels dipped a little but then came back up. "What you got, I can take."

"I've got maybe three hundred tops in my right pants pocket. My partner's got sixty more, if that. But we came here hoping to buy something for important money, and somehow I don't think any of us'd call three hundred and sixty bucks important."

The shotgun barrels dipped slightly again and this time stayed dipped. "You're looking to buy what exactly?"

"Information."

"About what?"

"The Goodisons, Pauline and Hughes," said Georgia Blue, who rose, then bent over to brush real or imaginary dust from her knees.

"I say you could get up, Slim?"

Georgia Blue straightened and said, "When money was mentioned you forgot about the sawed-off."

"You wish," Cullen said, again aiming the shotgun at her.

Overby then rose and also bent over to brush dust from

127

the knees of his blue London suit. While still dusting, he said, "You know the Goodisons, Colleen? Say yes and you get a thousand dollars."

"We met," Cullen said.

"That's one thousand," said Overby, straightening up all the way.

"How much if I got 'em locked in the cellar?"

Overby, taking his time, examined her for signs of trick and guile. Finding none, he said, "Too bad you don't."

Colleen Cullen lowered the shotgun, turned and went to a large round oak table that held a brass lamp with a bowl shade of green glass. Also on the table were a bottle of Virginia Gentleman, four tumblers and a pitcher of water.

"I was about to have a toddy," she said, placing the shotgun on the table. "You guys drink bourbon?"

"Now and then," Overby said.

Cullen poured generous measures into three tumblers, added a little water and, carrying two of the tumblers in one hand, served Georgia Blue first, then Overby.

"Sit down if you want to," she said, returning to the table and pulling out a chair for herself. Overby and Blue joined her.

"Lemme guess," Colleen Cullen said, staring at Blue. "You used to be some brand of cop, right?"

Blue answered by tasting the bourbon and water.

"But you, Ace," Cullen said, turning to Overby. "I think your main job's staying away from cops, right?"

Overby's tiny smile revealed nothing at all.

"If I tell you about them, the Goodisons," Cullen said, "how much do I get?"

"You've already made one thousand."

"All I got so far is say-so."

"Tell us what you know about them, you get another thousand. Tell us where we can find them, two thousand."

"Four thousand in all?"

Overby nodded. "Four in all."

"Who told you about me?"

Overby frowned, as if reluctant to betray his informer.

Then the frown gave way to a sigh and a look of regret as he said, "Dickie Brackeen."

"The dirty-movie man?"

Overby nodded.

"Tell us about the Goodisons," Georgia Blue said.

"You're not much for gossip, are you, sis?"

"The Goodisons," Blue said.

"Okay. The Goodisons, Hughsie and Paulie. Brother and sister. They fuck each other, but I guess you know that?"

Overby nodded.

"There at the last, they even tried to get me into bed with 'em."

"Exactly when was 'there at the last'?" Blue said.

"There at the last was a week ago tomorrow."

"Let's go back to the beginning."

"What about my money?"

Overby leaned forward, placed a possessive hand on the shotgun and said, "When my partner gets the sawed-off, you get some money."

Cullen blinked rapidly more times than Overby could count. "Not to keep, she don't."

"Okay. You keep the sawed-off but she gets the shells."

Without waiting for more debate, Overby slid the shotgun across the table to Georgia Blue, who broke it open, removed the two shells, put them in her purse, then slid the still-broken-open shotgun back to Cullen.

Cullen put a hand on it, looked at Overby and said, "My money."

Overby reached into a hip pocket and removed ten pre-counted hundred-dollar bills. He handed them to Cullen, who counted them slowly twice, then looked up and said, "When'll I get my next thousand?"

"After you tell us about the Goodisons."

Colleen Cullen drank some of her bourbon and water, tossed black hair out of her eyes and said, "They rolled up unannounced and unexpected right out front two weeks ago tomorrow in a big old black limo."

Georgia Blue gave Overby a triumphant half-smile. He

ignored it and said to Cullen, "Okay. They get out of the limo. Then what?"

"They say the secret password."

"Which is what?"

"Five thousand a week."

"For both of them?" Georgia Blue said.

"Each."

"Christ!" Blue said.

"That's with full board, sis."

"What else do they get for ten thousand a week?" Overby asked.

"Guaranteed money-back privacy."

Overby nodded comfortably, as if he found the price high but not excessive. "How often do the deputies drop by?"

"Every other Tuesday."

"And go away with what?"

"A thousand each—and that thousand each's still gotta be paid even if I'm empty."

"Okay," Georgia Blue said. "The Goodisons check in. Then what?"

"They stay in their room for three days—even take their meals there. The TV's going twenty-four hours a day, nothing but MTV shit, although it ain't loud. It's sort of like they wanted background noise. But it sure wasn't loud enough to drown out the sounds they made humping away on the bed."

"Why'd they use their real names?" Overby said.

"With those limey accents? Shit. The second they open their mouths, I go, 'Lemme see some passports.' "

"They tell you they were brother and sister?"

"Said they were married. I think, Sure you are, kiddies. You just happen to have the same noses, mouths, eyes and ears. But if kinfolks wanta fuck each other, it's none of my business, so I call him Mr. Goodison and her Mrs. Goodison—at least 'til they say they want me to call them Hughsie and Paulie."

"Was there a phone in their room?" Overby asked.

"Only one phone in the whole house and it's locked up."

"They ever ask to use it?"

"Once."

"They get any calls?"

"Be hell to pay if they did."

"When did they turn off the TV and the MTV noise?" Blue said.

"Who says they did?"

"I'm guessing."

"They turn it off at the end of the third day and never turn it back on. They come out of their room that night and start getting friendly—too friendly. First him. Then her. Then both of 'em together. Touchy-feely stuff. They like to shuck off their clothes, too. He's finally down to nothing but Jockey shorts and she forgets to put on anything but a little old bra and panties and for all the good they did, she might as well've left them off. I don't mind a three-way now and then but not with those two sickos. I'd as soon jump into bed with a snake and an alligator. So I posted me some new rules."

"Which were what?" Georgia Blue asked.

"Rule One: Keep Your Hands off the Landlady. Rule Two: Cocks and Pussies Must Be Covered at All Times."

"What'd they do?" Overby said.

"They just giggled and I don't see much of 'em after that except at meals 'til the morning they left."

"A week ago tomorrow?"

"That's right," Cullen said.

"They tell you they were leaving?" Georgia Blue asked.

Cullen shook her head. "They just came downstairs with all their stuff. One big old leather suitcase and two weekend carryalls made out of canvas or that new stuff mountain climbers use. And they're all dressed up, too—except they *look* like they're all dressed up—know what I mean?"

Overby nodded.

"So I come out with something like, 'Ya'll leaving so soon?' And Hughes, he turns all serious and says they're sorry, but it's time to move on—or some such shit. Then he says he's wondering if I might sell him some personal protection and I say I don't carry condoms."

Cullen grinned. Overby grinned back. But Georgia Blue said, "Go on."

"Well, Pauline blows up. She starts yelling that I'm too fucking dumb to know the difference between guns and condoms. I tell Hughes the longer she hollers the higher the price. He hauls off and knocks her down and while she's down on her butt, still howling at me, Hughes and I dicker over two hardly used Chief Specials that wind up costing him seven-fifty apiece and would've been only five hundred apiece if Pauline hadn't thrown her fit."

Overby nodded thoughtfully and said, "How much'd two thirty-eights cost us?"

"Six hundred each."

"We'll think about it," he said, then asked, "How did they leave?"

"In that same old black limo with the same driver."

"Then it was prearranged," Georgia Blue said.

"Had to be and where's my money?"

"You don't know where they went?"

"I didn't ask, they didn't say."

"Okay, Colleen," Overby said. "Here's the deal. You already got one thousand. We'll pay you another thousand for what you told us about the Goodisons. We'll pay you a third thousand for two pieces—providing they're in good shape. And we'll also pay you a thousand for the limo's license number. That all adds up to four thousand, just like I said."

"What makes you think I know the license number?"

Overby shrugged. "You do or you don't."

"Well, why the hell not?" Cullen said, rose and reached for the shotgun but Georgia Blue's hand was faster. "Better leave that here," she said.

Cullen thought about it, then shrugged and left through a door at the rear of the parlor. While she was gone, Georgia Blue took the two shells from her purse and reloaded the shotgun, snapped it back together and cocked both hammers.

When Colleen Cullen returned five minutes later, a Smith & Wesson .38 caliber revolver dangled upsidedown by its trigger guard from each forefinger. She stopped and stared at the shotgun Georgia Blue aimed at her.

"You gonna do me, Slim?"

"I don't know yet."

Still staring at Georgia Blue, Cullen went slowly to the table and carefully placed one of the pistols on it. Overby picked it up. Cullen then put the other pistol on the table, again looked at Georgia Blue and asked, "Now what?"

"The license number," Georgia Blue said.

After Colleen Cullen rattled it off, Georgia Blue uncocked the shotgun, broke it open, removed the shells, put the shotgun on the table and said, "Pay her, Otherguy."

Twenty

In his role as a Malibu newcomer, Booth Stallings spent nearly two hours that same afternoon and early evening introducing himself to his somewhat dumbfounded neighbors or their completely dumbfounded Latina maids.

He was invited in three times; told to go away twice; had two doors slammed in his face; experienced cool brief chats on four thresholds, and once was listened to politely, if with total incomprehension, by a vacationing woman from Düsseldorf who spoke only German except for the phrase "Okay, swell," which she used over and over again, smiling all the while.

The neighbors who did talk to him knew nothing pertinent about the late William A. C. Rice IV—at least nothing they would confide to Stallings—until he rang the bell of the duplex directly across the highway from the house where Rice had died.

The man who opened the door of the two-story canary-yellow duplex was at least 74 or 75. He was also barefoot and wore a short green terry-cloth bathrobe and apparently nothing else except a cigarette, aviator sunglasses and the amber drink he held in his left hand. Still, Stallings thought there was something vaguely familiar about the craggy face with the cigarette stuck in the left corner of the wide bitter mouth.

The cigarette jiggled a little when the man spoke before Stallings could even say hello. "You really think they'll send you to Hawaii for two weeks?"

"Who?"

"The crew chief who's got you out peddling magazine subscriptions door-to-door old as you are."

"Not selling anything, friend," Stallings said with what he trusted was a reassuring and even ingenuous smile. "The name's Booth Stallings and I'm just paying a friendly call on account of I'm your new neighbor."

"Which house?"

"The one right across the street that belonged to poor Mr. Rice."

The man nodded, removed the cigarette, had a reflective swallow of his drink, stuck the cigarette back in place and said, "Billy Rice was a lot of things, but poor sure as shit wasn't one of 'em."

"Knew him pretty well, did you?"

"You a drinking man?"

"I have to confess I am."

"Well, come on in and I'll pour us one and you can get acquainted with the neighborhood's friendliest neighbor, Rick Cleveland."

There was a brief, not quite imperceptible, pause before Cleveland stuck out his right hand. It was as if he were hoping Stallings would match the name with the face. After grasping the hand, Stallings took a chance and said, "Hell, you're in pictures."

There was a slight nod followed by a small relieved smile as Cleveland, turning to lead the way into the living room, said, "Yeah, but I haven't worked much for a couple of years."

Suspecting it was more like ten years than two, Stallings said, "Been in Malibu long?"

"Since fifty-one and in L.A. since thirty-seven," Cleveland said, picking up a half-empty bottle of Vat 69 from a marbletop table. "Scotch okay?"

135

"Fine."

"Water?"

"Some."

"You need ice?"

Since none was visible, Stallings said, "Got out of the habit."

Once he had his drink, Stallings turned to the large window that offered a view of the Pacific Coast Highway, the Billy Rice house and, when he went up on his toes, a very small slice of the Pacific Ocean.

"View's better upstairs," Cleveland said as he eased down into a gray club chair. Stallings chose the low pale blue couch in front of the window, tasted his drink, gave his host another neighborly smile and said, "You must've seen some changes."

"Yeah, but that's because I go back to the Flood—or to *GWTW* anyway. Remember all those young southern bloods hanging around Scarlett in the first few scenes? Well, I was the one who got to say, 'You're welcome, Miss O'Hara,' or maybe it was, 'You're welcome, Miss Scarlett.' Can't even remember which now. But who the hell cares?"

"Film buffs maybe?"

"Fuck 'em."

After another polite swallow of his drink, Stallings said, "See much of your late neighbor?"

Cleveland put out his cigarette and lit a new one before replying. "I sued the son of a bitch for ruining my view. But he had a fix in with both the county and the Coastal Commission and I found out pretty quick that only damn fools sue anybody who's sitting on top of a billion bucks."

"You guys weren't too friendly, then."

"I went to see him in his Century City office when I learned how high he planned to build his goddamned house. He told me to talk to his lawyers. That was our first and last conversation."

Stallings glanced over his shoulder at the Rice house. "Ever been inside it?"

"Nope."

"Not the coziest place I ever stayed."

"Then why'd you rent it?"

"The outfit I work for's based in London and they're thinking of expanding to L.A. The two principal partners thought they might need to do a little entertaining. That's why I snapped up a two-month lease on the Rice house—because it looks like it was designed for a never-ending party."

"Well, he did give a lot of 'em," Cleveland said. "But you'd never know it. There wasn't any noise to speak of because the partying was all done on the beach side. And you couldn't complain about the parking or the traffic because he always had a valet service that drove the guest cars off and hid 'em someplace. But I used to see her car parked in the courtyard. A lot of times it'd be there all night."

"Whose car?"

"Ione Gamble's—the one who shot him, God bless her."

"Think she really killed him, do you?"

"She sure as hell had the opportunity. Had two of 'em, in fact."

"Why two?"

"I don't sleep so good anymore," Cleveland said and reached for the bottle of Vat 69 to top up his drink. After adding at least one and a half ounces, he put the bottle back on the marbletop table. "And even when I do get to sleep, I have to get up every couple of hours or so and go pee because of my goddamn prostate. Well, when I'm standing there peeing in the upstairs john, which takes forever, I like to look out the bathroom window at the ocean because it's always more interesting than looking down at what I'm doing or trying to do, right?"

Stallings nodded sympathetically.

"So I'm standing there peeing New Year's Eve about eleven-thirty when I notice her car parked in Rice's courtyard. She's got one of those fancy new Mercedes roadsters that sell for close to a hundred thousand a pop. But I don't think anything about it and head on back to the bedroom for my traditional New Year's Eve celebration, which means lying up in bed with a bottle and watching strangers making damn fools of themselves on TV. Then about twelve-thirty, after I'm fairly sure I've made it through another year, I gotta go take another leak. And that's when I notice it."

"Notice what?" Stallings said.

"That her car's gone. Ione Gamble's."

"So?"

"So I thought it was kinda funny she didn't stick around for New Year's Eve or, if she did, only spent half an hour of the new year with her former fiancé. But what the hell. It wasn't any of my business so I went back to bed. Then around five in the morning, I have to pee again. And there's her car back, its horn tooting away. Then she pops out of it and yells something I can't hear. And that's when she goes inside the house either to shoot him or make sure he's really dead."

"I'll be damned," said Stallings. "How'd you see all this at night? Did Rice keep his outside lights on like I do as a kind of burglar insurance?"

"He didn't just have his regular lights on. He had all his Christmas lights on, too."

"What'd the cops say?"

"When?"

"When you told 'em what you just told me?"

"Nothing. They wrote it all down and then wanted to know how much I'd had to drink New Year's Eve and if maybe it wasn't time I started going to meetings again."

"Couldn't it have been somebody else that first time?" Stallings said. "I mean somebody else driving a car just like hers?"

Cleveland shrugged. "That's exactly what the cops said and I'll tell you what I told them. The odds are a hundred to one against it."

There was a silence that Stallings finally broke with a final question. "So what do you think'll happen to her?"

"What do I think or what do I hope?"

"Either one."

"I hope they give her a medal," Rick Cleveland said. "But I don't much think they will."

Twenty-one

During what Georgia Blue later called the Colonel Sanders Seminar, Booth Stallings's report on the old actor's two sightings of Ione Gamble's roadster caused what should have been a stunned silence. And it would have been if a heavy surf hadn't been hammering the beach just below the huge living room where Wu, Durant, Overby, Blue and Stallings were dining on $73 worth of Kentucky fried chicken.

Booth Stallings, the designated provisioner, had bought the chicken at the local franchise and served it without apology just before Wu and Durant reported on their hypnotism session with Ione Gamble. This was followed by Georgia Blue and Otherguy Overby with reports on their respective meetings with Jack Broach, the agent, and Richard Brackeen, the dirty-movie man. Blue and Overby then spelled each other in the telling of their joint encounter with Colleen Cullen at her lie-low bed-and-breakfast inn.

Stallings made his report last, smiled at its effect, dipped a hand into a bucket of chicken, withdrew a drumstick and gnawed it while waiting to see who reacted first.

It turned out to be Artie Wu, who, after shifting around

in the big dark red leather chair, cleared his throat and asked, "You say this Mr. Cleveland's an actor?"

His mouth still full of drumstick, Stallings only nodded.

"How old is he?"

Stallings chewed some more, swallowed and said, "About ten years older than I am, which places him right on senility's front stoop."

"And you also say the sheriff's investigators weren't as much interested in what Mr. Cleveland said as they were in how much he'd been drinking?"

"The guy's a pacer, Artie. I'd guess he didn't drink much more the night he saw Ione Gamble's car twice, if he did, than he would any other night."

"His memory's unimpaired, then?"

"I didn't say that. He admits he can't exactly remember his one line to Vivien Leigh in *Gone With the Wind*. But he told me to an inch how high this house is and to a penny what it cost him to sue Rice because of it."

Durant had been standing at the huge window, staring at the lights of Santa Monica. He turned, dropped a chicken bone into an empty KFC bucket and said, "Maybe you didn't take Ione Gamble back far enough, Artie."

"Maybe I didn't," Wu said.

"But maybe the Goodisons did," said Georgia Blue, who again was seated on the long couch with Stallings, a bucket of chicken between them.

Wu looked at her, smiled slightly and said, "Is there more, Georgia?"

She first patted her mouth with a paper napkin, then said, "Pure speculation."

Wu sighed. "Pure or impure, let's have it."

"Okay. Ione Gamble told you she didn't let the Goodisons hypnotize her, right?"

Wu nodded.

"Did you find it difficult to put her into a deep trance?"

"No."

"Let's say the Goodisons are as adept as you are."

"Let's say they're more so."

"Then can we assume the Goodisons might've hypnotized Gamble during their second session with her—the one where nobody else was present—without her realizing or remembering it?"

Wu only nodded.

"And while in a deep trance could she have told them about her two trips to Rice's house—providing, of course, there really were two trips?"

"Let's pretend there were," Durant said.

Georgia Blue agreed with a nod. "All right. On her first trip, she's already smashed. She shoots Rice after an argument, goes home, drinks some more and passes out. When she wakes up, she's suffering from a blackout and remembers nothing—except that she's still mad as hell at Billy Rice." Georgia Blue looked at Wu again. "Is that possible?"

"Barely."

"Then it's also barely possible that Gamble gets so mad at Rice all over again that she drives back out here, shoots the Chagall instead of Rice, finds him dead, but still doesn't remember shooting him earlier. She dials 911, blacks out for the last time and wakes up remembering nothing."

"You're guessing that the Goodisons, at their second session with her," Durant said, "got every word down on tape, right?"

Georgia Blue nodded. "Maybe even on videotape."

Durant turned to Wu. "Well?"

Artie Wu examined the high living room ceiling for a long moment. "Ione's extraordinarily easy to hypnotize. As for them taping it—" He broke off, brought his gaze down and looked at Durant. "But you weren't talking about that, were you?"

"No," Durant said. "Because if they did hypnotize her, they damn well taped her."

"If we assume they did tape her," Georgia Blue said, "then we'd better assume the Goodisons are going for blackmail."

"Blackmail's just their first bite," Overby said. "They'll probably send her a copy of the part of the tape where she doesn't talk about anything but shooting the painting and finding Rice dead. That's the tease. Then they'll send her the part where she tells how she blew Rice away. Okay, it's not admissible evidence. But it could sure get the cops busy. So she agrees to pay and the Goodisons take her for every last dime including her house."

"But they don't stop there, do they, Otherguy?" Durant said.

"Course not. All blackmailers are greed freaks. They never know when to quit because it's all so easy, so . . . effortless. Once the Goodisons squeeze Gamble dry, they'll try and peddle a copy of their tape to one of the supermarket tabloids. And if they've also got her down on videotape, like Georgia says—you know, with a camcorder—they can try and peddle that to one of the sleazoid TV shows and millions can watch a hypnotized Ione Gamble tell how she shot and killed her billionaire novio last New Year's Eve. By then, the Goodisons oughta be medium rich."

"That how you'd work it, Otherguy?" Durant asked.

Overby gave Durant a carefully chilled stare. "That's how guys both you and I know'd work it."

"We should hope that much of what both Georgia and Otherguy suggest is true," Wu said with a small wise gentle smile that Booth Stallings thought some of the smarter saints might envy.

Overby's answering smile was two parts knowing and one part wicked. "They don't get it yet, Artie."

"I think Georgia does—don't you, Georgia?"

"Sure."

"Quincy?"

Durant only nodded.

"Booth?"

"Haven't a clue."

"When the Goodisons attempt to blackmail Ione Gamble," Wu said, "which I now believe they will, what's the first thing she'll need?"

"Money?" Stallings said.

"She'll also need an intermediary," Wu said.

Stallings nodded. "A go-between."

"Who do you have in mind?" Durant asked.

"Georgia, of course," Wu said, sounding surprised that anyone would ask.

"Of course," Durant said, his voice flat and toneless.

"Get to the good part, Artie," Overby said. "The money part."

"It's occurred to me," Wu said, "that Wudu, Limited, of Berkeley Square, London, should let it be known it's in temporary residence in Malibu and anxious to acquire searing, shocking and even salacious true-life tapes—video preferably, but audio in a pinch—for a worldwide, multilingual, exposé-type TV show. For the right tape, it's prepared to pay what? Up to a hundred thousand dollars?"

"Why not pounds?" Durant said.

"Better yet."

"What're you going to do, run an ad in *The Hollywood Reporter*?" Stallings said.

"I think we should depend entirely on word of mouth," Wu said. "And I can think of no one better to serve as our town crier than Otherguy. Any objections?"

Overby sent a glare around the room that encountered no resistance. The glare quickly disappeared, replaced by his familiar hard white grin.

"But please remember this," Wu said. "We're being paid to find the missing Goodisons, who obviously don't want to be found. If Georgia's theory is correct, and again I'll say I think some of it is, the Goodisons will try to blackmail Ione Gamble. If they do, they'll have to deal with one of us as the go-between. If they try to sell tapes, audio or video, we'll've already made what I hope is a preemptive bid—and again they must deal with us. Would anyone like to add or ask something?"

"Who does what?" Durant said. "Spell it out."

Wu closed his eyes briefly, then nodded at something, which Booth Stallings guessed was the order of battle. After opening his eyes, Wu looked at Georgia Blue. "As I said, Georgia, you'll be Ione Gamble's go-between. But until you're needed for that job, you'll continue looking into the life and

143

times of Jack Broach. Otherguy, for now, will be our town crier and the putative buyer of whatever the Goodisons have to sell. Quincy and I will follow up on a couple of things, including the license number of the limo that carried the Goodisons off."

"That leaves me," Stallings said.

Wu gave Stallings a smile of genuine affection. "You'll be our Mr. X, Booth—the secretive emissary from the mysterious Mr. Z, who's retained Wudu, Limited, to scour the world for sensational videotapes."

"In other words, I sit by the phone and wait for somebody to try and sell me something," Stallings said.

"The answering machine can take care of that," Wu said. "What we need is a utility chameleon—someone who can step in and play any role at a moment's notice. I think you're ideal. Any objections?"

"None," Stallings said, "as long as you don't ask me to handle a juvenile part."

Twenty-two

T he tiny frame house on the eastern edge of Venice sat on a twenty-five-foot lot and the 1982 black Cadillac limousine, parked out front, looked longer than the lot was wide. The limousine license plate read, "LUXRY 3," implying that there might be a fleet of them. The implied claim was supported by a small, nicely painted wooden sign that was nailed to a porch pillar. It advertised "Luxury Limos" and listed a phone number that was as large as its name.

The small front yard was split by a concrete walk that left enough room on the right for some grass and five ruthlessly pruned rosebushes. The other half of the yard, the left half, was dominated by an ancient bougainvillea that had swarmed up and over the small front porch and onto the roof as if intent on devouring the chimney.

The bougainvillea concealed much of the roof but the part still visible revealed old composition shingles of a faded green. The rest of the house had been painted not long ago in two shades of yellow—a very pale shade for the clapboard siding and a much darker shade for the trim. Durant thought the house looked both cozy and bilious.

He got out of the Lincoln Town Car on the passenger side

and Wu got out from behind the wheel. After they reached the porch, they heard a telephone begin to ring inside the house. Durant knocked. When no one came to the door and the phone rang for the ninth time, Durant gave the brass doorknob a halfhearted twist and was surprised to find it unlocked.

The door opened directly into a living room. The ringing phone was on a small gray metal desk in the room's far left corner. Between the front door and the phone was a Latino in his late twenties or early thirties who lay on a braided oval rug with his throat cut. Durant stepped over the man, took out a handkerchief and used it to pick up the still-ringing phone.

"Luxury Limos," Durant said.

There was a silence until a woman asked, "Carlos?"

"He can't come to the phone right now," Durant said in what he discovered was rusty Spanish. "Any message?"

The woman hung up.

Artie Wu was now on the other side of the desk, turning the pages of a black-bound ledger with the tip of a ballpoint pen. "His logbook," he said without looking up. "All of February's missing."

"Let's go," Durant said.

Wu nodded and closed the ledger with the pen.

Durant again stepped over the dead man, but Wu knelt beside him. The man wore dark blue pants, well-polished black loafers, a white shirt and a black clip-on bow tie. Both tie and shirt were soaked with blood. A small leather-bound notebook or diary peeked out of the shirt's pocket. Wu fished it out, wrapped it in a handkerchief and shoved it down into his hip pocket. He then rose and hurried out the front door, followed by Durant, who paused only long enough to smear the inside and outside doorknobs with his handkerchief.

Just as they reached the Lincoln they saw a dark-haired woman hurry out of a house that was across the street and four or five doors up. The house was a brown twin of the yellow one that served as headquarters for Luxury Limos. The woman wore jeans, a white T-shirt and white sneakers. From a distance she could have been either 20 or 30 but she moved as if she were 20.

As Wu and Durant hurried into the Lincoln, the woman started racing toward the yellow house. Just as the Lincoln pulled away she reached the giant bougainvillea and stopped, staring at the accelerating Lincoln. In its rearview mirror, Artie Wu saw her lips move and assumed she was memorizing the car's license number.

"Who rented this thing?" he asked Durant.

"Booth."

"Call him and ask him to report it stolen."

"Where should we lose it—a shopping mall?"

"Why not?"

*　　*　　*

They found a parking space on the fourth level of the Santa Monica Place mall at Third and Broadway, which was only a short walk to the edge of the continent. They rode escalators up and down until they found a floor that featured a string of ethnic-food stands where Wu bought two cups of espresso and carried them over to a table Durant had claimed.

After Wu sat down, he took out the handkerchief-wrapped notebook that had "1991" stamped in gold on its black leather cover. The handkerchief had soaked up virtually all the blood and Wu used a paper napkin to wipe away what little was left. He then wadded his handkerchief up into the paper napkin, enclosed both in yet another napkin, rose and dropped everything into a nearby trash bin.

Wu sat back down, opened the notebook and began turning pages. Durant sipped his espresso and decided it was too weak. Wu reached for his cup, sipped it, went back to the notebook and murmured, "Good coffee."

Durant rose. "I'll go call Booth."

Wu nodded, completely absorbed by the notebook.

Durant finally found a bank of pay telephones only to discover he no longer remembered what it cost to make a call. Was it a quarter or thirty-five cents? He dropped in three quarters and tapped out the Malibu number with its 456 exchange. When Stallings answered on the third ring, Durant identified himself and said, "We have to lose the Lincoln."

"What d'you want me to do?"

"Call the rental agency—which one is it?"

"Budget."

"Tell them it was stolen last night and you just discovered it missing."

"Where'd you lose it—just out of curiosity?"

"On the fourth level of the Santa Monica Place mall with its windows up and doors locked."

"Then they'll find it this afternoon," Stallings said. "Want me to rent you another car?"

"Get something grander—since Artie might have to put in an appearance as the mysterious Mr. X."

"I'm Mr. X," Stallings said. "He's Mr. Z. What about a Mercedes—a big one?"

"Perfect," Durant said.

When Durant returned to the table, he found Wu sitting with his clasped hands resting on the leather-bound notebook. "Booth's getting us another car," Durant said. "A Mercedes."

Wu nodded and said, "His name was Carlos Santillan. He would've been thirty-one in May. He owed seventy-six thousand on his house, around twenty-six hundred on that old Cadillac, and both monthly payments amounted to around nine hundred and something. He was single but the person to be notified in case of accident or death is Rosa Alicia Chavez, whose address is just four doors up from his house on the other side of the street. She must be the woman who came running to see what'd happened. Miss Chavez is twenty-six."

"How do you know?"

"He wrote her birthday right after her address and phone number."

"He write everything down?" Durant asked.

"His car and house were insured by Allstate. He banked at Security Pacific. He was a 1978 graduate of SaMoHi."

Durant frowned, then nodded. "Santa Monica High School."

"He was five-eleven," Wu continued, "weight one-sixty-one, had brown hair, brown eyes, and was scheduled to have his teeth cleaned in two weeks."

"He did write it all down," Durant said.

"Everything. A week ago yesterday he had an appointment to pick up Mr. and Mrs. Goodison at Cousin Colleen's Bed and Breakfast Inn in Topanga Canyon. There's nothing in his notebook about where he was to take them. I don't think he knew."

"Maybe he talked to somebody about them?" Durant said. "God knows they're weird enough."

"By somebody, you mean Rosa Alicia Chavez."

Durant nodded.

"If we tried to talk to her, she'd yell for the cops," Wu said. "At least I hope she would."

"Did his notebook list any organizations he belonged to— a union, business association, maybe a fraternal order?"

"You mean one that might provide his survivors or heirs with a small death benefit?"

"Say, two thousand dollars," Durant said.

"I think the ILOA might," Wu said. "That's the Independent Limousine Operators Association, which just this moment sprang into existence."

"Who d'you think—Otherguy?"

"Otherguy could handle it nicely," Wu said. "But Booth would do even better. He's older and more, well, grandfatherly, although I don't think he'd appreciate the description."

"Sure he would," Durant said. "Booth likes being the oldest. He's got fifteen or twenty years on us and Otherguy and a lot more than that on Georgia. And although he enjoys being the in-house patriarch, the real reason he likes hanging out with us is because he thinks we're all fellow anachronisms."

"The hell he does," Wu said. "You ever think of yourself as an anachronism?"

"No, but some days I do feel kind of quaint."

"Yes, well, some days so do I."

Twenty-three

The first thing Georgia Blue had done that morning, even before she drank any coffee, was call the Department of Motor Vehicles and use a cold formal tone and some Secret Service jargon to demand and receive the name and address that belonged to the LUXRY 3 license plate.

She handed the information to Durant, who had just poured his first cup of coffee in the late William Rice's elaborate kitchen that was almost large enough for a small hotel. Durant looked at the slip of paper, grunted his thanks and headed for the deck, where he could drink the coffee alone without having to talk to anyone.

Blue found a Thermos in a kitchen cupboard, poured two cups of coffee into it, picked up a mug and carried both mug and Thermos into her bedroom. She drank one cup of coffee, showered, ran a comb through her hair, which had grown nearly half an inch since the Philippines, and again put on the Anne Klein dress and the Joan & David shoes. She then sat on the bed next to the telephone, poured her second cup of coffee, picked up the phone and tapped out a number she had written down the night before.

After the call was answered by a cheery "Jack Broach and Company," Georgia Blue said, "My name's Margo Dawson and I'm a vice-president with the Mitsu Bank in Beverly Hills. The reason I'm calling is to find out if we might land some of Jack Broach's business."

"You'd have to talk to our comptroller, Mr. Corrigan."

"Is he in?"

"He usually gets in around nine-thirty."

"Maybe you could give me a hint. Is Mr. Corrigan happy with your present bank?"

"I guess so. Sure."

"Bank of America, right?"

"Security Pacific."

"The one on Wilshire just off Doheny?"

"The one just off La Cienega."

"Thanks very much. I'll try Mr. Corrigan later."

She used GTE information to get the Security Pacific branch phone number. Her call was answered by a recorded actor's voice that started giving her instructions about which numbers to tap if she wanted to know her checking account balance. Georgia Blue broke the connection and called GTE information again. After lowering her cold Secret Service tone to freezing, she told the operator she wanted to speak to a human voice, not a recorded one, at the Security Pacific branch. The operator gave her a different number.

When it was answered by a live female voice, Georgia Blue said, "I'd like to speak to one of your new business officers about opening a commercial account in the mid six figures."

She was quickly transferred to a Mr. Davidson, who wanted to know how he could be of assistance.

"This is Georgia Blue. I'm vice-president of Wudu, Limited, an American-owned, London-based consulting firm. We're in the process of opening our L.A. branch and we're looking for a bank. One of your customers mentioned yours."

"Which customer?"

"Jack Broach."

There was a slight hesitation before Davidson said, "I see. Is your company also in the entertainment business, Ms. Blue?"

"Good God, no. We're security consultants and awfully good at putting an end to chain-store shoplifting and such.

But our real specialty is designing programs to prevent industrial espionage."

"How do you spell Wudu?"

Georgia Blue spelled it and added, "Our address in London is Eight Bruton Street, Berkeley Square, London west one. We bank with both Westminster and Barclays. Our initial deposit with you would be a quarter of a million. Sorry, that's pounds, not dollars."

Davidson's tone grew noticeably warmer when he said, "I'm sure we can provide what you need. Like to drop by this afternoon?"

"This morning's better for me."

"What time?"

Georgia Blue looked at her $36 watch. It read 9:22. "Eleven-thirty?"

"See you then," Davidson said.

*   *   *

Only Booth Stallings was in the living room when Georgia Blue entered it seven minutes later. He was reading the editorial page of the *Los Angeles Times* but looked up and offered her the hard-news section.

She shook her head and said, "I don't know the players."

"Same old crowd."

"How goes the war?"

"We're being brave. They're being cowardly."

"That's good. What's it about?"

Stallings looked at her but she seemed genuinely curious. "Some say oil," he said. "Others say it's about stopping naked aggression and restoring democracy in Kuwait."

"Since when was Kuwait a democracy?"

"Since the war started."

"How long will it last?"

"Until the first or second week in March. This country can't stomach a long ground war with lots of dead American kids. So we'll get it over with, pack up and go home, have ourselves a nice patriotic orgy and leave the Middle East pretty much like we found it—except for a bunch of dead Iraqis."

Georgia Blue seemed to tire of the war talk because she glanced around the room and asked, "Where is everybody?"

"Wu and Durant went off to track down the guy who drove that limo. Otherguy's off on Otherguy business."

"And you?"

"I'm in reserve."

"I need some more money."

Stallings nodded. "How much?"

"A couple of thousand. I've got one dress, one pair of shoes, and it looks like rain."

Stallings reached into a pants pocket and brought out a large roll of $100 bills. "I didn't ask what for; I asked how much." He counted out twenty $100 bills, paused, counted out five more and handed them to Georgia Blue.

"You're sweet," she said.

"Given a choice, I'd rather be sexy than sweet."

"We'll see about sexy tonight."

"Sounds like a real date."

"It is."

Stallings rose. "You going into town?"

"Need a lift?" she asked.

"To Santa Monica and Wilshire. That's where Budget rents its fancy cars."

"What're you getting?"

"A Mercedes for Wu and Durant."

"What happened to their Lincoln?"

"I guess the cops are looking for it by now."

"Sounds like progress," Georgia Blue said.

"Yes," Stallings said, "doesn't it?"

*　　*　　*

She dropped him off at Budget's fancy rental car place that seemed to offer everything from Miatas to Lamborghinis. Ten minutes later she was back in Neiman-Marcus, where she bought a bluish-gray silk and wool suit and a pearl-gray Aquascutum raincoat. The same woman who had sold her the Anne Klein dress wanted to know if she'd ever been a model. When Georgia Blue said she hadn't, the woman said that was too bad because she could have been big-time. "I mean very big-time."

* * *

Georgia Blue entered the Security Pacific Bank at 11:28 A.M. Three minutes later she was sitting beside the desk of Harold Davidson, who introduced himself as the branch assistant manager. Davidson had a long big-chinned brown face with shrewd dark eyes and a mouth with corners that hooked up at the end, giving him a smile that apparently wouldn't go away. Although not yet 40, he didn't have much hair but still had the big gawky frame of a college basketball player who wasn't quite quick or tall enough for the pros. Davidson helped her off with her raincoat and hung it carefully on a hatrack that held no hats. Georgia Blue suspected it had never held any.

"London," Davidson said after she was seated and he had lowered his six feet three inches into his chair.

"London," she agreed.

"Sort of like London out there today, isn't it? The rain."

"I don't know," Georgia Blue said. "For the past five years I've been Wudu's permanent representative in Manila."

"The Philippines," said Davidson, cocked his head to the left, let his smile grow a little and asked, "Was Wudu by any chance in on the hunt for the missing Marcos billions?"

"Let's just say I performed various tasks for Mrs. Aquino's government."

"And now you're in L.A.," Davidson said. "Found yourself some offices yet?"

"No, but we've temporarily leased a house in Malibu through a real estate man called Phil Quill, who'll probably handle our office space."

"Quill," Davidson said. "Phil Quill. That somehow rings a bell."

"He used to play football for Arkansas."

"All-American, wasn't he?"

"I don't follow football."

Davidson nodded understandingly. "I think you said Jack Broach recommended us."

"I said he mentioned you."

"He a client of yours?"

"No. But we're indirectly doing some work for a client of his, Ione Gamble. I want to emphasize that neither Mr. Broach nor Ms. Gamble is our client. Our only client in this particular instance is Enno Glimm."

Davidson was impressed. "The *Camaraderie!* Glimm?"

Georgia Blue nodded.

Davidson picked up a pen and pulled a notepad closer. "Just what kind of banking services will you be needing, Ms. Blue?"

"The usual. Mostly, we'll want you to handle a fluctuating payroll of anywhere from ten to seventy employees. You'd issue the bimonthly checks and see to the state and Federal withholding plus the usual FICA and SDI stuff. It'll all be routine although sometimes we might require sizable amounts of cash on short notice."

At the mention of cash, Davidson put down his pen and said, "May I ask if you know Mr. Broach personally?"

"He and I had a meeting yesterday."

"How did he . . . seem?"

Georgia Blue stared at him for several seconds before she said, "I don't understand the question. If you're asking about his health, he seemed fine. But that's not what you're asking, is it?"

"Jack Broach is an old and valued customer," Davidson said. "But when you mentioned Enno Glimm, I thought you might've been assessing the Broach agency for a possible buy-out, merger or even an infusion of capital."

"Enno Glimm has no interest in the Broach agency."

The corners of Davidson's mouth almost turned down. "I see."

"We're a small firm, Mr. Davidson. But if you want our business, you'd better level with me. Is Jack Broach and Company broke—or just suffering from a temporary case of the shorts?"

Davidson frowned, started to speak, changed his mind, then changed it again and said, "I really can't say more than I've said."

Georgia Blue rose. "Then I'm afraid we won't be doing business after all."

She went to the hatrack, removed her coat, draped it over her left arm and turned to Davidson, who was getting to his feet. "I'm sorry you feel that way," he said.

She stared at him, then said, "Jack Broach and Company's down the tubes, right?" When Davidson made no reply and looked at his watch instead, Georgia Blue said, "That's what I thought."

After she turned and walked away, Davidson reached for his phone, picked it up, tapped out a number and returned his gaze to Georgia Blue's back. Just as she walked out the bank's front door, Davidson's call was answered with a cheerful "Jack Broach and Company." Davidson identified himself and asked to speak to Mr. Broach.

Twenty-four

After Georgia Blue had let him out at the intersection of Santa Monica and Wilshire Boulevard in Beverly Hills, Booth Stallings made an anonymous phone call to the Santa Monica police and told the woman who answered that she could find the stolen Lincoln Town Car on the fourth level of the Santa Monica Place mall's garage.

Stallings then found a nearby cafe, went in and breakfasted on waffles, sausages and coffee. After paying the bill, he strolled down Wilshire until he came to a bank, where he purchased a certified check in the amount of $2,000 made out to Rosa Alicia Chavez.

Coming out of the bank, Stallings noticed a quick-service printshop that didn't look busy. He went in, smiled at the owner, laid two $100 bills on the counter and said he'd bet $200 the shop couldn't provide him with a dozen business cards in thirty minutes. "You lose," the owner said as the $100 bills vanished into his pocket. Thirty minutes later Stallings walked out of the shop with a dozen business cards that read: "Jerome K. Walters, Executive Vice-President, Independent Limousine Operators Association." There was also a made-up address on Colorado Boulevard in Santa Monica and some equally fictitious phone and fax numbers.

158

Fifteen minutes later Stallings walked into the Budget office and identified himself as the renter of the stolen Lincoln Town Car. The clerk was a pretty young woman in her mid-twenties who seemed to be brimming over with goodwill. She told him her name was Gloria and that the Santa Monica cops had just called to say they'd found the Lincoln, practically undamaged, in the Santa Monica Place mall.

"What d'you mean 'practically'?"

"Well, we had to send a locksmith and the cops are going to keep it a few days to check for prints and stuff."

"That's not going to cost me extra, is it?"

"Course not, silly."

"Good," Stallings said, then frowned and added, "Look, Gloria, I've got my president and vice-president in from London and they aren't exactly overjoyed to wake up their first morning in Malibu and find their wheels gone. So I think I'd better rent 'em something that's not so easy to steal—maybe even something foreign and fancy."

"We have a pretty white Bentley."

"Too much flash for them. What about a nice black Mercedes?"

"Well, we have a black 500SL, a black 300E and one that's really nice, a black 560SEL."

"I'll take the 560."

"You want full coverage this time?"

"You bet," Stallings said.

*　　*　　*

On the eastern edge of Venice, Stallings got out of the big Mercedes sedan, went up the short concrete walk and onto the porch. There he knocked at the door of the brown house that was the dark twin of the small yellow one across the street and five doors down. A plump middle-aged woman in curlers opened the door.

"Miss Chavez?" Stallings said, knowing it wasn't.

"Whaddya want?"

"You are Miss Chavez?"

"No, I'm Helen from next door. Rosa's still all shook up."

159

"Poor Carlos," Stallings said with a doleful headshake. "Poor Miss Chavez. We're all so very, very sorry."

"Who's we?"

"The ILOA."

"What's that?"

"The Independent Limousine Operators Association."

Helen from next door turned her head to call, "Rosa. Some guy's here from the limo drivers." She turned back to Stallings and said, "You better come on in."

Stallings went in and found himself back in the early 1960s. On the floor was a Stonehenge cotton shag rug in shades of white, red, brown and black that was a duplicate of one Stallings and his late wife had bought in 1961 at the Hecht Company in Washington, D.C.

There was also a tweedy couch on chrome legs and a wing-back chair upholstered in a nubby green fabric. The coffee table was of oiled teak and its smaller cousin, a side table, was placed next to the green chair. Scandinavian modern thirty years later, Stallings thought as he sat down uninvited in the wingback chair.

The young woman on the tweedy couch wore a plain black T-shirt and black jeans. She sat, her knees pressed together and clutching a balled-up handkerchief. She had a pretty oval face despite her swollen eyes, a too-pink nose and no makeup of any kind. Stallings guessed she was 23 or 24. She stared at him, sniffed and asked, "You knew Carlos?"

Stallings handed her a business card. She read it carefully, then looked at him and said, "He didn't tell me he'd joined anything."

"He only joined last month, around the first of the year."

"And you came by to say you're sorry he's dead. That's nice. I thank you."

"I also came to tell you about the death benefits," Stallings said and shot a go-away look at the still-hovering Helen from next door.

Helen said, "I'll be back in a few minutes, hon."

After she left, Stallings took out the certified check, rose and presented it with some formality to Rosa Alicia Chavez.

"*Two thousand?*" she said with disbelief.

Stallings shook his head regretfully, sat back down and said, "I'm sorry it's so little, but he was a member for such a short time."

"So much," she said.

"I know this is difficult, Miss Chavez, but one of the main reasons for the limo drivers association is to look after each other and stop terrible things like this from happening."

She nodded, again studying the check. "You wanta ask me some questions, right?"

"If it won't upset you too much."

She looked up. "I can tell you what I already told the cops."

"That'd be fine."

Rosa Alicia Chavez talked for nearly five minutes about the Lincoln Town Car she had seen speeding away from Carlos's house. She gave its year of manufacture, its color, its probable Blue Book value and its license number. She then talked about the man she called "*el chino grande*," and also the other one, who she said was real tall and dark and mean-looking. She described how they had rushed out of Carlos's house, sped off in the Lincoln and what she would like to do to them—especially *el chino grande*. Stallings took notes.

After she finally ran down, he said, "Did Carlos recently mention any strange or difficult clients?"

She shook her head. "Just the *ingleses*."

"The English?"

She nodded with an expression that was a curious mixture of revulsion and fascination. "A man and a woman who tell Carlos they are Mr. and Mrs. But he tells me they look like twins."

"You mean brother and sister?"

"Yes, brother and sister," she said, shuddering slightly.

"Did he mention their names?"

"No, he just says he drives them to a place in Topanga Canyon and then goes back and gets them maybe a week later and drives 'em someplace else."

"He say where?"

"To a motel."

"In L.A.?"

"In Oxnard."

"Did he say which one?"

She studied the check again, then looked up and said, "All he tells me is they're locos and he drives 'em to Oxnard, a motel there. You think maybe these locos are mixed up with the big Chinese and the tall guy with the real dark tan?"

"I don't know. It's possible, of course."

"So if I don't tell you what motel Carlos took 'em to, you're gonna take back the check, right?"

"No."

She waved the check a little, almost admonishing Stallings with it. "Look. If this is some kinda trick or joke, I don't think I can stand it."

"It's no trick or joke and you have our deepest sympathy," Stallings said and rose.

She looked up at him and said with great formality, "I thank you for coming and for the money. You're a very nice man. Can I offer you something to drink—some coffee maybe?"

He smiled. "Thank you, no."

"Can I ask one more question?"

"Of course."

"How long were you a limo driver?"

"Over thirty years."

She nodded gravely and said, "I thought it must be something like that."

Twenty-five

It took Otherguy Overby less than half an hour to win nearly $500 at the draw poker club in Gardena. He won by playing what he thought of as "sullen style"—never speaking other than to say "three cards" or "fold" or "raise ten" or "call." He also kept looking over his left shoulder.

The player to his right was a fiftyish woman with a 30-year-old body and a face that too much sun had baked into a filigree of fine lines. She wore a blue tank top and a Dodgers baseball cap with the bill turned sideways to the left. After Overby looked over his shoulder for what could have been the sixteenth time, she said, "You expecting reinforcements?"

"A guy's supposed to meet me here."

"Way you're squirming around, he must owe you a bundle."

"I'm looking to pay, not collect—if he ever shows up."

The woman lowered her voice and leaned toward Overby. "If you're really hurting, I can give you a number."

Overby scowled at her. "I look like a doper?"

"Who mentioned dope? But come to think of it you do look like every narc I ever saw."

Overby made his scowl go away. "I buy home videos."

They played two more hands before the woman asked, "Home videos of what?"

"Of people doing things they shouldn't."

"You mean sex stuff?"

Overby glared at her again. "What's with you, lady? First I'm a doper. Then I'm a narc. And now you've got me in the porn business."

She leaned closer to him and whispered, "What about a video of a couple trying to drown their four-month-old baby?"

Overby's glare changed into a speculative gaze. "You want a cup of coffee?"

"Sure," the woman said and gathered up her chips.

*   *   *

She said her name was Cheyne Grace. She spelled Cheyne and told Overby it was pronounced like Shane, the old movie, or Shayne, the old detective.

"What old detective?" Overby asked.

"Michael Shayne, private eye. What's his name, Lloyd Nolan, used to play him in pictures."

Overby stirred his coffee for almost fifteen seconds, looked over his left shoulder and said, "Tell me about the baby-drowning video."

"This guy I know says he knows somebody who saw it."

"Maybe I oughta talk to him—this guy you know."

"I'm sort of his agent."

"Sort of?"

"Okay, I'm his agent. You wanta talk to him, you talk to me first."

Overby nodded, looked over his shoulder again, leaned toward the woman, lowered his voice and said, "Okay. Here's how it works. I represent a guy I'll call Mr. Z—okay? Mr. Z is outta London—in England—and he's putting together a TV show for worldwide syndication. It won't need any actors and hardly any voice-over because everything'll explain itself. That's because it'll all be home videos of real shock stuff."

"Like what?" she said.

"Like the one Mr. Z paid a hundred thousand pounds for."

"What's that in American?"

"About a hundred and eighty thou." He looked over his shoulder again and dropped his voice into a confidential murmur. The woman leaned toward him. "There was this murder that happened in London two years ago," Overby said. "A guy comes home from a business trip to the States and finds his wife and mother-in-law with their heads chopped off."

The woman's eyes went wide. "You got all that on tape?"

Overby sighed, looked over his shoulder again and said, "Of course we haven't got it on tape. What we've got is a home-video tape of the killer confessing and then turning on the gas and sticking his head in the oven. We left his confession pretty much the way it is but edited the oven scene down to six or seven seconds—just long enough to make impact."

"Who was it?" she asked.

"Who was what?"

"The killer?"

"Yeah, well, it was the husband. He was in Washington, D.C. Bought or stole himself an American passport, flew the Concorde both ways, chopped their heads off with an ax and got back to Washington before anybody knew he was gone. Then he flew economy-class back to London thirty-six hours later, discovered the bodies and called the cops. Perfect crime, perfect alibi."

"Why'd he kill 'em?" Cheyne Grace asked.

Overby decided to go with the standard motive. "Money, what else? His mother-in-law was kind of rich and his wife was her only heir. So he kills the mother-in-law first, makes his wife fix them both something to eat, then kills her an hour later. The autopsy proves the mother-in-law died first and that means her daughter inherits everything. So the husband inherits it all from his dead wife. The mother-in-law left a real nice little place down in Torquay near the water and that's where the husband taped his confession and then stuck his head in the oven."

"How much did he inherit?" Cheyne Grace asked.

"It was about four hundred thousand pounds," Overby said after deciding to make it less than a million.

"Who'd you buy the confession tape from?"

Overby smiled for what he thought must be the first time in three hours. "That's confidential."

She nodded her understanding, then said, "That drowning-the-baby thing. I just made that up."

"No kidding?"

"Yeah, but this guy I know does know lots of weird people, know what I mean?"

Overby only nodded.

"So how do we contact you—in case he's got something?"

Overby recited the 456 number of the William Rice house. "Four-five-six," Cheyne Grace said, impressed. "That's Malibu."

"It's Mr. Z's place," Overby said. "But don't ask for him, ask for Mr. X."

"That's you, isn't it—Mr. X?"

Before Overby could reply a big hand landed on his left shoulder. He jumped, then looked up and around at a man who was well over six feet tall and wore a tightly belted tan bush jacket, dark aviator glasses, a pigskin hat with its brim turned down and a beard that had been growing for at least three days.

The man spoke in a low rumble that was half-accusation, half-threat. "You said you'd be alone, man."

"I am," Overby said.

"Then who the fuck's that?"

Overby looked at Cheyne Grace and shrugged an apology. "You mind?"

"No," she said, rising quickly. "Not at all."

When she was gone, the man sat down at Overby's left and said, "She's still watching us."

"Good."

"How'd I do?"

"You were perfect."

"I tried to put a lot of menace into that second line: 'Then

166

who the fuck's that?' I started to say, 'Then who the fuck's she?' but that sounded too stilted, don't you think?"

"It was exactly right," Overby said, reaching into the inside breast pocket of his jacket. "She still watching us?"

"Yes."

"Okay. I'm going to give you an unsealed brown envelope. Inside is three hundred in twenties. I want you to count it, but inside the envelope. Take your time. Then I want you to give me a nod."

"Just a nod?" the man said. "No line?"

"No line."

"I think I can put a lot into that nod."

"I know you can," Overby said and handed him the brown envelope.

*   *   *

At 1 P.M. Overby treated himself to a pre-lunch martini at a Manhattan Beach bar and grill he had once frequented when financial reverses in 1985 had forced him to become "House-sitter to the Stars." The fortyish bartender-owner slid the drink over and said, "I got a little something that might interest you, Otherguy."

"Yeah, what?"

With his elbows now on the bar, the owner looked left, right, then at Overby. "Some London TV biggie's in the market for videotapes—homemade stuff. I hear he's offering fat money."

"You mean homemade porn?" Overby said, looking at his watch. It was 1:05 P.M. and exactly two and a half hours since he'd left the poker club in Gardena.

"More like true confession stuff is what I hear," the owner-bartender said. "Stuff like, 'I killed the wife, the kids and the dog and now I'd like to show you where I buried them.' "

"I'd watch that," Overby said.

"All you really need is a camcorder and a script."

"And maybe an actor," Overby said.

"You want the phone number?"

Overby nodded.

The owner wrote it down on a beer coaster and slid it to Overby. He glanced at it and saw it was the 456 number at the Rice house in Malibu.

"Ask for Mr. X," the owner-bartender said. "And don't forget I'm still paying dues to SAG."

Overby tucked the coaster away in a jacket pocket and said, "You done anything lately?"

"Got a commercial coming up next week."

"I may be in touch," Overby said, finished his martini, placed a twenty-dollar bill on the bar and left.

Twenty-six

At 11 A.M. that day, Georgia Blue had called Jack Broach to suggest they have lunch. He quickly agreed and recommended a currently popular Alsatian restaurant on Sunset in Beverly Hills. After they agreed to meet at 1 P.M., Broach called a prospective client and cancelled their lunch date. This caused the prospective client, a moody actor, to accuse Broach of fickleness. Since the actor's career was going nowhere, Broach cheerfully pled guilty to the charge and hung up.

Arriving at the Alsatian restaurant fifteen minutes late, Georgia Blue gained an immediate audience as she followed the maitre d' to Broach's table. Most men looked at her face, most women at her clothes. Then all of them, or nearly all, noticed the white streak of hair and the long sure stride and her obvious indifference to their curiosity.

They were still watching when she reached Broach's table. By then Broach had decided that the stares and speculation were worth more than all the commissions he might have earned from the moody actor, who hadn't worked in eight months anyway.

Georgia Blue didn't apologize for being late. After she was seated, Broach asked if she would like a drink. She asked for a glass of the house red, if there was such a thing. When the drinks came, she glanced at the menu and ordered the special cassoulet, which Broach guessed was at least three thousand calories. He ordered soup and salad.

After the waiter left, she sipped her wine, smiled at Broach and said, "Did that nice Mr. Davidson at Security Pacific call you?"

Broach nodded.

"I hoped he would."

Suspecting he was supposed to ask why, Broach decided not to ask and see whether silence would provoke elaboration. It didn't. Instead, Georgia Blue sipped more wine, glanced around the room and said, "Some of them look familiar. Should they?"

"A few of them."

"I haven't seen a movie in five years. Did I miss much?"

"It depends on what you like."

"Ironic ones with lots of talk."

"You haven't missed anything."

"What do you like about your business, Mr. Broach?"

"The money. The deals. And now and then the people and the product."

"I take it you're still Ione Gamble's best friend?"

"I certainly hope so."

"Then you should know I'm to be her go-between."

"You'll go between what or whom?"

"Between her and whoever's going to blackmail her."

Broach leaned back in his chair and studied Georgia Blue. Finally, he said, "If there were any blackmail attempt, I'm sure she would've talked to me about it."

"She doesn't know about it yet."

"Who do you think or suspect is going to blackmail her?"

"Hughes and Pauline Goodison."

"And what exactly would you do as Ione's go-between?"

"Buy back stuff that could ruin her reputation and destroy her career."

"Then you have my blessing."

"Good. Now we can talk about money."

"The money to pay the blackmailers."

"Yes. That money."

"If the Goodisons are the blackmailers, you're talking to the wrong guy. You should be talking to Enno Glimm."

"Because he's guaranteed to indemnify her against any damage or loss the Goodisons might cause?"

"That's what the contract says."

"But we only suspect the Goodisons are the blackmailers," Georgia Blue said. "What if they're not? What if they're perfectly innocent?"

"Then why did they disappear?"

She shrugged. "Maybe something or somebody made them disappear. Until you prove the Goodisons are the blackmailers, I don't think Mr. Glimm will pay anything."

"Which means Ione will have to come up with the money."

Georgia Blue nodded.

Jack Broach tasted his drink for the first time, then set it aside as if he had no intention of picking it up again. "How much money are you talking about?"

Staring at his left eye, Georgia Blue said, "I'd guess a million."

"That's why you paid my bank a visit, right?"

She then began an examination of his right eye and said, "We need to know if there's enough to make the payoff."

"And is there?"

"Mr. Davidson was very circumspect."

"Do you think there's enough?"

"No."

"Why not?"

She ended her eye examination, drank the rest of her wine, smiled at him and said, "The Daumiers. In your office. I mean the fake Daumiers. The moment I spotted them I wondered why a guy like Jack Broach would hang fake Daumiers on the wall. My answer: he had to sell the real ones because of hard times in Hollywood." She rested her elbows on the table, leaned toward him a few confidential inches, smiled again and said, "You are broke, aren't you, Jack?"

"Am I?"

She straightened, shrugged and looked over his right shoulder at something that might have been halfway across the room. "I could sniff around some more. But to save time I could also have Howard Mott tell Ione Gamble that he needs a financial statement of her assets, liabilities and cash on hand."

There was a long silence before Jack Broach said, "Why the warning?"

She stared at him with complete indifference. "Self-interest."

"Go on."

"Let's try a worst-case scenario," she said. "Suppose the blackmailer—singular or plural—demands a million. Ione Gamble agrees to pay and turns to you for the money—or, more precisely, for the money she's entrusted to you. What then?"

"It's your scenario."

"You tell her you'll have to sell or hock everything to come up with a million. She says fine, do it. Could you raise a million, Jack—in cash?"

Broach said nothing.

"Well, could you raise—say, three hundred thousand? I think you could. So what you do is raise the three hundred thousand and tell Ms. Gamble the million's ready for the go-between. You then hand me the three hundred thousand and I eventually hand you or Ione Gamble the incriminating material along with a guarantee that the blackmailer or blackmailers won't ever bother her again."

"What if they ask for less—say a half a million?"

"The price is still three hundred thousand. I don't haggle."

"What good is your guarantee?" he said. "I'm no criminal defense lawyer, but the best of them tell me blackmailers never know when to quit."

"They do when they're dead," said Georgia Blue.

Twenty-seven

The two-room, $350-a-day suite Howard Mott had rented was on the fifth floor of a ten-story hotel on Ocean Avenue in Santa Monica. The suite's living room, now turned into an office, afforded a view of the ocean and the long, long narrow strip of green grass lined with tall palms that was called Palisades Park.

Often encamped beneath the palms was an assortment of throwaway people, whose current euphemism was "the homeless." These consisted in part of the deranged, the jobless, the muddled, the addicted, the dispossessed, the senile—plus a variety of other mendicants who ranged from journeyman panhandlers to novice bums.

Santa Monica, a notoriously softhearted town, had at first pitied and tolerated its homeless, even supplying them with shelter and hot meals. But the city was wearying of its burden and now hoped, maybe even prayed, that its permanent underclass would migrate elsewhere, ideally to some spot far, far away such as Wyoming or Alaska or even Palm Springs.

As Wu and Durant turned the corner of Broadway and Ocean Avenue, heading for Mott's hotel, they were set upon by a band of alms seekers. After he and Durant ran out of money, Wu ducked into a bank and returned with fifty dollars

173

in one-dollar bills. He gave roughly half of them to Durant and by the time they reached Mott's hotel six blocks later, Wu had three ones left; Durant had none.

* * *

Howard Mott guided Wu and Durant past his two secretaries, who were busy at their word processors, and into the bedroom, where Booth Stallings sat, drinking coffee, on the edge of the remaining twin bed.

"Want some?" Stallings asked, indicating his cup.

Before Wu or Durant could answer, Mott said, "I think they'd prefer a beer, right?"

Durant said, "If it's no problem."

"It'll only take a couple of minutes," Mott said. "Maybe three." He left the bedroom, carefully closing the door behind him.

"I think Howie doesn't want to hear what maybe he shouldn't hear," Stallings said.

"And what's that, Booth?" Wu said.

"I rented you guys a new car—a black Mercedes sedan, the 560. It's even got a telephone. I also gave Rosa Alicia Chavez a certified check for two thousand dollars along with the sympathy of the Independent Limousine Operators Association. She was most grateful and told me she'll never forget the two guys who killed her intended. She especially won't forget the big fat one she called 'el chino grande.'"

"How'd she describe me?" Durant said.

"Tall, dark and mean-looking."

"What'd she say about the Goodisons?" Wu asked.

"All her late fiancé told her was that both Goodisons are locos and that he picked them up by prearrangement at the bed-and-breakfast place in Topanga Canyon, then drove them to a motel in Oxnard. She didn't say which one because he didn't tell her. I found Oxnard on the map and it's about thirty miles up the coast from Malibu. I called its Visitors' Bureau and they told me they have a couple of dozen motels."

"What about Otherguy?" Durant said.

"When last heard from, he was spreading the word about

the booming new market for home videos of people doing awful stuff they shouldn't. He said he'd begun at a poker parlor in Gardena and was working his way back."

"Oxnard," Wu said to Stallings. "Why don't you and I run up there this afternoon and check out some motels?"

Stallings nodded and was about to add something when the door opened and Howard Mott came in with three open bottles of Mexican beer. He kept one for himself, served the others to Wu and Durant, then asked, "Who wants to go first?"

"Why don't you?" Durant said when everyone was seated— Mott behind his desk, which occupied the space where the missing twin bed had been, and Wu on the bed next to Stallings. Durant half sat on the windowsill.

Mott took a long drink of beer from the bottle as if he were parched, then said, "We have a problem. The sleaze media's staked out Ione's house and she has to go to the dentist."

"Sounds like a job for Jack Broach, super agent," Durant said.

"He's having a long lunch with your Ms. Blue—or so his secretary says."

"I take it this isn't just Ione's regular six-month checkup?" Wu said.

"It's an impacted wisdom tooth that has to come out before it develops an abscess," Mott said. "She'd drive herself but they're going to give her sodium Pentothal to knock her out. The dental surgeon insists somebody has to drive her home and Ione insists somebody trustworthy has to be on hand to monitor her babbling while she's under the influence of what she calls 'the truth serum.' "

"When's her appointment?" Durant asked.

"Two."

"I'll drive her, if her car's out of impound."

"It is," Mott said.

Durant asked, "What else, Howie?"

"They traced the murder weapon—that Beretta semiauto-matic—to its previous owner, which turns out to be Para-mount Studios. It was stolen from a movie set there nine years ago. Fortunately, Ione didn't do anything at Paramount that year."

"What movie was it?" Stallings asked.

"A TV pilot that none of the networks picked up. Something called *The Keepers*. I have copies of the script and the names of everyone in the cast and crew. I have a videotape of the pilot itself and I'm told that everyone connected with it who's still alive is being questioned by the sheriff's investigators."

"Could I get copies of everything you have?" Stallings said.

"Ask Mary Jo," said Mott.

"She the blonde?"

"The brunette."

Wu rose. "Anything else?"

Mott nodded. "Enno Glimm."

"He called?" Durant said.

"No, but Jenny Arliss did. She and Glimm're flying in late tonight. But there's no need to meet them because she's arranged a limo that'll whisk them out to the Malibu Beach Inn, which she thinks'll be quite convenient for all concerned."

"She say why they're coming?" Durant asked.

Mott nodded. "She says Glimm wants to know how you're spending his money."

*　　*　　*

The *paparazzi* had gathered at the northwest corner of Seventh Street and Adelaide Drive in Santa Monica. They had arrived in three vans and five cars and positioned themselves less than a block from Ione Gamble's house. Durant, with Gamble beside him, backed out of her driveway in her almost new Mercedes 500SL roadster and started around the curve where the photographers waited. Durant automatically counted the number of what he thought of as the opposition, if not the enemy, and came up with seventeen—five of them women. Six were armed with camcorders and the rest had one or more 35mm cameras. They were uniformly young, uniformly scruffy and, Durant decided, about as congenial as sea gulls.

"What should I do—duck?" Gamble asked.

"Ignore them."

He stopped the Mercedes in the center of the street, shifted into neutral and raced the engine up to five thousand revolutions per minute. The *paparazzi*, unfazed, formed a wavering line across the street a dozen yards ahead. His left foot firmly on the brake, Durant shifted into low, raced the engine again and took his foot off the brake.

The Mercedes leaped forward, its fat rear tires clawing at the asphalt. The acceleration slammed Durant and Gamble back into their seats. Durant had read somewhere that the 500SL could accelerate from 0 to 60 in less than seven seconds. The claim was apparently valid.

The line of *paparazzi* wavered—then broke mostly to the right, the passenger side. They had less than a second to aim and shoot as the roadster flashed by, its passenger staring straight ahead. By the time the photographers had piled into their cars and vans, the Mercedes had disappeared around the corner and was racing south on Seventh Street.

Ione Gamble's destination was a medical building on the southwest corner of Wilshire Boulevard and San Vicente. But instead of taking the most direct route, which would have been east on San Vicente, Durant used tree-lined side streets, turning south or north at almost every intersection, but bearing always east.

Ione Gamble finally said, "You seem to know the way—sort of."

"Wu and his wife used to live in Santa Monica."

"And you?"

"In Malibu—Paradise Cove."

"Where the rumrunners used to unload," she said. "During Prohibition."

"I missed that by about fifty years."

"You were there in the seventies, then?"

"In the late seventies," he said. "For a while."

"How long've you lived in London?"

"Nearly five years."

"You like it?"

"I haven't decided yet."

"Listen," she said. "No matter how much they bitch, I want you with me every second we're there."

"You won't say anything."

"How d'you know?"

"Because he'll have both hands in your mouth."

*   *   *

Dr. Melvin Unger didn't want any spectators. Ione Gamble told him that unless Mr. Durant were present, her impacted wisdom tooth would stay right where it was. Dr. Unger, a pale, very thin man with soft brown eyes that were either extremely sad or extremely kind, remained adamant for nearly ten seconds before he relented and agreed that Durant could stay.

A practitioner of four-handed dentistry, Dr. Unger let his dental technician inject the sodium Pentothal. Ione Gamble was now almost horizontal on the dental chair. Just as the needle went into a vein in her left arm, she was asked to count backwards from ten. She reached six before she went under and out.

The extraction of the impacted wisdom tooth took less than ten minutes. Durant calculated that Dr. Unger, working at top speed, could gross around $7,200 an hour. Ione Gamble was still out when Durant helped the dental technician half walk, half carry her into the quiet room where they eased her onto a narrow couch.

The technician handed Durant a box of Kleenex and said, "There shouldn't be any more bleeding, but if there is, give her some of these."

"What about pain?"

"No pain," she said. "Just some mild discomfort."

"When can she eat?"

"An hour or two from now. But I'd suggest soup, medium warm. Later this evening, anything she wants within reason."

After the technician left, Durant sat down next to Ione Gamble, watched her for several seconds, then said, "Ione?"

"Yes," she said, her eyes still closed.

178

"Did anyone borrow your car New Year's Eve?"

"No."

"Did you go out to Billy Rice's house twice that day—once in the late afternoon or evening and again early the next morning?"

"No."

"Did you shoot Billy Rice?"

"No."

"Do you know who did?"

"No," she said just as the dental technician bustled in and asked, "She coming around?"

"Seems to be," Durant said.

"Let's have a look." She bent over Ione Gamble and, using a voice she would use on someone hard of hearing, said, "Miss Gamble? Can you hear me?"

Ione Gamble opened her eyes and said, "Is it over yet?"

The technician smiled. "All over and everything's fine."

"God, that Pentothal's wonderful stuff."

The technician beamed. "Isn't it, though?"

Gamble turned her head and found Durant leaning against a wall. "I say anything?"

"Nothing I could understand," he said.

Twenty-eight

After they left the medical building, Durant followed Ione Gamble's advice and took San Vicente Boulevard all the way to Ocean Avenue in Santa Monica. After two acute right turns he drove up the short steep incline that was a seldom-used back way into Adelaide Drive.

This stretch of the drive had been transformed into a one-way street by those who lived in the huge houses that lined its right side. To the left of the street the land fell sharply away, almost straight down, and provided a see-forever view of canyon, mountains and ocean.

At the end of the one-way section was a white-painted steel barrier that blocked two-way traffic and gave the long row of huge houses the air of a gated community. As he squeezed the Mercedes past the steel barrier, Durant noticed a group of six or seven fit-looking men and women in their early twenties. Some were doing cramp-relieving exercises. Others were gulping Evian water from one-liter plastic bottles. Nearly all were wearing shorts, tank tops, running shoes, and sweating at half past three on a late February afternoon with the temperature in the low sixties and falling.

"They still bounce up and down those steps?" Durant asked.

"Night and day," Gamble said. "One hundred and eighty-nine steps up from the floor of the canyon and one hundred and eighty-nine down. The same as in a fourteen-story building. A few of them make three or four round trips a day. Some of them even do it two steps at a time."

Because Durant couldn't think of anything to say except "Ah, youth," he said nothing. His silence provoked a smile from Gamble. "They make me feel the same way and you've got ten years on me."

"More like fifteen," Durant said.

They were both silent for almost a block until they turned into her driveway, stopped, and she asked, "Is Pentothal like opium?"

"Why?"

"If it is, then I finally figured out why the British fought the opium wars with China."

"To corner the euphoria market, right?"

"Sure, but what I felt at the dentist's was ten notches up from euphoria. What I felt was, well, perfection."

"I'll remember that the next time they try to give me novocaine," Durant said, switched off the engine and handed her the keys. He had his door half-open when he turned back to ask, "Any letdown? Pain? Discomfort?"

She shook her head. "A slight twinge now and then—just enough to make you wonder if getting up for a couple of aspirins is worth the effort." She opened her own door, paused and said, "Why not come in for a drink and some almost instant mock Senate bean soup?"

Durant said it sounded interesting.

*　　*　　*

He sat at the kitchen table with a Scotch on ice and watched her open a large can of Great Northern beans. She dumped the contents into a saucepan and placed it on the stove over low heat. She found some garlic, then located a large onion, cut it in half and removed its outer skin. She didn't bother with the outer skin of the garlic.

After Gamble had butter melting in a small frying pan, she

181

tossed the garlic and onion into a mini-Cuisinart, gave it a couple of bursts, then another one, and dumped the chopped results into the now sizzling butter. Once the garlic and onion turned golden brown, she spooned them, butter and all, into the simmering beans, stirred, added salt, a little water, lots of · pepper and a dash or two of Tabasco. She almost forgot the bay leaf but tossed it in at the last minute, admitting it provided more style than flavor.

She found two soup bowls, two napkins, two soup spoons and a loaf of dark rye bread sliced at the bakery. She then asked Durant if he wanted anything besides Scotch to drink. He said he didn't.

After serving the soup, she sat down, picked up her spoon and said, "This recipe was taught me a long time ago by a very young one-term congressman from L.A. who, when last heard of, was living in semi-permanent exile just outside of Lisbon."

"Chubb Dunjee," Durant said and tasted the soup.

She halted her spoon a few inches from her mouth. Her eyes widened. "You know him?"

"Artie and I ran into him down in Mexico years ago. Chubb certainly knew some . . . shortcuts."

"What were you guys doing in—"

The kitchen's wall telephone rang, interrupting her question. Gamble rose, crossed to the phone, put it to her left ear and said, "Allo," in what Durant thought must have been a perfect imitation of her Salvadoran housekeeper.

Gamble then listened to the voice on the phone for nearly fifteen seconds before she said, "*Un momento, por favor.*" Again, the accent was perfect.

She used her right hand to indicate the telephone, then used the same hand to point at the hall leading into the living room. Durant nodded, rose and hurried into the living room where he picked up an extension phone with his right hand and looked at his watch. It was 3:13 P.M. Just as the phone touched his right ear, he heard Ione Gamble say, "Who's this?"

"Recognize the voice, love?" a British tenor said.

"Hughes, you dipshit. What the hell happened?"

"Paulie and I went on a retreat—to sort out our options," said Hughes Goodison.

"Why call me?"

"Because we've decided you're our best option—although we do have several others."

"You're not making sense."

"Of course I am, love. And you'll understand perfectly once I play a tape of you talking to Paulie and me while you were deep in hypnosis. It's just a tiny bit of a much, much longer tape, but, still and all, rather a fair sample."

The next voice was Gamble's, but filtered by tape and telephone. Her voice was also deeper than normal and nearly toneless. "I wanted to kill him," she said.

Then Hughes Goodison's voice, similarly filtered, asked a question: "Billy Rice?"

"Yes."

"Did you?" Goodison's voice asked.

A long pause, followed by Gamble's uninflected answer: "Yes."

"That's it, Ione," Goodison said in his normal voice. "We want you to know we're willing to sell all forty-nine and a half minutes of the tape you just heard."

"You mean you want to sell me one of the God knows how many copies you've made."

"Lord, no. Paulie and I are risk avoiders, not risk takers. Whoever pays our price buys the original. There are no copies. None."

"Bullshit."

Goodison giggled. "Believe what you like. But I'll say it again. There is only one copy. Just one."

"How much?" Gamble asked.

"One million—dollars, of course. Cash."

"What happens if I can't or won't buy?"

"Then we sell to the highest bidder. Only today we heard about a mysterious Mr. X who's in town looking for confessional-type videotapes of, you know, people doing naughty things—and that's exactly what we have to sell."

"You told me there's only one tape."

"One audiotape—and one videotape. Those camcorders are such a marvelous treat. But you get both tapes for the same low, low price."

"I'll go two hundred and fifty thousand."

"Don't be tiresome, Ione."

"Five hundred thousand."

"Sorry."

"Okay," she said with a long sigh. "One million—but it'll take time to raise that much cash."

"You have four days. No more."

"What if I can't raise it in four days?"

"I happen to know you can," Goodison said. "But if you *won't*, I'll have to get in touch with Mr. X and then people all over the world can sit in their most comfy chairs, watching Ione Gamble, movie star, confess to the murder of poor Billy Rice."

"Where do I call, if I manage to get the money together?"

"You're being tiresome again, Ione."

"Okay. You call me. But let's get something straight, Hughes. You're a slimebug and your sister's a certifiable weirdo and I won't come anywhere near either of you. So if I do get the money, I'll send somebody with it, somebody who'll insist on inspecting the merchandise before paying for it."

"Who is he?" Goodison demanded, his voice almost cracking on the "he."

"Who said anything about a he?" Ione Gamble said and hung up.

*　　*　　*

When Durant returned to the kitchen, she was again seated at the table, head bowed, hands folded in front of her, the bowl of soup shoved to her right.

"You were fine," Durant said as he sat down, picked up the spoon and tasted his soup again. "In fact, you were perfect."

She looked up. "Really?"

"Absolutely perfect."

She looked around the kitchen curiously, as if seeing it for the last time. "I'll have to sell it."

"What?"

"The house."

"Why?"

"You heard him. If I don't buy, they'll sell to Mr. X or Y or Z—whoever. To the sleazoids. And I can't raise a million cash unless I sell the house."

Durant had two more spoonfuls of soup, nodded appreciatively, then said, "The Goodisons won't sell to anybody else and you'll never pay them a dime."

Ione Gamble, dry-eyed and skeptical, stared at Durant for moments before she pulled her soup bowl back and began eating hungrily. Moments later she looked up at him, frowned, then grinned and said, "Why the fuck do I believe you?"

Twenty-nine

Artie Wu remembered the Oxnard of nearly thirteen years ago as a small, agriculturally dependent city with a predominantly Mexican flavor and a Japanese mayor. But after he and Booth Stallings paid gruff calls on four of the city's twenty-four motels, Wu read a tourist leaflet and discovered Oxnard had transformed itself into a diversified business center that boasted industrial parks, a new museum of muscle cars from the fifties and sixties and an almost new passenger train depot, which Booth Stallings claimed was the only passenger train depot built in the United States since 1940.

It was around 4 P.M. when they reached the ninth motel. Wu was wearing a blue blazer, khaki pants, a white shirt open halfway down his bare chest and, on his feet, plaintoed black oxfords with white socks. Stallings had suggested a cheap gold chain to go with the open shirt but Wu said he didn't want to soften his image. Stallings himself wore a gray suit, white shirt and a dark gray tie with maroon polka dots.

After they got out of the rented Mercedes at the ninth motel, Stallings said, "I'm damn near out of business cards."

"Maybe we'll get lucky," Wu said and led the way into the motel office.

Redundantly named "The La Paz Inn," the motel was independently owned, fairly new, and offered a small coffee shop, an equally small swimming pool and, Wu guessed, about three dozen units. Behind the reception counter was a stocky man in his late fifties with thin silky gray hair, bifocals and the suspicious pursed mouth that many motel owner-operators seem to acquire after only a year or so in the business. The man stared at Wu for a moment, dismissed him as a potential lodger and turned to Stallings, who was now leaning on the counter.

"Help you?" said the man in a twangy voice that dared Stallings to sell him something.

"Hope so," Stallings said and handed over one of the last business cards that claimed he was Jerome K. Walters, executive vice-president of the Independent Limousine Operators Association.

The man read the card, handed it back and said, "Don't get much call here for limos."

Stallings straightened, glanced around the room, nodded understandingly and said, "Didn't think you would. But that's not why we're here." He looked around the room again, then leaned toward the gray-haired man and used a soft conspiratorial tone to say, "We're here on an in-ves-ti-ga-tion." Stallings pronounced each syllable of investigation lovingly, as if he liked the word's sound.

The man behind the counter frowned. "Investigation of what?"

"One of our owner-operator members, a fine young man of Mexican descent, drives a couple up here from L.A. Just before the couple checks into a motel—not yours—they give our member twenty dollars to go buy 'em a bottle of drinking whisky."

"So?"

"So our fine young man, glad to be of service, heads for the nearest liquor store. But when he comes back with the

187

booze, the couple's skedaddled. Never checked in. And that leaves our fine young man stuck with a two-hundred-and-thirty-five-dollar tab he'd run up driving them all over L.A. and then on up here."

"That's one pitiful story," the man said.

"The thing is, Mr.—?"

"Deason."

"The thing is, Mr. Deason, my organization's bound and determined to put a stop to this sort of thing. We want to prosecute those two thieves—and that's what they are, thieves—to the full extent of the law. But cops don't get too excited about some Mexican limo driver who's been stiffed for a couple of hundred bucks. So we in the ILOA are offering a five-hundred-dollar cash reward for any information leading *not* to the arrest and conviction of this thieving pair, but just to their present whereabouts."

"They got names?" Deason asked.

"Yes, sir, they do. Their real names are Hughes and Pauline Goodison."

Deason looked down at the counter, then up at Stallings, shook his head regretfully and said, "Never registered 'em."

"In their late twenties or early thirties?" Stallings said. "Both blond and look a lot alike on account of they're brother and sister but claim they're man and wife? Talk with a real strong English accent?"

Something changed in Deason's face. His eyelids drooped and his pursed mouth formed a crafty smile just before he said, "British accents, you say?"

"English. British."

"Both kinda tall and skinny and blond?"

"Exactly."

"What'll you do with 'em?"

"Me and my associate here, Mr. Chang, will pay 'em a call. We'll ask for a full refund of the fare they stole. Then we'll make sure they settle their bill with the innkeeper. You. Then we'll put 'em in that black Mercedes out there and give 'em a fast ride to the police station." Stallings paused. "In other words, Mr. Deason, we'll make a citizen's arrest."

"What about the five-hundred-dollar reward?"

"It'll be paid on the spot. Cash. No receipt required."

Behind closed lips, Deason ran his tongue back and forth across the front of his lower teeth. Artie Wu decided it was part of a decision-making process.

"Room four-twenty-four," Deason said. "Been here since last Friday. Registered as Mr. and Mrs. Reginald Carter of Manchester, England. Don't know what they came in, but they didn't have a car and I never like the look of that. Had one big suitcase and two small carryalls. Nothing else. But listen, I don't want no damage. They paid me three days cash in advance and I just want the rest of what they owe me and the reward you promised. Once you ride off with 'em, you do what you please."

"I wish everyone was as public-spirited, Mr. Deason," Stallings said and turned to Wu. "Pay the man, Mr. Chang."

Wu scowled. "I think we oughta wait and see if they're really in four-twenty-four. I think he oughta give us a key. I think we oughta surprise 'em. And if they're the ones, then I think we oughta give him his five hundred."

Stallings nodded in judicious agreement. "Mr. Chang here has had himself a whole lot of experience in stuff like this. So maybe you oughta give him the key to four-twenty-four like he says."

Deason made no reply. Instead, he ran his tongue over the front of his lower teeth again, half turned, took a key from a slot, placed it on the countertop, stepped back quickly and said, "I don't want nothing busted up, understand?"

Wu picked up the key, examined it suspiciously, examined Deason the same way, scowled again and said, "You mean you don't want none of the furniture busted up, right?"

"Especially the TV set," Deason said.

"Don't worry," said Artie Wu, aimed a nod at the door and told Stallings, "Let's go get this crap over with."

Thirty

Artie Wu would later say that the car was a black Chevrolet Caprice sedan. Booth Stallings would later say that although he could identify any American car manufactured between 1932 and 1942, he could no longer tell one postwar car from another. But he agreed with Wu that the black car had been a sedan and that the low-in-the-sky, 4:12 P.M. February sun had splashed a blinding reflection across the car's windshield, making it impossible to identify the driver who tried to run them down.

The car had backed out of a space at the bottom of the motel's U-shaped layout as Wu and Stallings walked toward unit number 424. They paid little attention to the car until it picked up speed and veered toward them at 30 miles per hour, according to Wu, and 50 miles per hour, according to Stallings.

They went to their left, but so did the black Caprice, and it was Stallings who first leaped between two parked cars, tripped, fell and landed mostly on his hands and knees. After Wu's great leap to the left, he stumbled over Stallings, fell, but bounced up and hurried out from between the parked cars to catch a brief glimpse of the black Caprice as it turned right and disappeared down the street.

Wu hurried back to Stallings and helped him to his feet. "Break anything?" Wu asked.

"Bruised some ego. You get the license?"

"No."

"Think it was them—the Goodisons?"

Wu shrugged. "Let's find out."

As they continued toward the bottom of the motel's U, Stallings wrapped a handkerchief around his left hand, which he had skinned on the asphalt. When they reached 424, neither was surprised to find that the black sedan had backed out of the space directly in front of the unit.

Although Wu had the room's key in his hand, he said, "Let's knock first."

"What for?"

"Never hurts to be polite."

Stallings knocked on unit 424's lime-green door with his undamaged right hand. When there was no response, he stepped back to let Wu open the door with the key. Wu went in first. Stallings followed, closed the door behind him and sniffed the room's air.

"Smell it?"

Wu only nodded.

"Exploded cordite," Stallings said. "That means somebody pulled a gun and shot at somebody. And if somebody got hit and killed, the next thing we'll smell is loosened bowels. Ever since the war, whenever I smell cordite, the next thing I expect to smell is shit. And somehow I know if I go through that bathroom door over there, I'll smell 'em both, cordite and shit, together again."

"Then stay here while I look," Wu said.

"Death, cordite and shit don't bother you, Artie?"

"Not as much as your babbling."

"My mouth runs when I'm nervous. Not scared. Just nervous. When I'm scared, I clam up."

"Stay here," Wu said, crossed the room, opened the bathroom door, looked inside, turned and said, "You'd better come look."

Stallings saw the woman first. She was huddled in the

191

southwest corner of the shower stall, her knees drawn up to her chest. She wore a white blouse, black jeans and tan sandals on bare feet. There was a small neat hole just above the bridge of her nose. Her eyes were open.

The man was scrunched up against the bathroom wall between the sink and the toilet. His hands lay in his lap. His face was turned up toward the ceiling. There was a neat hole in his left temple and his eyes were also open. So was his mouth.

"They do look alike, don't they?" Stallings said.

"Very much."

Stallings, who had been holding his breath, sniffed twice, then began breathing through his mouth. "God, I hate that smell."

"Don't leave any prints," Wu said.

"Hadn't planned to," Stallings said, then asked, "Now that we've found them, what next?"

"Let's see what else we can find."

Two minutes later, Stallings discovered a crumpled-up computer-produced receipt in a wastebasket beneath four empty diet Coke cans. He lifted the empty cans out with a handkerchief, picked up the receipt with his fingers, smoothed it out, read it and handed it to Wu. The receipt was from an Oxnard company called The You Store. After deciphering it, Wu said the Goodisons apparently had rented a store-and-lock compartment for a month at a cost of $106.50. They had paid cash. The number of their storage space was 3472.

"Think that's where they stashed the tapes?" Stallings asked.

"Probably."

"Think they're still there?"

"Probably not."

"So how do you figure it?"

"The same way you do, Booth. The shooter killed one of them, then promised not to shoot the last one left if he or she would tell where the tapes were hidden. The one still alive told all and was shot dead."

"Then the last words of the last one left weren't words, just numbers."

"Maybe not," Wu said. "Maybe the last words were 'Please don't' or 'Please don't kill me' or just 'Please.' " He turned toward the motel room's door and said, "Let's go."

"What about the dead folks?"

"We'll stop by the office, pay Deason his five hundred and tell him that the Goodisons—what'd they call themselves?"

"Mr. and Mrs. Reginald Carter."

Wu nodded. "That the Carters must have stepped out. We'll also tell him to call us at that fake number on our business card when the Carters return."

"The shooter killed the young limo driver, right?" Stallings said. "He made the kid tell him where he'd driven the Goodisons, then cut his throat."

"What makes you so sure the shooter's a he?" Wu said.

*   *   *

As they drove through east Oxnard toward The You Store, using directions Stallings had extracted from a sullen gas station attendant, the same thought occurred to them simultaneously.

"The driver of that black car—" Stallings began.

"Knew us," Wu said. "One of us anyway."

"Unless he thought we were cops."

"We don't look like cops. You're too old and I'm too, well, too exotic—especially with my shirt open halfway to my navel."

"Undercover vice cops maybe?" said Stallings hopefully.

"Okay. We're vice cops. You're pretending to be the aged john and I'm pretending to be the fat Chinese pimp who's steering you toward an afternoon of sensual delight with a couple of thirteen-year-old demi-virgins. If whoever was in the black Chevy thought that, he'd've driven right past us. But he didn't and that means what?"

"That he not only knew us, but we also know him. Or one of us does."

"Or her," Wu said.

"I keep forgetting the ladies," Stallings said. "Even though the size of the wounds back at the motel are small enough to suggest what a sexist would call a lady's gun."

"Probably a twenty-two- or a twenty-five-caliber revolver—which is also a favorite of the professional shooter."

"Why not a small semiautomatic?"

"No shell casings. I looked."

"Maybe he or she picked them up," Stallings said. "There were only two."

Wu sighed. "Maybe."

Stallings glanced out the passenger window, saw the street number of a machine shop and said, "It should be two blocks up on the right."

"Good."

"How do we play it?"

"Just follow my lead," Wu said.

*   *   *

Before they got out of the Mercedes, Wu borrowed Stallings's necktie and put it on. Stallings kept his own shirt buttoned all the way up, at Wu's suggestion, and unzipped his fly—also at Wu's suggestion.

The You Store office was in a small mobile home. The storage spaces themselves were metal shipping containers, almost the size of boxcars and painted in gaudy reds, blues, greens and yellows. Wu guessed the containers occupied at least two acres.

Taking Stallings by the left hand, Wu led him up three steps and into the mobile home office. A young redheaded woman stared up at them from behind a gray metal desk. Wu smiled at her reassuringly, let go of Stallings's hand, turned to inspect him and murmured, just loudly enough for the woman to hear, "Frank, you forgot to zip."

Stallings giggled, looked down, zipped up his pants and, when Wu turned toward the woman with an apologetic smile, zipped them down again. The woman pretended not to notice.

Still smiling at the woman, Wu said, "Good afternoon."

194

She didn't return the smile. "Can I help you?"

"I'm the Reverend Dudley Chang of the Roundhill Methodist Church and I'd like to rent storage space for one of the members of my congregation who'll be going away to—uh—rest for a while. He's Mr. Jeffers here. Mr. Frank Jeffers. While he's—away, he'd like to store his belongings."

"Leakproof," Stallings said. "Gotta be leakproof. Ratproof, too. Don't wanta find rat shit all over everything when I come back."

"Do you have space available?" Wu asked with a faint embarrassed smile.

"Depends on how much you need," she said. "We only rent whole containers. They're each eight by eight by forty and provide twenty-five hundred and sixty cubic feet. If you've got a lot of stuff, they're fine."

"I got sixty-five-fucking-years' worth of stuff, little lady," Stallings said.

"He can use an entire container," Wu said. "But there's a small problem."

"How small?"

"Mr. Jeffers believes in numbers."

"Sorry," she said. "I don't get it."

"Numbers, little lady," Stallings said. "Numbers control our lives, direct our destinies, determine our future. Use the right numbers and you've got it made. I've used numbers all my life and they never let me down yet."

This time Wu's smile was one of sincere apology. "We understand your containers are numbered?"

"Yeah. They are. So?"

"The number he wants is the same number of his combination lock in junior high school."

"Three right, forty-seven left, two right," Stallings chanted. "Three right, forty-seven left, two—"

"Please, Frank," Wu said. Stallings fell silent, hung his head and stared at his shoes.

"The number he wants, if it's available, is thirty-four seventy-two. I do hope you'll be able to indulge him."

"How long's he want it for?" she asked.

195

"Till two thousand twenty-six," Stallings said. "When I hit a hundred."

"Six months," Wu said.

The woman turned to her computer, tapped out some numbers, studied them briefly, turned back to Wu with a cool smile and said, "You're in luck. Three-four-seven-two just came vacant this afternoon."

Wu turned to Stallings with a broad smile. "Hear that, Frank? It's available. Old three right, forty-seven left, two right."

Stallings gave him a sly look. "Wanta see it first. Wanta make sure everything's all hunky-dory."

"Zip up, Frank," Wu said, turned back to the woman and whispered, "How much for six months?" He put a finger to his lips. She nodded and wrote a number on a pad, then turned it around so Wu could read it. The number was $100 per month plus tax.

After glancing at Stallings, who was now engrossed in pulling his zipper up and down, Wu reached into a pocket, brought out some crumpled bills and handed the redheaded woman $700.

Wu whispered, "I'll pick up the change later."

She used a whisper to ask, "What's wrong with him?"

Wu smiled sadly and whispered, "Just age."

She handed over a key along with a photocopy map of the container's location and, no longer concerned that Stallings could hear her, said, "I've got a granddaddy just like that."

*   *   *

The color of the storage container was green and there was nothing in it. Stallings and Wu wandered around inside for a few minutes, but there was nothing to see, nothing to pry into. When they came out, Stallings said, "Well, what d'you think, Reverend?"

"Two things," Wu said. "One, Ione Gamble's going to be hearing fairly soon from whoever was driving that black Caprice. And two, you'd better zip up your pants."

Thirty-one

Otherguy Overby, seated in the late Billy Rice's big port-wine leather chair, picked up the console phone just before its third ring, said hello and heard an electronically distorted male voice say, "Mr. X, please."

"Lemme get to the other phone," Overby said and sent a look and a nod to Georgia Blue, who rose from the long living room couch and hurried into the kitchen. Overby, staring at his watch, noted that the time was exactly 5:03 P.M. when he heard her pick up the kitchen's wall phone. It was then that Overby said, "That's better," into his own phone and, in turn, was treated to a bass chuckle that sounded like tired thunder.

"Put somebody on the extension, did you?" said the man with the distorted bass voice. "Well, that's fine. Means you're careful."

Overby made no response and let the silence build. While waiting, he decided the caller's altered voice sounded as if it were coming from the bottom of a steel oil drum. The caller was in no hurry to end the silence because it went on and on until the reverberating voice finally said, "I hear you're interested in videotapes."

"Depends," Overby said.

"On what?"

"On quality."

"What's the quality market's top price?"

"For prime stuff," Overby said, "up to a hundred thousand pounds—about a hundred and seventy-five or eighty thousand U.S."

"Listen," the distorted voice said.

First, there was a very soft click—much like the sound a mercury light switch might make. Then a male voice with a pronounced British accent said, "Tell me your name."

A woman's voice that to Overby sounded either sleepy or tired said, "Ione Gamble."

After a too-long pause, which Overby blamed on incompetent splicing, the British-accented male voice asked, "When you learned Billy Rice wasn't going to marry you or let you star and direct his *Bad Dead Indian* picture, how did that make you feel?"

There was only a slight pause this time before the woman's voice said, "I wanted to kill him."

"Did you?" the male voice asked.

"Yes," said the woman who claimed she was Ione Gamble.

After a final soft click, the caller's distorted voice rumbled up out of the oil drum again. "Like the quality?"

"Seemed a little short."

"That's just a taste, a sniff," said Oil Drum, which was the name Overby had now given him. "I've got forty-nine and a half minutes of stuff just as rich. Maybe even richer. Interested?"

"Could be," Overby said, "if it's really on video and not just audiotape and I get to screen it first."

"I'll get back to you," Oil Drum said.

"When?"

"Eight tomorrow morning. By then I'll've figured out a way to set up a screening."

"What if I gotta get in touch with you before that—in case something comes up?"

Oil Drum chuckled again. "Nice try," he said and broke the connection.

Georgia Blue waited for Overby to hang up before she replaced the kitchen wall phone and returned to the living room. She was wearing the jeans and a white sweatshirt she had bought that afternoon during a seven-minute shopping spree at the Gap on Wilshire in Santa Monica. On her feet were a pair of sockless dark blue Keds that were also new.

Overby was frowning at the phone console when Blue sank cross-legged to the floor, looked up at him and said, "How're you going to work it?"

"What?"

"The fuck-him-over."

"Won't be easy. Not old Oil Drum."

"Oil Drum," she said. "I like it. Why d'you think he altered his voice? Because he thought you might be taping him?"

"Or that I might recognize it."

"Did you?"

"No. Did you?"

"No," she said. "But it must've been Hughes Goodison's voice asking Gamble those questions. And that could mean the tapes've been sold or stolen or the Goodisons have taken in a new partner."

Overby frowned. "He didn't even mention blackmail, did he, Oil Drum?"

"No."

Overby frowned again, obviously concentrating until the frown disappeared, replaced by his hard white grin. "If I was them, the Goodisons, I know what I'd do. I'd collect as much as I could from Ione Gamble and then use somebody else, somebody like Oil Drum, to peddle the videotape to the highest bidder." He nodded comfortably at the scheme and said, "Very rich and very nice. It's got, you know, symmetry."

"Oil Drum would handle both the blackmail and the videotape sale?" Georgia Blue asked.

"Sure."

"Then the Goodisons would never see a dime, would they?"

199

"Of course not," Overby said. "They're amateurs and too much money's up for grabs. What they should've done is got in and out for a quick two hundred and fifty K. If they'd done that, they could already be spending it somewhere nice."

"What did you think of the tape?" she asked.

Overby shook his head dismissively. "It'd been doctored by somebody who didn't know what the fuck they were doing. Take that question Goodison asked Gamble about how she felt after Rice dumped her and she said she wanted to kill him. Then Goodison asks, 'Did you?' and she says, 'Yes.' That was all spliced together by somebody in a hurry."

"They must have something else they're banking on."

"Sure they do," Overby said. "They got the videotape. Audio's simple. If you know what you're doing, you can make it say damn near anything. But video's different because it's lip-synched and then there're the expressions and eye movements and body language and all that to worry about. But if you find yourself a real good cutter, the best, you can still do a hell of a lot with videotape."

Georgia Blue stared up at him. "You already have it all planned out, don't you?"

"What?"

"The Otherguy angle."

Overby examined her for several moments before he shook his head. "Not this time, Georgia."

"Bullshit."

Overby shifted in his chair and studied her some more before he said, "How long've we known each other?"

"Half my life."

Overby ran the years through his mind, added them up, then nodded in agreement. "I'm gonna give you some advice and that's something I seldom do because I don't like it when people give it to me. Okay?"

She shrugged.

"If you're thinking of setting up a sideshow, Georgia, that's fine—as long as it doesn't affect my cut. Just make sure you don't get Durant pissed off at you. All that stuff you pulled in Manila and Hong Kong's still eating at him and he's just waiting for you to give him an excuse. If you get him really pissed off, even Artie can't stop him. So if you're considering a solo, think about Durant."

"I've had five years to think about—"

She broke off because Booth Stallings came into the living room, followed by Artie Wu. After a quick glance around, Wu asked, "Durant's not back yet?"

"Not yet," Overby said.

"He still at Ione Gamble's?"

"Far as I know."

Wu went to the phone, picked it up, looked at Overby and said, "What's her number?"

Overby took a three-by-five-inch card from his shirt pocket and ran a forefinger down a list of a dozen or so neatly printed names. When he came to Ione Gamble's, he read it off. Without repeating the number, Wu dialed it.

*   *   *

Ione Gamble rolled over, picked up the bedside telephone on the fourth ring and said, "Yes?"

"This is Artie Wu. Is Quincy Durant still there?"

"I'll see," she said, covered the mouthpiece with a palm, looked to her left and said, "Artie Wu."

"Right," Durant said, rose naked from the bed, went around it, took the phone from Gamble and sat down on the bed, his back to her. She ran a gentle forefinger over the thirty-six crisscrossed scars on his back, wondering how and where he had got them and decided to ask him someday.

Instead of saying hello into the phone, Durant said, "I was just leaving."

"Good," Wu said. "We have some news."

"So do I."

"Then perhaps you might share it with us."

"I'll be there in twenty minutes," Durant said, hung up the phone, turned to Gamble and kissed her. When the long kiss ended, she said, "Thanks for all the comfort and solace."

201

"Is that what it was?"

"That's sometimes what sex is between friends."

"Between good friends anyway."

Her smile turned into a grin. "I'd say we were pretty good friends by now."

Thirty-two

At the 26-foot-long, 459-year-old oak refectory table where the late Billy Rice's guests had once dined, the five current residents of his beach house were gathered around $81.56 worth of Mandarin-style, MSG-free Chinese food that Booth Stallings had ordered from The China Den, a Malibu restaurant-carryout that years ago, according to Overby, had been called The China Diner.

Artie Wu, who had never cared for Chinese food, was the first to finish. He pushed his plate away, lit a cigar and began a report on his and Booth Stallings's visit to Oxnard. When he described how the black Chevrolet Caprice sedan had tried to run over him and Stallings, Georgia Blue and Durant stopped eating.

And after Wu said, "Booth and I then found Hughes and Pauline Goodison shot dead in their motel bathroom," Overby, who was enormously fond of Chinese food, put down his chopsticks. Only Booth Stallings continued to eat, using a spoon to scoop up the last of his shrimp with lobster sauce.

Wu answered the quick hard questions that followed and then told of the trip he and Stallings had made to The You Store, where they found nothing. There were more questions, which Wu patiently answered, before he looked around the table and asked, "Okay. Who's next?"

"Me, I think," Overby said and gave a nearly verbatim account of his phone call from Oil Drum, whose disguised voice had offered to sell him a videotape of Ione Gamble confessing to the murder of Billy Rice.

After Overby finished, Wu asked, "Your friend Oil Drum said he'd call back tomorrow morning?"

"Eight sharp."

Durant turned to Wu and said, "What time did you and Booth find the Goodisons?"

"Around four-fifteen, wasn't it, Booth?"

"Probably a minute or two earlier."

"Maybe at four-thirteen exactly?" Durant said.

"Maybe," Stallings said. "Why?"

"Because I'm looking for something extraordinary or peculiar and I'm not finding it. Exactly one hour earlier, at three-thirteen, is when Ione Gamble got a call from Hughes Goodison, offering to sell her almost exactly the same stuff that Otherguy's new phone pal, Oil Drum, now wants to sell him."

"Then you heard the conversation between Gamble and Goodison?" Wu said.

"On her extension."

"She agreed to pay, I hope?"

"She told Goodison she needed time to raise the money and he gave her four days."

"Let's get all the times straight," Wu said—again to Durant. "You picked up Gamble when?"

"We left her house at about twenty 'til two and arrived at the dental surgeon's at two straight up. Her wisdom tooth was out by two-twenty. It took another ten or fifteen minutes for the Pentothal to wear off in the recovery room. But before it did, I decided to find out how effective a truth serum Pentothal really is and asked her if anyone'd borrowed her car New Year's Eve. Or if she'd gone out to Billy Rice's house twice that same day and night. Or if she'd shot him. She answered no to everything."

"Why're you so sure it was exactly three-thirteen when Goodison called Ione Gamble?" Wu said.

"Because when I picked up the extension I looked at my watch," Durant said.

Wu decided to examine the ceiling. "Goodison calls Gamble at three-thirteen and is dead by four-thirteen." He brought his gaze down. "Can any of you make something out of that?"

When no one spoke, Wu looked to his left and said, "You're next, Georgia."

Her face was expressionless and her tone neutral when she said, "Jack Broach's company is nearly bankrupt."

Artie Wu leaned back in his chair at the head of the table, clasped his hands across his belly, smiled contentedly and, around his cigar, said, "There's more, I trust."

"There is," she said. "I checked with Broach's bank first and they're not happy with his business. Then Broach and I had lunch in Beverly Hills. During lunch I told him why I thought he was almost broke and, after the coffee came, I made a suggestion."

"I bet you did," Durant said.

"Let her tell it," said Overby.

After a shrug from Durant, Georgia Blue stared directly at him and said, "When I finished telling Broach why I thought he was broke, I asked him what would happen if Ione Gamble told him to raise, say, one million in cash to pay off a blackmailer. Could he or couldn't he, yes or no? He said nothing, not a word, which didn't really surprise me. So I said all right, if he couldn't raise a million, could he raise three hundred thousand? If yes, he could tell Gamble that the million in cash was ready for her go-between, me. In exchange for the three hundred thousand, I offered to hand over all incriminating blackmail material along with a personal guarantee that the blackmailer, singular or plural, would never bother her again. Broach said he didn't have much faith in such guarantees because he'd always heard that blackmailers never quit. I said they do when they're dead."

There was a long silence. During the silence, Otherguy

Overby's slight smile widened into his white hard grin. Durant stared at her without expression—except for the thin compressed line his lips made. Artie Wu nodded several times, as if to himself. Booth Stallings poured himself a cup of lukewarm tea, added sugar and drank it down, staring at Blue over the rim of the cup.

Ignoring them all, Georgia Blue picked up her chopsticks and used them to transfer the last dim sum to her mouth. She chewed slowly, almost thoughtfully, swallowed, put the chopsticks down and used a napkin to pat the corners of her mouth. She then leaned back in her chair, smiled politely, as if there had been a lull in the conversation and she was now waiting for someone to say something interesting.

Artie Wu ended the long silence with a question. "What was Mr. Broach's reaction?"

"I've been hoping he would've called Ione Gamble by now," Blue said. "Or her lawyer, Mr. Mott. Or maybe even you. Apparently, he hasn't."

"Come on, Georgia," Durant said. "Did he say, 'That's one hell of an idea, Ms. Blue'—or 'I don't know what the fuck you're talking about and don't want to know'—or even, 'You'd better watch your mouth, lady'?"

"What he did," she said, ignoring Durant and speaking directly to Wu, "was sign the check, add a twenty percent tip, smile and say, 'We'll have to do this again very soon.'"

"When did the lunch begin and when did it end?" Wu asked.

"It didn't begin until one-fifteen because I was late and it ended at two."

"Where'd you go then?" Durant said.

"Shopping. I bought some things at Saks and some jeans and a sweatshirt at the Gap. I also stopped at a store in Santa Monica and bought a pair of blue Keds. Then I drove home, arriving here around four forty-five or four-fifty. Otherguy was already here."

"Did you tell him about Jack Broach?" Durant asked.

"Not a word," Overby said.

Stallings was still frowning at Georgia Blue when he said, "If I got it right, you offered to kill the blackmailers, singular or plural; retrieve the stuff they were blackmailing Gamble with, and provide both of these services for a flat fee of three hundred thousand dollars, right?"

"Wrong," she said.

"Let me, Georgia," Artie Wu said. "What she did, Booth, was exactly what I asked her to do: check Jack Broach out all the way. What she discovered is that he and his agency are in rotten financial shape. Just how rotten we can judge from his reaction, or lack of reaction, to Georgia's intriguing suggestion. He didn't reject it out of hand. He expressed no indignation. He didn't even remind her that, as a lawyer, he's an officer of the court—nor did he threaten her with the cops. To me, his silence speaks or even shouts of interest—although an understandably wary interest because he may've suspected a setup or entrapment or even that Georgia was wearing a wire."

"There's more to it than that, Artie," Overby said. "You or Quincy told me Broach handles all of Gamble's money, right? I mean he's her agent, business manager and personal attorney. He looks after her investments, pays her bills—credit cards, charge accounts, insurance premiums, mortgage payments, utilities—everything—and maybe even keeps her personal checking account topped up at around five or ten thousand dollars. In fact, she doesn't have to even think about money. I mean ordinary money. All the money she has to worry about is if they're going to pay her two, three or five million to act in their next picture. Right?"

Wu nodded.

"Let's suppose Broach has made some bad investments for her and maybe even for himself. Say he shorted some stocks and now has to cover his shorts. Or maybe he's even dipped into Gamble's assets to get himself out of some other kind of bind. But he wasn't worried about it because his number one client was about to star in and direct a megabucks picture and marry its billionaire producer and never worry about money again—not that she's had to worry about it lately. Then all of a sudden Billy Rice is killed and Gamble is arrested and Jack Broach finds himself scrambling to raise money for bail and lawyers and hypnotists. And to top it off, here comes some blackmailer demanding a million or so. The only one not pressing him for money yet is Gamble herself. So when Georgia comes up with her goddamned elegant no-risk plan that offers him a chance to write off seven hundred thousand of what he borrowed from Gamble—okay, stole— he doesn't say yes, he doesn't say maybe, but he sure as hell doesn't say no."

Booth Stallings, wearing a frown, stared at Georgia Blue and said, "I'm really curious about Broach's reaction to your offer. How'd he take it? Like it was merely another offer from some reputable member of the nation's burgeoning service economy?"

Artie Wu smiled and said, "What *did* you say to him, Georgia? You must've rehearsed it."

"He said he was no criminal defense lawyer, but the best of them had told him that blackmailers never quit. All I said was, 'They do when they're dead.' And that's when our lunch came to its sudden end."

"Perfect," Wu said. "Absolutely perfect." He looked at his watch. "Booth and I can discuss ethical nuances in the morning. But it's getting late and Quincy and I still must meet with Enno Glimm and Ms. Arliss. Then at eight tomorrow morning Oil Drum, our putative blackmailer, is due to call. Perhaps we should gather at, say, seven for breakfast." He looked at Stallings. "What may we expect in the way of breakfast, Booth?"

"Coffee, juice and Egg McMuffins."

"Excellent," said Wu as he rose.

"Before we go," Durant said, "I have two questions for Georgia."

She hesitated, then shrugged, and Durant said, "What made you suspect Jack Broach was broke or nearly so?"

"I spotted three fake Daumiers hanging in his office."

Durant nodded thoughtfully. "That's a good answer. My

208

other question is: why tell us about the offer you made him? If you hadn't, you might've walked away with three hundred thousand tax free."

"No matter what I say, Quincy, you won't believe it."

"That's also a very good answer," Durant said.

Thirty-three

They decided to walk the three quarters of a mile or so from the Rice house to their meeting with Enno Glimm at the Malibu Beach Inn. They walked because Wu claimed it would burn off most of the Chinese dinner's calories. He then confided that after the meeting with Glimm he planned to replenish the burned-off calories with two Big Macs, a small chocolate milkshake and possibly an order of French fries.

Durant was only half listening to Wu's thoughts on diet when he noticed the black sedan parked one hundred feet or so up from the Rice house. He noticed it not because of its make, model or color, but because long ago he had decided you should give long odds that four grown men sitting in a parked car at night are intent on either arrest, robbery or mayhem.

The sedan's four doors flew open when Wu and Durant got within ten feet of the car's left front fender. Four white males all dressed in black stepped out. None was more than 30 and all wore matching black pants, running shoes and sweatshirts. Even their baseball caps were black.

When Wu and Durant reached the car, the two who had emerged curbside took up posts to Durant's left. The second

210

pair had popped out of the car on the street side and hurried around its front, heading for Wu. When they drew near, Artie Wu smiled and said, *"Buenas tardes, señores,"* which caused the closer man to hesitate just long enough for Wu to kick him in the testicles. The man hissed and bent over, clutching himself.

Durant, his eyes on the other pair, turned parallel to a knife thrust, grabbed the knife hand by the wrist, found the key nerve with a thumb and squeezed. The man yelled, dropped the knife and sank to his knees. Durant released the wrist, kicked the man in the head, scooped up the switchblade and threw it at the second man, who was trying to tug something from his right hip pocket.

The hilt of the switchblade struck the man in the chest, then fell to the concrete with a clatter. The man looked down, as if to make sure the knife blade really wasn't embedded in his heart. Before he could look up, Durant slammed his cupped palms against the man's ears. Openmouthed now and screaming silently, the man dropped to his knees, curled up on the sidewalk and began to whimper softly, hands to his ears.

Durant spun around to find the first of Wu's would-be assailants still cradling his testicles and crooning to himself. The other one was struggling to breathe because of the massive forearm that had been clamped around his neck from behind.

"If you talk, you breathe," Wu said, loosening the hold slightly.

The man gasped three times first, then said some guy'd hired them for $500 each to wait outside the beach house in the car for a real tan tall guy and a big fat Chinaman to come out.

Wu increased the pressure on the man's throat, asked, "Then what?"—and relaxed the hold.

The man sucked in more air and used it to say, "If you drove off in a car, we were gonna follow and force you over and, you know, maybe mess you up a little."

"A little or a lot?"

"Maybe a little more'n a little."

"Who was he—the guy who hired you?"

The man said he didn't know, honest to God he didn't. Wu increased the pressure, eased it and asked, "How'd he pay you?"

"He said the money'd be in the glove compartment of the car and the car'd be in the parking lot of a Carl's Junior—the one at La Brea and Santa Monica where all the kiddy fags hang out."

"How'd he tell you?"

"On the phone, how else? He said the car was hot and we could keep it, lose it, whatever."

"When did he call you?"

"Real late this afternoon—around six."

"How long were you going to wait outside the beach house?"

"Till two A.M. Then we could split and try again tomorrow night for another five hundred each in another hot car the guy said he'd find us."

Wu removed his forearm, pointed the man at the black Caprice and said, "Take off. All of you. But when he calls again, tell him the Chinaman knows who he is."

*   *   *

"So who is he?" Durant asked as they watched the black sedan pull slowly away from the curb.

"The same guy who killed the Goodisons this afternoon and tried to run over Booth and me," Wu said, turned and resumed walking toward the Malibu Beach Inn.

"You didn't see the driver this afternoon," Durant said as he fell into step.

"No, but it was the same car—same make, model, color, everything—and I made the logical conclusion."

"More of a logical leap," Durant said. "How many black Chevrolet Caprices do you think GM turned out last year?"

"More than they sold probably."

212

"Which is still plenty because it's very anonymous, very comfortable and much favored by cops, cabbies and old folks who like a mushy ride. Too bad you didn't get the license number in Oxnard."

"Why too bad?"

"Then we could be sure it was the same car."

"What good would that do, if it's a stolen car?"

"It would at least prove your powers of observation."

"I see no need to prove anything," Wu said and increased his pace.

*   *   *

The only noticeable change in Enno Glimm was the garish green and red Hawaiian shirt he wore, tails out, over pants that seemed to belong to a blue pinstripe suit. Glimm sat in an easy chair in the sitting room of his two rooms on the inn's third floor. To his left on a couch was Jenny Arliss, wearing white duck pants and a navy-blue T-shirt. Wu and Durant, after a perfunctory greeting from Glimm, chose a pair of matching armchairs.

Once they were seated, Glimm said, "This place hasn't got a restaurant."

"You can send out for a pizza," Durant said.

Glimm ignored the suggestion. "Okay. Let's hear it. What've you done right so far?"

"So far," Wu said, "we've discovered the murdered bodies of Hughes and Pauline Goodison—thus completing the task you set for us, which essentially was, 'Find the Goodisons.' "

Jenny Arliss murmured, "My God."

All Glimm did was rise, move to the window and pull a drawn curtain back just far enough to peer out at the miles-away lights of Santa Monica. While staring at them, he said, "They claim there's a hell of a daytime view from here. Too bad I won't get to see it." He let the curtain go, turned to Arliss and said, "Get us on the next flight to New York."

"I think we should hear the rest first," she said.

"Make the fucking reservations," Glimm said, went back to

his chair, sat down, aimed his pale gray gaze at Wu, then at Durant, and said, "Okay. Let's have it."

It took them thirty-six minutes to tell it. During the first seven minutes, Jenny Arliss spoke quietly into the room's telephone, then interrupted Wu to tell Glimm she had made first-class reservations for them on a 1 A.M. flight that would get them into Kennedy at 9:30 A.M. with a 12 noon connection to Heathrow. Glimm only nodded and told Wu to keep talking.

By then, Wu was describing his hypnosis of Ione Gamble. Glimm listened silently to everything, asking no questions, not even when Durant described their discovery of the murdered limousine driver, Carlos Santillan. Or the possible bankruptcy of Jack Broach & Co. Or even the failed four-man attack on him and Durant not ten minutes before they arrived at Glimm's suite. During all but the first seven minutes of the joint recitation, Jenny Arliss made rapid shorthand notes in a spiral notebook. Durant assumed it was a verbatim account.

After Wu and Durant finished, there was a long silence until Enno Glimm asked, "How much?"

"How much what?" Durant asked.

"How much'll the blackmailer ask for those tapes the Goodisons made and he stole?"

"Probably a million," Durant said. "That's almost the standard asking price. People can comprehend it. Divide it easily. And it's still just enough to make them believe it'll solve all their problems—even though it's no more than three hundred thousand was in seventy-three."

Glimm snorted something in German that sounded derisive, then went back to English. "You say Gamble didn't kill what's his name, Billy Rice?"

"We don't believe she did," Durant said.

"But the Goodisons' tapes say she did."

"We think they've been doctored."

"You think?"

"Suspect," Durant said.

214

"Well, Christ, if they were doctored, can't you and Howie Mott prove it?"

"Not until we get our hands on them," Wu said. "And if Ione Gamble doesn't buy them, the blackmailer will probably sell them to the news media that dote on sleaze. If the tapes are printed or broadcast before her trial—the blackmailer claims to have her on both audio- and videotapes—the publicity could affect the trial's outcome, regardless of the tapes' accuracy or their inadmissibility as evidence."

"She willing to pay the million?" Glimm asked.

"Providing she can raise it," Durant said.

Glimm looked at his right hand, nodded more to himself than to the others, then asked, now looking at his left hand, "But you say this guy, Jack Broach, might've lost all her money and his, too, right?"

"We think so," Durant said.

Glimm stopped looking at his hands, rose, went back to the window and again peered out at the lights of Santa Monica. He stared at them for nearly a minute before he turned, looked first at Wu, then at Durant and asked, "You two wanta make some more money?"

"How much more?" Durant asked.

"Another five hundred thousand U.S."

"We're interested," Wu said.

"Okay. You'll get the extra five hundred thousand, on top of what we've already agreed to, if you do two things. One: you keep me out of it. I'm not just talking no stain now. I mean no connection whatever. And two: get Ione Gamble off the hook. Prove she didn't kill what's his name, Rice." He then looked at Jenny Arliss and said, "Tear up all your notes and burn 'em."

Arliss nodded, closed her notebook, put away her ballpoint pen, looked at Durant and said, "I think we should hear a bit more about your Georgia Blue. From what you've said, she seems to be your weak link."

"She's my responsibility," Durant said.

Artie Wu smiled slightly and nodded several times, the way

he almost always did when shocked or surprised. No one seemed to notice except Durant.

"The way you guys told it," Glimm said, "your Ms. Blue could gum up the works."

"She's the best there is," Durant said. "And that makes the risk worthwhile."

"You're saying she's the best woman?" Jenny Arliss asked.

"She's the best anybody," Durant said.

"How long've you known her?"

"Seventeen or eighteen years."

"How old is she?"

"Thirty-six or -seven."

Arliss's left eyebrow rose. "A teenage girlfriend?"

Artie Wu slipped into the conversation before Durant could answer. "I agree with Quincy that Georgia's the best there is. I must also stress that it was my decision that she join us. And that makes me equally responsible for her actions."

"Except neither of you trust her around the corner, do you?" Glimm said and chuckled. He had nearly chuckled during his first visit to Wudu, Ltd., in London, and Durant had then wondered how it would sound and suspected it would be a dry scratchy noise—like something small and vicious trying to claw and bite its way out of a cardboard box. He now discovered he was right.

The chuckle over, Glimm said, "Don't worry. I've hired guys just because they're the best—even though I wasn't sure I could trust 'em. It's probably why I hired you two."

"How kind," Artie Wu said.

"We got a deal?" Glimm said as if he already knew the answer.

Durant nodded first. A moment later, so did Wu.

Looking almost satisfied, Glimm turned to Arliss and said, "Call down to the desk and tell 'em we're checking out and to get us a limo."

He turned back to Wu and Durant to study them carefully for almost thirty seconds before he rose, gave them a farewell nod and their final orders: "Do it right." Enno Glimm then disappeared into the adjoining bedroom.

VOODOO, LTD.

Durant rose and went over to Jenny Arliss just as she put down the phone. He held out his hand and said, "I'll take the steno book."

She handed it to him, then asked, "You don't really trust anyone, do you?"

"Not often."

"Good," she said.

Thirty-four

At shortly after midnight, Booth Stallings lay propped up in bed, reading copies of documents given him that afternoon by Mary Jo something, the brunette legal secretary who worked for Howard Mott.

The first document he read was a Los Angeles Police Department report on the semiautomatic 9mm Beretta that had been stolen February 2, 1982, from the set of the television pilot, *The Keepers*, while it was being filmed at Paramount Studios.

Written in what Stallings judged to be standard copese, the report said the TV pilot's property man put the gun down somewhere on the set when summoned by the director just after the day's shooting ended. When the property man returned for the gun it was gone, as were the cast and crew. The theft was reported immediately, investigated and eventually forgotten until the Beretta resurfaced as the gun that killed William A. C. Rice IV.

The next item Stallings read was a list of the cast and crew's names. None of the crew's names caught his eye, but three other names jumped out at him. The first two jumping names belonged to Rick Cleveland and Phil Quill. Cleveland was the

218

old actor who'd had a bit role in *Gone With the Wind* and who, in *The Keepers* pilot, played "Father Tim Murray, an aged priest." Phil Quill, the Malibu real estate man and former Arkansas quarterback, played "Joe Lambert, a compulsive gambler." Both lived in Malibu in 1982 and listed their agent as Jack Broach & Co., which was the other name that had caught Stallings's eye.

The L.A. County Sheriff's investigators had questioned all three men after Rice's death. Someone had boiled the interviews down to three summary paragraphs. Broach came first, either because of alphabetical order or, more likely, Stallings thought, because of his position in the industry's pecking order.

"Broach says his agency no longer represents either Cleveland or Quill," the report read. "Broach also says he has only 'a dim recollection' of the TV pilot, *The Keepers*, and never visited the set. Broach says he doesn't know if his former clients, Quill and Cleveland, are friends but doubts it because of their age difference. Broach also denies any knowledge of how his present client, Ione Gamble, came into possession of the murder weapon."

Richard Cleveland—or Rick, as he'd introduced himself to Stallings—was next. "Cleveland gives his age as 75," the report read. "He was arrested for DWI 3-5-72 and 8-2-84. No other priors. Alcohol noted on his breath during interviews 1-3-91 and 2-9-91. Cleveland says he played 'a dumb old priest' in *The Keepers* pilot and 'carried a cross, not a pistol.' He admits knowing Phil Quill and describes him as 'a better ball player than actor and a better real estate salesman than either.' Cleveland called Malibu Sheriff's substation on 1-3-91 to report seeing Ione Gamble's black Mercedes 500SL parked in William Rice's driveway at around 2300 on 12-31-90 and again at approximately 0513 on 1-1-91. Cleveland admits suing Rice for blocking his (Cleveland's) ocean view. He says he met Rice only once, didn't like him and isn't sorry he's dead. Questioned about his drinking, Rice says he is a charter member of the Malibu AA chapter and volunteered his opinion that Gamble murdered Rice 'because he jilted her.' He also volunteered an opinion that Gamble is a fine actress, but a mediocre director."

Phil Quill received less space. "Quill," the report read, "says he played the heavy in the TV pilot, *The Keepers*. He says the 9mm Beretta semiautomatic was used only by Jerry Tinder, who played the film's lead role (Tinder died, New York, 3-15-88, of AIDS, according to NYPD). Quill says he is not a close friend of Richard Cleveland but sometimes sees him in the Hughes supermarket, Malibu, 'to say hello.' Quill is a licensed real estate broker in Malibu and says he never met William A. C. Rice IV although Rice's attorneys retained his real estate company to provide maintenance of the Rice property in Malibu until probate is completed."

After Stallings stuffed the reports back into the manila envelope and placed it in a nightstand drawer, he heard the soft knock at the bedroom door. He looked at his watch. It was 12:43. Stallings rose, went to the door and opened it. Georgia Blue entered the bedroom, wearing her new raincoat as a bathrobe and carrying two glasses and a bottle of J&B Scotch.

"I thought we'd have a nightcap," she said, placing the glasses and bottle on the dresser. "Water?"

"In the bathroom."

She poured two generous measures of whisky, carried the glasses into the bathroom, added a little cold water, then returned to the bedroom and handed Stallings one of the drinks. He sat down on the bed. She sat next to him and said, "It's started."

"What?"

"The ground war."

"Huh."

"You don't sound surprised."

"Well, they've been building up to it for what—six months—and they've bombed the shit out of Iraq and've got all the troops and tanks and planes and artillery and ships they can use. It'll probably end pretty soon—like I said."

"You don't sound very interested."

"If there was any danger of losing, I might get interested. To me it's just another dumb war with a foreordained outcome being fought by some young mercenaries or professionals we call volunteers. This country'll never lose another conventional war. If it looks like we might lose, we won't fight."

"Especially if they're white folks," Georgia Blue said.

Stallings grinned. "Haven't fought any of them since forty-five."

"What happens next?" she said.

"You still talking about the gulf war?"

"No."

"L'Affaire Gamble?"

She nodded. "When it's over."

"I expect we'll all wander off again."

"Wu with Durant, you with Otherguy?"

Stallings shook his head slightly, smiling at what might have been fond memories. "After five years, I think Otherguy's ready to dissolve the old firm. I know I am."

"He likes you."

"Otherguy was—is—" Stallings paused to search for the right words. "—a postdoctoral education."

"What'll you do?"

He looked at her. It was a look of cool examination. "What d'you suggest?"

"We could team up," she said.

"And do what? Run variations of the Lagos Bank Draft on rich old marks in Palm Springs?"

"I'm not talking about forever," she said. "I'm talking about six months—a year at the most."

"Living in fancy hotels, drinking fine wines?"

"Why not?"

Stallings rose, went to the dresser, poured more Scotch into his glass, sipped it, turned back to her and asked, "What would I have to do?"

"I'm not sure yet," she said. "Maybe nothing."

"But probably something."

"Probably."

"Just because I'm stuck on you, Georgia, doesn't mean I'm simple."

"I know."

"What if Durant finds out?" he asked.

"He won't."

"But if he does?"

She shrugged slightly, put her drink down on the bedside table and began loosening the belt of her raincoat. "Durant won't care," she said.

"I won't cross him," Stallings said. "Or Artie."

"We won't cross them," she said as she undid the raincoat's buttons.

"Otherguy?"

"Not Otherguy either."

"So who do we cross?"

"Jack Broach and Company."

"Jesus, you're not back on that 'dead blackmailers can't blackmail' pitch again, are you?"

Georgia Blue undid the last of the raincoat's buttons as she rose, let the raincoat slip to the floor and said, "You still don't quite get it, do you?"

Stallings paid no attention to the question as he stared at the perfect body, remembering it, rediscovering it and refusing to analyze his nearly adolescent surge of eroticism. Instead, he set his drink down and hurried to her. There was a brief stare of either accommodation or understanding before the kiss began—a very long and nearly savage kiss that featured clicking teeth and what Stallings thought of as dueling tongues.

When the kiss ended, both were gasping, but Georgia Blue managed to ask a question. "Well, is it?"

"Is it what?"

"Like a real date?"

"Exactly," Booth Stallings said.

Thirty-five

A t 7:59 the next morning the five of them were again gathered around the long refectory table in the dining room, waiting for the telephone to ring. The wrappings and remains of their Egg McMuffin breakfasts had been pushed into a neat pile by Otherguy Overby. Georgia Blue rose, picked up a carafe of coffee from the sideboard and warmed the cups of Overby, Durant and herself—Wu and Stallings declining with headshakes.

The telephone on the long table rang just as Blue sat back down. Wu let it ring four times before he picked it up and said hello.

The electronically distorted voice of the man Overby called Oil Drum said, "You don't sound like Mr. X to me."

"I'm Mr. Z, the yes-or-no man," Wu said.

"I think you're maybe a cop."

"What a terrible thing to say."

"So what the hell're you doing at the phone number of Billy Rice's beach house? Answer me that."

"Mr. X and I're also the go-between people."

"Between me and who else?" Oil Drum asked.

"Between you and whoever buys what you've got to sell."

"Yeah, well, I've already told your Mr. X what I've got to sell."

"And now you can tell me."

"I got audio- and videotapes of a hypnotized Ione Gamble confessing to the murder of Billy Rice. That's what I got."

"You mentioned a screening to Mr. X," Wu said.

"I changed my mind. No screening."

"Why not?"

"Because there's only one videotape and the only way you could look at it is if I made a copy and messengered it to you. But if I did that, you'd have everything I've got and could go peddle it for a bunch of money."

Wu sighed. "How much do you want for your pig in a poke—a hundred thousand?"

"Now you're wasting my time," Oil Drum said. "I can make one call to Florida and they'll fly a guy out this afternoon, be here by two P.M., with three hundred thousand in cash."

"Who're the they in Florida?"

"One of the supermarket rags."

"Then why don't you?"

"I want a fast in-and-out deal," Oil Drum said. "So I figure I might as well sell it all to Gamble herself."

"For how much?"

"One million."

"Impossible," Wu said.

"Okay. You just said no, so I'll say goodbye."

Wu spoke quickly. "How much time do we have?"

"It's a one-day sale."

"You can't expect her to raise that much cash in one day."

"Why not? Banks open at nine and close at four—some of 'em at five or six. She's got till six P.M. We agree to do it by then or not at all."

"Call me back at five," Wu said.

"Same number?"

"Same number."

"Okay," Oil Drum said. "But at five it's go or no-go. I don't want any maybes."

"No maybes," Wu promised just before Oil Drum broke

224

the connection. Wu hung up his telephone, pushed it away, rested his elbows on the table and looked at Overby.

"That was Oil Drum, Otherguy," Wu said. "Ione Gamble has until this evening to raise one million dollars."

Overby's mouth curled down at its ends in grudging respect. "So he's going for it all?"

"Apparently."

"What happened to him and the sleazoids?"

"They're his fallback and threat."

Overby nodded his professional approval and said, "Makes sense."

Wu turned to Georgia Blue. "You'll be our go-between, Georgia. Quincy will be your backup. I'll call Howard Mott and tell him we've heard from the blackmailer, who's demanding one million for the tapes."

"That means we go through Jack Broach," said Georgia Blue.

"Yes," Wu said.

"Who can raise maybe three hundred thousand tops, if that."

"So you've told us," Wu said.

"He'll hand it to me with a wink and a nod—the three hundred thousand."

"Precisely."

"And I'll hand it to Oil Drum, who'll want to count it."

"I don't believe you and Quincy will let it get quite that far," Wu said.

There was a short silence before Durant said, "Then I'll need a piece."

"Here," Overby said. He reached into his hip pocket, produced the .38-caliber revolver he had bought from Colleen Cullen, and slid it across the table. Durant picked it up, examined it, slipped it into the right pocket of his jacket and said, "What about Georgia?"

"She's already got one," Overby said.

Before Durant could comment, Blue said, "All you have to do is watch my back, Quincy."

"And my own," he said.

225

Artie Wu cut off further bickering with an announcement. "I have some good news about money."

Everyone looked at him except Durant, who continued to study Georgia Blue.

"Last night," Wu continued, "Enno Glimm made us a rather interesting proposal. If we can quietly resolve this entire matter and keep him and his companies out of it—which, of course, means absolving Ione Gamble of Rice's murder—Glimm will pay us an additional five hundred thousand. If we succeed, Quincy and I feel that this fresh money should be divided into equal shares—one hundred thousand each. You might think of it as an incentive bonus."

"Or a don't-stray bonus," Durant said, still studying Georgia Blue.

This time it was Overby who blocked any retort from Blue with a question: "Didn't Glimm agree to indemnify Ione Gamble for any and all losses the Goodisons caused her?"

"Right," Wu said.

"Then what Glimm's really doing is spending half a million on us to keep from coming up with the million Oil Drum's asking. Or am I wrong?"

Wu smiled. "Some such thought may indeed have crossed his mind."

"So even if we clear Gamble of Rice's death, she can still sue Glimm for a bundle."

"On what grounds?" Durant said.

"How the hell should I know?" Overby said. "That'd be up to Howie Mott. Loss of income. Mental suffering. That's what you hire lawyers to do."

"What an interesting notion, Otherguy," Wu said. "You can try it on Ms. Gamble herself later this morning."

Instantly wary, Overby asked, "What d'you mean?"

"I mean you're going to be her personal security."

"Not me."

"Why not?"

"I'm no rent-a-cop."

"You are now," Durant said.

Overby started to protest again, but changed his mind, slumped back in his chair and glowered at anyone who looked at him. A new silence began that was ended by Georgia Blue's amused laugh.

"What's so funny?" Overby demanded.

"Artie's funny," she said. "Everybody gets a nanny. Artie watches Booth. Quincy watches me. And Ione Gamble watches you."

Wu gazed at her with a fond smile and asked, "Should we have taken a vote on who does what, Georgia?"

"A secret one?"

"Of course."

"Who'd count the votes, Artie?"

"I would," he said, still smiling. "Who else?"

*   *   *

After Artie Wu tapped out Howard Mott's telephone number, he listened to the rings while looking at Booth Stallings, now the last one left at the old refectory table. "You didn't say much during discussion period, Booth," Wu said.

"Believe I said, 'Please pass the salt.' "

Before Wu could continue, Howard Mott answered the phone with a grumpy "What is it?"

"It's Artie Wu."

"You woke me up. If I sound testy, it's because I am."

"Late night?"

"I dictated till three. Maybe three-thirty."

"I have some news."

"Good or bad?"

"I'll let you decide," Wu said. "The blackmailer called."

"Ah."

"He disguises his voice with some kind of electronic device. Otherguy calls him Oil Drum."

"Because he sounds like he's talking from the bottom of one," Mott said.

"Exactly," said Wu, happy as always when a bright mind required no explanation. "He wants to sell Ione video- and

227

audiotapes of her confessing under hypnosis to the murder of Billy Rice. The price is one million. He wants—I should say demands—a yes or no by five P.M. today."

"You know she can't raise a million that quickly, Artie. So what are you really calling about?"

"A proposal."

"I may not give you a reply."

"Perhaps, but I propose that you call Jack Broach and tell him Ione needs a million in cash by four P.M. today and why. Then merely listen to what he says."

There was a very long pause until Mott asked, "You think Jack, instead of saying, 'Impossible,' will say, 'Okay, fine,' don't you?"

"Should he say yes or, 'Okay, fine,' tell him Georgia Blue will be picking up the money."

"All by herself?" Mott said, then quickly added, "Never mind. I don't want to know."

Wu said nothing and there was another long silence that Mott ended when he asked, "What's going on, Artie? Nothing specific, please."

"Something that might exonerate Ione."

"Might?"

"That's as specific as I can get," Wu said. "But there's one thing you must do and that's to give Ione some sense of progress. Simply call her and say that Durant and Georgia are dropping by to bring her up to date and introduce her to her new bodyguard."

"Who is?"

"I'm not quite sure yet."

"The hell you're not."

"Bear with me, Howie."

Another very long pause was followed by a grunt from Howard Mott, who then changed the subject and asked, "How was Enno Glimm?"

"Nervous," Wu said. "He offered us an additional five hundred thousand to keep him all the way out of it and get Ione off the hook. Then he flew back to London."

"Artie," Mott said.

"Yes?"

"I really don't need to hear everything," Mott said and broke the connection.

Wu recradled the phone, frowned at it for a moment, then turned to Stallings. "What d'you think, Booth?"

"I think your phone pal Oil Drum not only stole the tapes but also killed the limo driver, Mr. Santillan, then did in the Goodisons and tried to run over you and me at the motel in Oxnard."

"How very neat," Wu said.

"It'd be even neater if he also killed Billy Rice," Stallings said.

"Except he didn't," Wu said.

"No."

"But you think you know who did."

"Maybe."

"Like to share your suspicions?"

"Depends," Stallings said.

"On what?"

"On what happens to Georgia," Stallings said.

Artie Wu tugged at his right earlobe as he seemed to examine something that was just beyond Stallings's left shoulder. "You think I've sent Georgia down the path to temptation rather than redemption, don't you?"

"You sure as hell've pointed the way."

"Then why would I send Quincy with her?"

"That stumps me."

"How does Quincy seem to you—compared to five years ago?"

Stallings considered the question. "He's turned sour and about as remote as the moon—although he never was what I'd call a bucket of laughs."

"And Georgia?"

"She's moved to the outback of remote."

"What I've done," Wu said slowly, "or what I hope I've done, is to send them on a cure together."

"A cure that can get 'em both killed—if they don't kill each other first."

"But the interesting thing is, Booth, they both know what I'm doing and neither objects."

"Maybe the cure will take and maybe it won't," Stallings said. "But as long as I know you're not setting Georgia up, I'll go along."

"I'm very fond of Georgia," Wu said. "You know that."

"Ever been stuck on her?"

"No," Wu said. "But then Agnes was already—present."

"Durant was once," Stallings said. "Stuck on her."

Wu nodded.

"So was Otherguy."

Wu moved his shoulders just enough to form a slight shrug.

"And now me," Stallings said.

"You're a lucky man, Booth," Wu said, paused, then asked, "About what you said earlier?"

"About who killed Rice?"

Wu nodded. "Is it a hunch?"

"More notion than hunch."

"Notions are good, too," Wu said with a couple of judicious nods. "Need anything?"

"Money, but I'll cash a check at the bank for five thousand."

"Want me to tag along?"

Stallings shook his head and rose.

"May I ask what you think you might come up with?"

"What about a signed confession?"

"That'll do nicely," said Artie Wu.

Thirty-six

The three of them were following the Salvadoran housekeeper and the flop-eared rabbit up the stairs to Ione Gamble's office when the 7-year-old shepherd-Labrador began its charge.

Otherguy Overby, bringing up the rear, turned just in time for eighty-two pounds of dog to spring and slam into his chest. A second later Overby found himself in a sitting position on the stair's fifth step, the shep-Lab licking his face and emitting yelps and whines of joy and delight.

Overby finally grinned, gave the dog a rough hug, pushed him away and said, "How the hell are you, Moose?" The dog replied with yet another wet lick, rested his head on Overby's knee and gazed up at him with what seemed to be total adoration.

It was then that Ione Gamble appeared at the top of the stairs and asked Durant, "What happened?"

"Your dog just took out your new bodyguard," said Durant and quickly introduced Gamble to Georgia Blue.

After the introduction, Gamble stared down at the back of Overby's head and called, "Are you okay?"

Overby rose slowly, turned around even more slowly, looked up at Gamble and said, "I'm fine."

"*Godalmighty*," she said. "It's Otherguy Overby himself."

Overby smiled up at her—a little wanly, Durant thought—and said, "Howya doing, Ione?"

"You've met, I see," Georgia Blue said.

Ione Gamble nodded, still staring down at Overby, whose faint smile had now almost faded away. "The first time was in seventy-four," she said. "I was eighteen and Otherguy was what—thirty-three?"

"Thirty," Overby said.

"As I said, thirty-three, and he was going to make me a star. Well, he did get me my first job—leading an iguana by a rope over to Cal Worthington in one of those 'My Dog, Spot' used-car commercials."

"You had to start somewhere," Overby said.

"And the next time?" Georgia Blue said.

"Ten years later."

"Eleven," Overby said. "Eighty-five."

"Okay. Eighty-five. I'd just bought this house and had to do a picture in London. I needed someone to house-sit and a friend recommended what she called 'this perfectly marvelous house-sitter.' So I said okay, send him around. Well, who shows up but Maurice Overby, House-sitter to the Stars."

"Tell 'em who saved the house, Ione," Overby said.

"You did. The firemen ordered him out because a fire was sweeping up the canyon. But Otherguy stayed on the roof all night with a garden hose and nobody got hurt and nothing got burned. But when he left six weeks later, my animals pined for him so much, especially Moose here, that they'd hardly eat. The bastard had alienated their affections and I had to pay him fifty bucks every Sunday for two months just to come over and play with 'em for an hour."

Overby shrugged. "Animals like me."

"If you don't want him as bodyguard," said Durant, "just say so."

"How long will I need one?"

"Two or three days, if that."

"If he stays more than three days, my animals will fall for him again. On the other hand, Otherguy's mean and crafty

232

and ought to make an okay bodyguard. So let's go on in the office and you guys can have a beer or something." She looked back down the stairs at Overby. "You, too."

Ione Gamble indicated the way to her office, which Durant already knew. He led the way, followed by Georgia Blue. When Overby reached the top of the stairs, trailed by Moose, Gamble looked over her left shoulder to make sure Blue and Durant were inside the office. She then turned back to Overby and said, "You going to give me a hug or not?"

After he gave her a quick hug and a kiss on the cheek, she said, "Why didn't you tell them you knew me?"

"It was a long time ago, Ione."

"Something told me to ride you a little. Was I right?"

He nodded. "As always."

"How are you—really?"

"Couldn't be better," he said, and intuition told Gamble that Otherguy Overby, for once, was probably telling the truth.

*   *   *

No one wanted a beer at 10:45 in the morning so the Salvadoran housekeeper served coffee to everyone except Gamble, who, seated behind her Memphis cotton broker's desk with the flop-eared rabbit in her lap, stuck to diet Dr Pepper.

After a sip of the soft drink, she looked at Durant and said, "I talked to Howie Mott. He called forty-five minutes ago and told me the blackmailer wants a million dollars for the Goodison tapes. I asked him what I should do and Howie said he's against paying blackmail in any form. But it's my reputation at stake and it has to be my choice."

"That's a nonanswer," said Overby, who was sitting in the businesslike armchair with Moose curled up at his feet.

"No, it's not," Gamble said. "Howie said that before I decided anything I should find out from Jack Broach if I can even raise a million dollars in cash by five this afternoon. If I can't, he says the question of payment is moot." She paused. "Academic?"

"Or irrelevant," Georgia Blue said. Durant, sitting next to her on the chintz-covered couch, agreed with a nod.

"Well, I called Jack and asked if it was possible and he said just barely, but I'd have to take a beating on some of my stocks and bonds and all my annuities. I told him to go ahead. Of course, he wanted to know what to do with a million in cash. I told him Howie said a Ms. Georgia Blue would be by to pick it up."

"What did Mr. Broach say?" Blue asked.

"He sounded relieved and said you were very competent."

"You have to sign anything?" Durant asked Gamble.

She shook her head. "Jack's got my power of attorney."

"I'd never give anybody my power of attorney," Overby said.

Ione Gamble dismissed Overby's comment with a derisive roll of her eyes and turned again to Georgia Blue. "You've had a lot of experience in stuff like this?"

"Yes."

"Georgia used to be a Secret Service agent," Overby said.

"Really?"

Blue nodded.

"What do you think I should do?"

"Get the tapes back. You don't have any choice."

"But they tell me they're inadmissible as evidence because I was hypnotized."

"This isn't about evidence anymore," Blue said. "It's about Ione Gamble, movie star. If you don't get the tapes back, they'll be sold to slash-and-burn TV shows and tabloids. They'll run tapes of you on TV saying God knows what—maybe describing the details of your sex life with Billy Rice. And everything they run on TV will be boiled down by the tabloids into three- and four-word Second Coming headlines that'll scream the whole story." Georgia Blue paused, then continued. "Okay. You're tough and you can take it. But it'll be an avalanche of pretrial publicity—all of it bad."

"Maybe it won't ever come to trial," Overby said.

"Maybe it won't," Georgia Blue said.

"What you're really telling me is that those tapes could help send me to the gas chamber."

"That's melodramatic," Blue said. "What I'm saying is that they can do you no possible good and could cause you a great deal of harm."

Gamble looked at Durant. "What d'you think?"

"I think Georgia's right."

Gamble seemed drawn back to Blue. "In the Secret Service you must've had a lot of experience protecting people."

Georgia Blue nodded.

"Anybody famous?"

"Imelda Marcos. Mrs. Bush—when he first became Vice-President. Some others."

"Then you're an expert."

"I was."

"Well, if I need a bodyguard, why is it Otherguy and not you?"

"You'll have to ask Mr. Durant," Georgia Blue said.

Gamble shifted her gaze to Durant, who said, "We don't know that your life's in danger. But we think it's a possibility and Otherguy is the precaution we've taken. And a competent one."

"As competent as Ms. Blue?"

"Nobody is."

Georgia Blue turned to stare at Durant, then looked quickly away.

"So you and Ms. Blue—"

"Better call me Georgia."

"So you and Georgia will buy the tapes from the blackmailer with my million dollars?"

"You tell her, Georgia," Durant said.

"When it's all over," Georgia Blue said slowly, "we plan to hand you the tapes and also your million dollars and possibly even the blackmailer."

Ione Gamble seemed to shrink back in her wooden swivel chair. "Possibly?" she said, almost whispering the word.

"It's possible the blackmailer will be dead."

Ione Gamble shrank even farther back in the chair, as if to get as far away from Blue and Durant as possible. She stared down at her desktop, stroked the flop-eared rabbit, as though for reassurance, then looked up at Overby and said, "I don't really want to hear any more, Otherguy."

Thirty-seven

It was 2:42 P.M. when Georgia Blue began counting the $300,000 in Jack Broach's Beverly Hills office. There were thirty bound packets of currency stacked on his eighteenth-century French desk, each packet containing $10,000 in hundred-dollar bills. Blue stood, counting silently. When done, she carefully packed the money into a dark blue nylon carryall she had bought at a Sav-On drugstore for $8.95 plus tax.

Broach sat behind his desk, not speaking until she zipped up the carryall. He then smiled and said, "One million exactly, right?"

Georgia Blue sat down in a chair in front of the desk, stared at him for a moment, then said, "Exactly."

"A receipt in that amount might prove useful someday."

"Useful to you, not to me."

"I thought it worth a try."

She shrugged. "Anything else?"

He leaned toward her, forearms on the ornate desktop, the well-cared-for hands clasped, a look of what seemed to be genuine interest, even curiosity, on his face. "I'd like to know how it'll work—the mechanics of it."

"The details," she said.

237

He nodded.

"That's normal," she said. "Most people become curious when they find themselves in a mess like this for the first time. They ask who-does-what-and-when questions—probably because so much money's involved."

"It does spark the curiosity," Broach said.

"All right. Here's how it'll work. When Oil Drum calls later this afternoon—"

"Oil Drum?"

"It's our name for the seller because of his electronically distorted voice."

"I see."

"When he calls—"

Again Broach interrupted. "Who'll be taking the call?"

"Artie Wu. I'll probably listen in on an extension. Quincy Durant might also listen in—or he might not."

Broach nodded, satisfied.

"Anyway," she said, "after Oil Drum calls, he'll be told the money's ready."

"The million?"

"The million. We'll then settle on where to make the buy. It'll be a quiet, out-of-the-way place."

"What kind of place?"

"A place where he can count the money in private and where I can check out the tape on a VCR."

"You have such a place in mind?"

"Yes."

"Where?"

"Sorry."

"Of course," Broach said. "Security."

"Common sense," said Georgia Blue. "Artie and Oil Drum will dicker about the place. Oil Drum'll turn our first suggestion down and we'll reject his alternate proposal. Artie'll then recommend the place we wanted all along and make it clear that unless Oil Drum agrees, the deal's off."

Broach frowned. "That sounds risky. All ultimatums do."

"Oil Drum's selling, we're buying and we have the customer's leverage. After he finally agrees, we'll haggle about the time. We'll suggest eight o'clock and he'll come back with nine or ten. We'll let him win because unless he has time to scout out the meeting place, he won't show and who could blame him for that?"

"Interesting," Broach said. "Will you be going alone?"

"Why?"

"Because it's occurred to me that if you don't go alone, then you'll have to share this—" He touched the carryall. "—with somebody else."

"I won't be going alone," Georgia Blue said, rose and picked up the carryall.

Broach also rose. "Who're they sending with you?"

"Durant," she said. "But he and I won't be sharing anything."

She turned then, strode to the door, the carryall in her right hand, opened the door, looked back, smiled and left. Jack Broach judged it to be another perfect exit.

*   *   *

Georgia Blue walked south on the west side of Robertson Boulevard, moving with long quick strides until she came to the rented Ford. She walked with the blue money bag in her left hand, her right one thrust deeply into her new over-the-shoulder Coach purse that contained the .38-caliber revolver she and Overby had bought from Colleen Cullen.

After reaching the Ford, she opened its front curbside door, tossed in the carryall, got quickly into the car, closed the door and locked it. Durant started the engine, glanced over his left shoulder, then pulled out of the metered parking space and asked, "How'd it go?"

"Fine," she said. "He was very interested in what he called the mechanics."

"Translated, I'd say that means: are you going alone or with somebody?"

"He also said that if somebody does tag along, I'll have to share this." She patted the blue moneybag.

"And you said?"

"I said Durant is coming with me but he and I won't be sharing anything."

Durant grinned, then chuckled. She frowned slightly and said, "That must be the first laugh you've had in a month."

"There haven't been any funny parts until now."

"Not even when you and the movie star were getting it on?"

He gave her a quick, not quite surprised look. "Were we now?"

"She was obvious about it, even if you weren't. But then you've had years and years of experience. I don't think anyone else noticed except Otherguy. Anyway, she's rather nice. I think I like her, although I still can't believe she's all that famous."

"She made it big during the last four or five years."

"Then perhaps I should go see some of her pictures."

"You don't have to *go* see them anymore," Durant said. "You can rent them on tape for two or three bucks. Play them at home on a VCR. Microwave your own popcorn. Fast-forward the dull parts."

"Is that the chief cultural advance I've missed?"

"I can't think of any others," Durant said.

After that, they drove in silence. Durant took the Robertson Boulevard on-ramp to the Santa Monica Freeway and headed west toward the Pacific Coast Highway. Three minutes later, Georgia Blue broke the silence. "We'd better— never mind."

"We'd better what?" Durant said.

"I was going to suggest we stop at the Bank of America in Malibu and get some money," she said. "But then I realized we already have three hundred thousand." She touched the carryall.

"Money for what?"

"Remember Otherguy telling you about Colleen Cullen and her lie-low bed-and-breakfast inn?"

He nodded. "Topanga Canyon."

"I think we'd better go rent it for the night. The entire place."

"How much?"

"She'll probably ask ten thousand. We'll offer her five and settle for seventy-five hundred."

"Where'll she be when it starts?"

"You haven't met her, have you?"

"No."

"When you meet her," Georgia Blue said, "tell me where you think she should be."

*   *   *

After riding a bus into Santa Monica, Booth Stallings took a taxi that let him out at the Beverly Hills Budget rental car outlet that specialized in exotic autos. On duty was the same clerk who had rented him the Mercedes 560SEL sedan that Wu and Durant drove. She looked up when he came in, smiled and said, "Hi, there, Mr. Stallings. Don't tell me somebody went and stole the Mercedes?"

Stallings, remembering that her name was Gloria, decided she still had yet to experience a moment of gloom. He returned her smile and said, "Not yet, Gloria." He paused then, frowned slightly and said, "What'd you tell me your last name was?"

"I didn't. But it's Ransome with an 'e'—at your service."

"Well, Ms. Ransome with an 'e,' I need me another car."

"Business must be good—whatever you guys are doing out there in Malibu."

"Picture deal," Stallings said. "A fat one."

"No kidding? That's wonderful. So what've you got in mind? Just remember we're talking car now."

"If you were a few years older, we might be talking Tahoe weekend."

"I've gone out with older guys."

"To Tahoe?"

"No, but there's always the first time."

"Tell you what, Gloria," Stallings said, leaning on the

counter, "after we sign this picture deal, I'm going to treat myself to both a weekend in Tahoe and a new car and probably could use some company."

"What kind of car?" she asked.

"I've been thinking about a Mercedes 500SL."

"Good Lord! You know how much those things cost?"

"About a hundred thousand. But what I'm more interested in right now is how much they rent for. I thought I'd test-drive one for a few days before deciding anything."

"Must be some picture deal."

"Like I said, it's fat. Real fat."

"Well, the 500SL rents for four hundred a day but you've got to put up a cash deposit."

"How much?"

"Five thousand."

"That's fine. You got one ready to go?"

"Let me check." She turned to her computer, tapped away for a few moments, studied the screen and said, "You're in luck. We've only got the one and it's available."

"You've only got one?"

"They're real expensive and we don't get all that many calls for it."

"Is it black?"

She nodded. "You got something against black?"

"No, I was just wondering if it's the same one a friend of mine rented last New Year's Eve."

"Like me to check that for you?"

Stallings gave her his warmest smile. "Only if it's not any trouble."

Thirty-eight

Quincy Durant didn't like the looks of Cousin Colleen's Bed & Breakfast Inn and said so. Georgia Blue replied that if he had seen it for the first time at night, he would've liked it even less.

Durant stopped the rented Ford sedan near the large sign where the red neon letters forever blinked "No Vacancy." He studied the huge old house in the distance and decided it looked like a place to store ancients until they breathed their last while watching black-and-white reruns of *I Love Lucy* and *Perry Mason*. As if reading his thoughts, Georgia Blue said, "It's just somewhere to lie low until the looted trust funds reach the Bahamas."

Durant grunted, then drove up the long brick drive, taking in the trees and drought-resistant flowers that he thought could use some moisture. In the fan-shaped parking area, Blue noticed that the elderly MG roadster was gone although the Toyota pickup truck remained.

Durant parked next to the pickup and said, "What d'you want to do with the money?"

"Lock it in the trunk?"

"Trunks take about three seconds to open."

"You carry it, then," she said.

When they were out of the Ford, Durant followed Georgia Blue up the nine steps to the porch. As they neared the doorbell, she also noticed that the stained-glass panel of a bowl of cherries, through which Otherguy Overby had rammed his elbow, had been replaced by one representing a bowl of purple grapes.

Blue gave the doorbell a five-second ring and waited. Ten seconds later, the heavy front door flew open and Colleen Cullen appeared, aiming her sawed-off double-barrelled shotgun at them. Durant automatically noted it was fully cocked and that she had fingers on both triggers.

"Whatever you want, Slim, the answer's no. *N-O*. No."

"We want the whole place for tonight," Georgia Blue said.

"Full up. Booked solid. No room."

"Tell her about the money," Durant said to Georgia Blue.

"Well, shit, he can talk," Cullen said. "Just opens his mouth and out it comes. Who's Mr. Tan Man, Slim?"

"My partner."

"What happened to Maw-reese?"

"All three of us are partners."

"Tell her about the money," Durant said.

"What you got in the bag, Mr. Tan Man?" Colleen Cullen said.

"Money," said Durant.

"Open it up and let's see," Cullen said.

"Not out here."

"I got a double-barrelled sawed-off that says open it up."

"Ms. Blue's hand is in her purse," Durant said. "In that hand is a thirty-eight I understand you sold her. It's aimed at your right eye. If you even think you're going to pull a trigger, you're dead."

Colleen Cullen and Durant stared at each other. Nobody moved or spoke or blinked until Georgia Blue said, "Let's go inside, Colleen, and have a drink and talk about money."

Still staring at Durant, Cullen said, "How much we going to talk about?"

"Enough," Blue said. "But inside."

"Okay," Cullen said and took two quick steps back, the shotgun still levelled at Durant. "But Mr. Tan Man goes first. Then you, Slim."

As she followed Durant through the door, Georgia Blue said, "To your right."

When they reached the closed sliding doors, Blue said, "Open them."

Durant slid the two doors back into their walled recesses, went into the large living room, looked around quickly, then turned to Colleen Cullen and said, "Hughes and Pauline Goodison were shot dead yesterday in a motel bathroom in Oxnard."

Cullen reacted with a clearly visible start. But the shotgun didn't waver. "That calls for a drink," she said. "Big round table back there's where the whiskey is. You pour, Mr. Tan Man. Three bourbons. Water. No ice."

Durant turned, went to the big round table, poured generous shots of Virginia Gentleman from the now half-empty bottle into three glasses, then added water from a glass pitcher. He did it all with his right hand, keeping a tight grip on the blue carryall with his left.

Once the drinks were poured he turned to look at Colleen Cullen, who was aiming the shotgun at Georgia Blue. "I'm going to open the bag and put something on the table," Durant said to Cullen. "If you don't like it, shoot her."

Without waiting for agreement, Durant zipped open the blue carryall, took out $10,000 worth of bound hundred-dollar bills and placed it on the table. He then picked up his drink and had a long swallow.

Cullen used the shotgun to herd Georgia Blue toward the table. When they reached it, Cullen picked up the bound packet of currency, flicked through it with one hand, her eyes shooting from the money to Durant to Blue and back to the money. It was an indifferent, even contemptuous gesture. Cullen then picked up one of the drinks Durant had mixed and tasted it while studying her guests over the rim of the glass.

245

She put the glass down, resumed her two-handed grip on the shotgun, backed away two steps and asked, "If I pull these two triggers, how much richer am I?"

"Three hundred thousand dollars richer during the second before we kill you," Georgia Blue said.

"What if I did you first, Slim?"

"Mr. Durant would shoot you in the left eye."

"You shoot folks in the right eye. He shoots 'em in the left. Those the rules or something?"

"Pick up the money and count it," Durant said.

"Shit, I don't need to count it. I know what's there. Ten thousand dollars. You think I don't know how high a ten-thousand-dollar stack in hundreds is?"

"Here's the deal," Durant said. "We'll pay you seventy-five hundred for the exclusive use of your house from seven to twelve tonight."

Cullen frowned. "What's the other twenty-five hundred for?"

"Security."

Cullen turned to Georgia Blue. "What the fuck's he talking about now?"

"If things fall apart," Georgia Blue said slowly, "he wants you to put them back together again."

Colleen Cullen turned, put the shotgun down on the big round table, pulled out a chair and sat down in front of her drink. She picked it up, had another swallow, then gestured for Durant and Blue to join her. They did—Georgia Blue on her right; Durant on her left.

"This ain't no drug buy, is it?" Colleen Cullen asked.

Georgia Blue shook her head.

"Blackmail payoff?"

Blue nodded.

"Something to do with those Goodison creepies?"

"A little," Blue said.

Cullen nodded slowly, then turned to look at Durant. "And you want me for backup."

"That's right."

"Where?"

"Outside."

"Suppose they kill you two, grab the money and run. What d'you expect me to do?"

"Kill them," Blue said.

"And the money?"

"Keep it," Durant said.

"All of it?" she asked.

"All of it," he said.

Thirty-nine

Booth Stallings came out of Johnnie's New York Pizza on the Pacific Coast Highway in Malibu carrying two 16-inch cheese and sausage pizzas, three quarts of mixed green salad and a six-pack of Mexican beer. After loading it all on the right-hand seat of the newly rented black Mercedes 500SL roadster, he went around the car's rear, got behind the wheel, started the engine and carefully nosed out into the highway traffic. A few blocks later, Stallings made a U-turn, parked the Mercedes at the curb and, now bearing early dinner for four, walked back a block and a half to the Rice house. He arrived at 4:52 P.M., eight minutes before Oil Drum, the blackmailer, was due to call.

By 4:59 P.M. Stallings had seen to the plates, silverware, napkins and glasses; Georgia Blue had served the pizza and salad, and Durant had opened four bottles of beer. Artie Wu sat at the head of the old refectory table, a telephone at his elbow. At 5:01 P.M. Wu took a large bite of pizza. Seconds later, his mouth still full, the phone rang. Wu continued to chew calmly as Georgia Blue rose and hurried to the phone in the living room. At the end of the fifth ring, she and Wu—

his mouth still half-full—simultaneously picked up their telephones.

"Yes?" Wu said.

"It's me," said the reverberating voice of Oil Drum.

"So it is."

"What about my money?"

"It's handy."

"So where d'you want to do it?"

"I'm open to suggestion," Wu said and had another large bite of pizza.

"There's a place out in the Valley—"

"The San Fernando Valley, you mean?"

"Yeah."

"Close to the Ventura Freeway?"

"Not far."

"Sorry," Wu said, paused to drink some beer, then continued: "Anywhere we meet will have to be at least ten minutes from any freeway. Otherwise, the temptation to smash, grab and tear off down the 101 or the 405 might be, well, irresistible."

"Who the fuck you think you're dealing with?" Oil Drum said.

"A blackmailer," said Wu. "But when you reconsider, you'll realize that the smash, grab and run temptation might be equally irresistible to us."

There was a pause before Oil Drum said, "Okay. Then you come up with a place."

"Topanga Canyon," Wu said. "About halfway between the Ventura Freeway and the PCH. It's a bed-and-breakfast inn devoid of guests. Privacy guaranteed. And it offers not only a place for you to count your million but also a VCR we can use to view the tape."

"And a real narrow twisty road perfect for a hijack," Oil Drum said.

"You're selling, we're buying," Wu said. "And our risk is considerably greater than yours."

"That sounds a whole lot like take it or leave it."

"A reasonable interpretation," said Wu and finished off the last of his pizza wedge.

There was another silence until Oil Drum said, "Okay. How do I get there?"

Wu took a three-by-five card from his shirt pocket and, without sounding as if he were reading, slowly read the directions to Cousin Colleen's Bed & Breakfast Inn. After Wu finished, Oil Drum repeated the directions without hesitancy or mistake and asked, "What time?"

"Eight o'clock?" Wu said.

"Too early."

"Ten," Wu said.

"I like nine better."

"All right. Nine."

"Who're you sending?" Oil Drum asked.

"Why?"

"What d'you mean why? Because I wanta know, that's why."

"Do you want to know who—or how many?"

"How many," Oil Drum said. "I don't give a shit who."

"Two," Wu said. "One to watch the other."

"Two, huh? Okay, then I'll bring somebody."

"I thought you might," Wu said. "At nine o'clock, then?"

"Nine sharp," Oil Drum said and broke the connection.

*   *   *

At 6:55 P.M. Georgia Blue rose from the refectory table and said she was going to lie down for a while. Ten minutes later, Durant got up and said he planned to do the same thing. That left Wu and Stallings seated at the table, their untasted third cups of coffee cooling in front of them.

Wu lit a cigar, blew smoke at the ceiling, then looked at Stallings. "I want you to do something that might sound a little underhanded, Booth."

Stallings only nodded.

"I suspect Oil Drum might bring more than just one other person along."

"Can't blame him—especially since Georgia and Durant'll

have what's her name, Colleen Cullen, staked out with a sawed-off."

Wu puffed on his cigar, examined its ash and said, "Before nine tonight it's quite possible that Oil Drum will get to Colleen Cullen with a better offer—or get rid of her altogether."

Stallings thought about it. "Possible or probable?"

"Possible," Wu said. "You have plans for this evening?"

"Not until later."

"Are you making any . . . progress?"

"Maybe."

"But nothing you'd care to talk about?"

"Not yet."

"I need an hour of your time," Wu said and blew a smoke ring off to the right.

"To do what?"

Artie Wu reached into his right rear pants pocket and brought out a small semiautomatic. It was a German-made Sauer, the one that held nine 7.65mm rounds, had an overall length of six and a half inches and weighed a little more than twenty-two ounces loaded. Wu slid the pistol over to Stallings, who picked it up, examined it carefully, tucked it away in his own hip pocket and asked, "Who d'you want me to shoot?"

"I want you to get it to Otherguy."

"When?"

"Now."

"What else?"

"Tell Otherguy to go to the Cullen inn as soon as possible."

"Before Durant and Georgia get there?"

"Yes."

"Why?"

Wu blew cigar smoke off to his left this time. "You were in the infantry during the war?"

Stallings nodded.

"A platoon leader?"

"Right."

"You sent out scouts?"

"I sent 'em out and sometimes they didn't come back."

"Which told you something was amiss up ahead."

"And why nobody ever wanted to be a scout. Otherguy won't either."

"But he'll do it," Wu said.

"What about Ione Gamble, whose body he's supposed to be guarding?"

"I'd like you to deliver her to Howie Mott and leave her with him until it's over."

"Howie know about this yet?"

"I'll call him."

"You going to tell Georgia and Durant about Otherguy?"

"No," Wu said, reached into a pants pocket, brought out some car keys and offered them to Stallings. "You'd better take the Mercedes."

Stallings shook his head and rose. "I rented myself a car this afternoon."

"Good."

Stallings looked down at Wu for several moments before he said, "Why aren't you going, Artie—instead of Otherguy?"

"Because I'm not needed."

"You hope."

"I hope," Wu agreed.

"Okay, so what else do I tell Otherguy besides all that 'scouts out' bullshit?"

"Tell him to fix it."

"Fix what?"

"Whatever breaks," said Artie Wu.

Forty

Ione Gamble, trailed by Moose the dog, reached the bottom of the staircase, turned right and entered her living room just as the seated Booth Stallings drew the Sauer semiautomatic from his right hip pocket and seemed to aim it at the standing Otherguy Overby.

"Oh, shit, please don't!" Gamble said in a cry that was almost a yell.

Stallings rose and turned, pistol in hand. It wasn't a quick turn but it was quick enough to terrify Gamble. Her eyes seemed to double in size, her mouth dropped open and her hands flew up, palms out, as if to ward off the aged assassin's bullet.

"For chrissake, Ione," said an exasperated Overby. "He's Booth Stallings—Howie's father-in-law."

The hands were slowly lowered. The mouth shut itself like a trap and the eyes returned to normal. A flush raced up her cheeks as she pried open her now grim and angry mouth just enough to say, "I don't like people waving guns around in my living room."

"I wasn't waving it around," Stallings said. "I was delivering it."

He turned and offered the Sauer to Overby, butt first.

Overby took the weapon, gave it a glance and dropped it into his jacket pocket as if it were something he did every morning just after he strapped on his watch.

Fresh anger streaked across Gamble's face and her voice turned bitter and accusative. "You didn't even have a gun? What kind of fucking bodyguard doesn't have his own gun?"

"Somebody you want me to shoot?" Overby said. Before Gamble could reply, he moved over to her and said, "Listen, Ione. There's something you've gotta do. You—"

She cut him off, not with words, but by sinking slowly into a chair, bending forward and burying her face in her hands. Her shoulders shuddered when she spoke in what was almost a murmur. A stage murmur, Overby thought.

"When he turned—with that gun—I was never so scared in my—"

Overby, unmoved, interrupted. "The thing you gotta do, Ione, is go upstairs and pack an overnight bag. Won't take five minutes. Then Booth here'll drive you to Howie's suite, where you'll spend the night."

She glared up at him. "Are you trying to dump me off?"

"Go pack the bag, Ione."

She rose instead and wandered over to Stallings, studied him for a moment, then gave him a smile that he felt was full of false promise. She reached up to brush an imaginary speck of something from his left shoulder just before she asked, "So what exactly do you do for Wudu?"

"I'm the wise old head. The bank of memory. I'm also chief provisioner, exchequer designate and general factotum."

"And before that?" she asked, still seeming to be deeply interested.

"Boy soldier. Professional graduate student, government consultant. Itinerant professor without hope of tenure. Frequent beneficiary of any number of think tank and foundation grants. And most recently, the aging but junior partner in Overby, Stallings Associates."

All of Gamble's real or pretended interest vanished, replaced by more rage. "You and Otherguy are *partners*?" she

said, making it sound, in Stallings's opinion, more like a fel-
ony than a misdemeanor.

"Ione," Overby said.

"What?"

"Go pack the fucking bag."

Gamble turned on him, obviously prepared to refuse, argue and even rant until Overby nodded just once toward the
door. Yet it wasn't really a nod, Stallings thought. It was
instead a silent peremptory command that brooked no re-
fusal. She hesitated, then turned, headed for the foyer, almost turned back, again changed her mind and hurried out
of the living room, Moose at her heels. After Overby made
sure she really had gone up the stairs, he came back into the
living room and asked, "Who's worrying Artie the most—
Durant or Georgia?"

"He only mentioned some slight misgivings about Colleen
Cullen," Stallings said.

Overby considered the Topanga innkeeper for a moment,
arrived at a conclusion and shared it with Stallings. "Yeah,
you could spin Colleen around for a price." He frowned then
and studied Stallings the way he might have studied some not
quite legible handwriting. "Tell me again what Artie said—
exactly."

"He said you're to fix whatever gets broken."

"You're sure he said 'what' and not 'who'?"

"He said 'what.' "

Overby's hard white grin came and went quickly, replaced
by a look of anticipation. "Know something, Booth? This
whole thing could turn out to be kind of interesting after all."

*   *   *

With Ione Gamble as passenger, Stallings drove his rented
Mercedes roadster south on Seventh Street to Montana Avenue, turned right toward the ocean, then turned south again
on Fourth Street because Gamble said Fourth was both the
quickest and safest way. She didn't speak again until they
reached Wilshire Boulevard.

"I have a car just like this," she said.

"Not quite. This one's rented. Yours isn't."

"What's her name—your daughter who's Howie's wife?"

"Lydia."

"She your only child?"

"I have another daughter. Joanna. But she's sort of bitchy."

Ione Gamble was silent again until they were a block from Howard Mott's oceanview hotel. "D'you think there's any chance of this turning out all right?"

"Like in the movies?" Stallings said. "No chance."

"I don't think so either," she said.

*   *   *

When it was 8:14 P.M. and time to go, Durant and Georgia Blue presented themselves to Artie Wu, who still sat at the head of the old refectory table, enjoying a cigar and a glass of excellent Armagnac. Wu had discovered a bottle of it hidden away by someone in an empty flour canister. Possibly by Billy Rice himself, Wu thought, because the Armagnac was far too good to share with anyone.

Georgia Blue was wearing black jeans from the Gap, a black sweatshirt from the same place and her dark blue Ked sneakers but no socks. She had concealed her reddish-brown hair with a turban fashioned out of a dark blue silk scarf. She raised her sweatshirt to reveal the .38 Smith & Wesson revolver that was clamped against her bare flat stomach by the tightly fitting jeans.

Wu nodded approvingly and turned to examine Durant, who wore a pair of gray-green tweed trousers with cuffs that evidently had belonged to an old but expensive suit. On his feet were a pair of weathered New Balance running shoes, and covering his upper body was a dark maroon sweatshirt that bore the Greek letters of the Phi Delta Theta fraternity.

"I never knew you were a Phi Delt," Georgia Blue said, not trying to hide her mockery.

"I found it on the top shelf of a closet," Durant said as he produced the other .38-caliber S&W revolver Overby and Blue had bought from Colleen Cullen. He checked it carefully, then shoved it back into a hip pocket and said, "The pants come from an old clothes bag in the garage."

"I was wondering," Wu said. "Now then. An announcement or two. If something rotten happens, try to get to a phone and call here. If nobody answers, call Howie Mott. If something good happens, do exactly the same thing—call here first and, if no answer, call Howie."

"What you're saying is you might not be here," Durant said.

"That's a possibility."

"If you've got nothing else to do, Artie," Georgia Blue said, "you can always tag along and backstop us."

"You don't need me," he said. "Together, you're better at this sort of thing than anybody. Notice I said together. Separately, you're very, very good but not quite—I hate to say it—tops. Because of that I strongly recommend the team approach—as distasteful as I know it must seem."

"Are you sick or something?" Durant said.

"Why?"

"Whenever you're sick you get preachy."

"I may be suffering from a slight premonition," Wu said.

"Which is the real reason you're not coming with us," Blue said.

"Exactly."

"What's the premonition, Artie?" Durant asked. "The sky beginning to fall?"

"If I told you, it would no longer be a premonition but a prophecy and I have no desire to be a prophet just yet." He looked from Georgia Blue to Durant, then back to Blue. "Anything else?"

"You can wish us luck," she said.

"I sincerely wish you won't need it," said Artie Wu.

Forty-one

After he left Howard Mott and Ione Gamble in the hotel suite discussing who would sleep where—or whether they would sleep at all—Booth Stallings stopped at the first liquor store he came to on the Pacific Coast Highway and bought a bottle of very expensive Scotch whisky.

Traffic began to slow when he was still half a mile from the Rice house. It then slowed even further and turned into stop-and-go. When Stallings finally crept around the last curve he saw flashing bar lights of black and white police cars. When he got closer he counted three black-and-whites belonging to the Los Angeles County Sheriff's Department and a pair of black matched sedans that he guessed were those of the sheriff's plainclothes investigators. The cars were parked just outside the Rice house.

Two uniformed deputies stood in the center of the highway, waving flashlights and trying to hurry the gawkers along. Since he was driving a $100,000 car, Stallings lowered its left window, stopped and used what he hoped was a $100,000 voice to ask the nearer deputy what the hell was going on.

The deputy was 30 or so and had grown the obligatory gunfighter mustache. "Just a little domestic disturbance," he said. "Nobody hurt. Nothing to see. Please keep it moving."

"That's Billy Rice's house, isn't it?" Stallings asked.

"I don't know whose house it is."

"That big producer who got shot dead New Year's Eve?"

"Please move your fucking car, sir. Now."

Stallings drove another one hundred feet, found an illegal parking space and pulled into it. Once out of the Mercedes he stuffed the brown paper sack containing the Scotch down into a jacket pocket, then darted across the highway and almost got hit by a car whose driver called him a dumb shit.

Stallings walked back toward the Rice house on the beach side of the highway and got there just in time to see Artie Wu, wearing exactly what he had worn at the early pizza dinner, being herded by two plainclothes investigators toward one of the unmarked sedans. Wu's wrists were handcuffed behind him. His face was impassive. One investigator opened the sedan's rear door and the other investigator put a hand on top of Wu's head to keep it from bumping into anything when he turned and backed into the rear seat. As Wu turned and lowered himself, his eyes met Stallings's. There was no flicker of recognition in the eyes of either man.

A small crowd of a dozen or so had gathered just outside the steel gates that guarded the Rice driveway. Stallings recognized a few of them as neighbors to whom he had paid, or tried to pay, courtesy calls. He avoided them and instead picked out the smartest-looking neighbor he hadn't met, sidled up to him and said, "I've seen that Chinese guy down at the Hughes market. What'd he do?"

"Killed some Mexican taxi driver."

"Huh," Stallings said. "He the only one they arrested?"

"So far."

"Bad-luck house, I guess. Billy Rice got his there on New Year's Eve and now this Chinese guy takes a fall."

"No telling who you're living next to out here," the neighbor said. "They let any asshole with a few bucks rent whatever he can pay for. I figure the Chinese guy for a coke dealer."

"Must've been, to afford this place," Stallings said and wandered away. When the stop-and-go traffic stopped again, he hurried across the highway to the yellow duplex and knocked on its door. It was opened seconds later by Rick Cleveland, the *Gone With the Wind* alumnus. Cleveland was still wearing a bathrobe but this one was canary yellow and came down to his calves. He also wore some new sandals along with a lighted cigarette in the left corner of his wide bitter mouth.

"Got some excitement over your way," he said around the cigarette.

"Damned if we don't," Stallings said. "Mind if I use your phone?"

"Help yourself," Cleveland said, opened the door wide, stepped back and then followed Stallings into the duplex's living room.

"It's right over there," Cleveland said and pointed.

Stallings took the sack-wrapped bottle of Scotch out of his jacket pocket and handed it to Cleveland. "Pour us one while I make my call."

The old actor slipped the bottle out of the sack and brightened at the sight of its label. "Jesus. I haven't had a jolt of this in years."

Stallings went over to pick up the phone and tap out Howard Mott's number. As it rang, he noticed that Cleveland had moved to within easy listening distance while working on the bottle's cork.

When Mott answered the telephone, Stallings said, "The sheriff's people just took Artie away in handcuffs. The rumor is that he killed a Mexican cabdriver."

"You're not alone, then," Mott said.

"No."

"Where'd they take him—the Malibu jail?"

"Probably."

"Then I'd better get busy—except we have a problem. Not enough baby-sitters."

"Tell you what," Stallings said, raising his voice slightly. "There's an actor friend of mine out here who might be willing to help out while you tend to Artie."

"You're up to something, Booth."

"I thought you'd like the idea. Let's see what my friend says."

He turned to Rick Cleveland, who had poured two stiff drinks and now stood no more than four feet away, sipping one of the drinks and holding the other in his left hand.

"You want to make five hundred bucks tonight?" Stallings said.

"How?"

"Help me bodyguard Ione Gamble."

"You're shitting me."

"Yes or no?" Stallings said.

"Hell, yes."

Into the phone Stallings said, "We'll be there in twenty or twenty-five minutes."

"After you get there, take a look in the lower left-hand drawer of my secretary's desk," Mott said.

"The blonde's desk?"

"The brunette's."

"One other thing, Howie."

"What?"

"Take Artie some cigars."

*   *   *

Rick Cleveland was wearing a tweed jacket, blue shirt and faded Levi's jeans when he and Booth Stallings reached the illegally parked Mercedes 500SL. Cleveland stopped and stared at the car. "Christ, that looks just like the one Ione Gamble drove that night."

"That's because it is the same one," Stallings said.

They drove to Howard Mott's hotel in twenty-one minutes. Mott opened the door to the suite, was introduced to Cleveland and, in turn, introduced him to Ione Gamble, who was seated in the lone easy chair in the secretaries' office. Gamble smiled up at the actor and said, "I must've seen you a hundred times on one screen or other. Funny we haven't met before this."

"Haven't been working much lately," Cleveland said and

looked curiously at the two desks and the two word processors.

"I must go," Mott said. "Good of you to accommodate us, Mr. Cleveland."

"Glad to help out," Cleveland said. "At least I think I am."

Mott smiled his goodbye and left. After the door closed, Ione Gamble looked up at Stallings and said, "So you and your young friend here are my new bodyguards."

Because it wasn't a question, Stallings made no reply. Instead, he went over to the blond secretary's desk and opened the deep bottom drawer. The only thing it contained was a .25-caliber semiautomatic.

It was a very small vest-pocket-size weapon of Italian manufacture that held five .25-caliber rounds. Stallings could almost conceal it with one hand. But he made a point of showing it to Ione Gamble. "It's a gun, Ione. I'm not going to shoot you with it. I just want you to know your new bodyguard is armed." He dropped the small gun into his jacket pocket.

"And with such a very little gun," she said. "What now?"

"We wait," Stallings said.

Rick Cleveland sat down behind the brunette secretary's desk. "Wait for what?" he asked.

"For whatever happens," Stallings said.

"Well, what d'you guys think's going to happen?"

"Something awful," said Ione Gamble.

Forty-two

At 8:49 that night, Otherguy Overby lay flat on the treehouse floor, peering down at Colleen Cullen as she ended her final security sweep through her five-acre grounds. In her left hand was a two-foot-long flashlight and, in her right, the sawed-off shotgun—aimed straight ahead—its shortened stock pressed hard against her right hip.

At 8:51 Cullen returned to the inn, mounted the nine steps to the porch and went inside. A minute later all the interior lights went out. The only lights left burning were the two 100-watt ones on the porch.

Overby had discovered the treehouse just after 8 P.M. as he slowly made his way through what he regarded as the forest primeval but was actually a well-tended three-acre stand of pines, sycamores, eucalyptus and a few rather old live-oak trees. Earlier, he drove past the entrance to the inn's long brick drive with its always lit red neon sign warning of no vacancy. He stopped a quarter mile farther up the narrow blacktop road, parked the rented Ford on the shoulder, got out, locked the car and disappeared into what he suspected to be the wildwood.

Eight minutes later he tripped on a root, tried to regain his balance, but fell on his butt and found himself staring up at the moonlit treehouse in the old sycamore. The tree was only a yard or so from the long brick drive and less than twenty yards from the inn itself. Overby guessed that the treehouse was fairly new and at least fourteen feet above the ground. Six 2×4s, each two feet long, had been nailed to the tree's thick trunk at two-foot intervals to provide a crude ladder. The treehouse itself wasn't a house at all but merely a platform in the form of a trapezoid that had been wedged into the sycamore's first crotch. Its floor was about six feet long by four to five feet wide. The support frame was more 2×4s; its flooring, 1×10 pine planks. It was obviously a place far too dangerous for kids, and Overby, who had never had a treehouse, wondered if Colleen Cullen had built it—or had had it built—because she'd never had one either.

Just before 9 P.M., a black Ford sedan sped up the brick drive, stopped, then backed into the fan-shaped parking area as if positioning itself for a getaway. Overby watched from the treehouse as Georgia Blue, illuminated by moon and porch lights, slipped out on the passenger side. She held a revolver with both hands and made a quick visual sweep of everything in front of her. Quincy Durant got out on the driver's side, a pistol in his right hand, the blue $8.95-plus-tax moneybag in his left. Durant hurried to the nine steps that led up to the inn's wraparound porch.

Georgia Blue, walking backwards, followed Durant—her eyes and weapon raking everything to his rear. When Durant reached the bottom step he stopped and said something over his shoulder that Overby couldn't hear. Durant then waited for Blue's back to touch his. Overby nodded his approval.

Durant took his time going up the steps. Georgia Blue, her back still to him, went up even more slowly, placing both feet on each step before moving up to the next riser. After they reached the front door, Durant rang the bell. A moment later every light bulb in every room on every floor of the old three-story mansion was ablaze. Overby, from his treehouse perch, liked Colleen Cullen's decision to light up the whole place all at once with the master power switch. Yet he wondered how she'd managed to keep the front porch lights on but everything else dark and decided to ask her.

Durant tried the front door. It opened and he went in. Georgia Blue backed in slowly, her pistol still in its two-handed grip and moving from side to side in a sixty-degree arc. After the inn's front door closed behind them, Otherguy Overby looked at his digital watch. The time was 8:59:33.

*   *   *

A familiar voice drifted down to them from the staircase. "Y'all are on time at least."

Durant and Blue looked up to find Colleen Cullen on the halfway-up landing and beginning her descent to the foyer with the sawed-off shotgun in the crook of her right arm. Her left hand trailed the banister. Durant thought it was an effective, even graceful entrance despite the shotgun and the black jeans and the black cotton sweater and the black athletic shoes with the high tops that had to be laced up.

"We're the first?" Georgia Blue asked.

"Just did my outside rounds," Cullen said. "Nobody out there but rabbits and raccoons."

"Where will we be?" Georgia Blue said.

"Be right where you were before—in the parlor," Cullen said, turned and led them toward the closed sliding doors.

When they reached them, Durant said, "You first, Colleen." She shrugged, shoved the left door back into its recess and went into the parlor followed by Durant, then Georgia Blue. Once all three were in the room and heading for the big round oak table where some drinks had been laid on, a man's voice behind them barked an order. "Hold it!"

Durant and Blue stopped immediately. But Colleen Cullen whirled around to aim her sawed-off shotgun not at the intruder, but at Durant and Blue.

"Do something with your hands," Cullen said.

Durant dropped the blue moneybag to the oak floor and raised his hands shoulder height. Georgia Blue merely held her arms and hands away from her body.

265

"Man behind you's got an Uzi," Colleen Cullen said. "You gotta know what that is." Her eyes flicked to Georgia Blue. "Now here's what you do, Slim. First, use two fingers of your left hand and pull up your front shirttail. Then use two fingers of your *right* hand to pull your piece out from between your tummy and your panties and lay it in my left hand."

Blue did as instructed. As the .38 revolver was deposited in Cullen's left hand, she gave it a quick glance of recognition and said, "Looks like I get to sell you one more time, sweet thing."

She shoved the revolver down into her own left rear pants pocket, then turned herself and the shotgun slightly toward Durant. "Same thing, Mr. Tan Man. Two fingers only."

"Mind if I use a thumb?" Durant said as he carefully took the revolver from his hip pocket, placed it on Cullen's palm, smiled and said, "Get a better offer, Colleen?"

"Sure did."

"How much better?"

"Too much for you to top it."

"Too late to try?"

"Way too late," she said. "Now I'm gonna turn around and go lay these pieces on the table and I expect you all to stay put on account of the Uzi back there. When I get rid of these, then we'll get down to—well, whatever it is we're gonna get down to."

Cullen turned and walked six steps toward the big round oak table. Just as she began her seventh step there was a short burst of automatic fire. Durant guessed four rounds but changed his mind when only three rounds pierced Cullen's black sweater just above her waistline and about where her spine was.

The rounds slammed her forward and her legs collapsed first. Before she reached the floor both barrels of the shotgun fired and tore two joined holes in the oak. The holes reminded Durant of a fat solid-black 8 that had fallen on its face.

Durant didn't move. But Georgia Blue did. She sighed first, turned, went to the nearest straight chair, sat down, crossed her right ankle over her left knee, used the knee to support her elbow, then cupped her chin in her palm, glared at someone other than Durant, then said, "That was a stupid fucking thing to do."

"One less witness," said the man who had ordered them to "Hold it."

"You can't kill everybody off," she said. "First the limo driver. Then the two Goodison twits up in what—Oxnard? And now Colleen. It's dumb."

"Only one to go," he said. "And you can do him."

"Why me?"

"To earn your money and share the liability, why else?"

"I don't think she'll do it," Durant said.

"Whyever not?" the man said.

"There's nothing in it for her."

"Three hundred thousand dollars isn't nothing."

"The blue bag at my feet," Durant said.

"The moneybag?"

"The moneybag," Durant agreed. "Except there's no money in it. Just magazines. Old copies of *Architectural Digest* mostly."

"You're lying, of course."

"Take a look."

"Lying or not, I'm afraid Georgia will still have to kill you as a kind of—what shall we call it—penance?"

"Penance is good," Durant said. "And she's got a lot to be penitent about. But it wouldn't be smart."

"Aren't we all just a bit past smart?"

"Probably," Durant said. "But if you want her to kill me, you'll have to let her handle a piece. And if you do that, she'll take you out first and then work something out with me to save her own ass. There's this about Georgia: she always knows when to cut her losses."

"Kick the bag out in front of you," the man said.

Durant took a step back and kicked the bag away.

"Take another step back."

Durant stepped back just as the man came into view. Durant grinned and said, "My God, it must be Jack Broach,

267

Hollywood super agent—and off to World War Two about fifty years late. Is it tonight we raid Calais, Jack?"

Broach smiled a charming smile. "I'd've liked to have done that, Mr. Durant. I really would."

Broach wore a knitted navy watch cap pulled down over his ears. He also wore a navy-blue turtleneck wool sweater and black pants that were bloused down over jump boots that looked as if they had been spit-shined. Although Durant thought the boots were a bit much he also thought that Broach handled the Uzi with disturbing familiarity.

Broach suddenly stopped smiling, knelt on his right knee beside the moneybag but kept his eyes and the Uzi on Durant. With his left hand, Broach felt for the moneybag's zipper, found it, tugged it open and glanced down. The open bag was stuffed with hundred-dollar bills.

When Broach looked down, Georgia Blue snatched the small .25-caliber semiautomatic from the ankle holster on her right leg—the same leg whose ankle she had rested on her left knee.

She shot the kneeling Jack Broach in his upper left arm. Broach grunted in either surprise or pain or both, dropped the Uzi, clapped his right hand to his wound and stared at Georgia Blue with astonishment. "You shot me," he said, making it both a question and an accusation.

Now on her feet and aiming the small weapon at Broach with both hands, Georgia Blue said, "Give it up, Jack."

But his right hand had already darted back to grip the Uzi he had dropped. "Maybe I'll shoot Mr. Durant myself after all."

"You can try," she said.

Broach frowned, as if both puzzled and saddened by events. "We did have a deal, you and I."

"Where're the tapes, Jack?"

"What tapes?" he said. "There were never any tapes—none we could use anyway because Ione didn't kill Billy Rice and don't ask me who did because I don't know."

"And the Goodisons?" Georgia Blue said.

"They became all antsy and wanted to pull out of our

blackmail deal and sell their story to some supermarket tabloid and, well, that had to be prevented, didn't it?"

"Make him drop the Uzi, Georgia," Durant said.

"A head shot, you think?"

"A head shot would be nice," Durant said.

"Of course," Broach said, "it was altogether different with you and me from what it was with me and the Goodisons. You and I are equals. And we made our deal as such."

"No tapes, no deal, Jack," Georgia Blue said. "Sorry."

Jack Broach shook his head as if disappointed. He rose with the Uzi in his right hand, pointed downward, his finger nowhere near the trigger. He seemed unaware of the blood that ran down his left arm beneath the sweater and dripped to the floor.

Clenching his teeth and barely moving his lips, Durant said, "Make him drop the fucking piece, Georgia."

"I'm leaving now," Jack Broach said and walked slowly toward the open sliding door. Just before reaching it, he stopped and looked back at Georgia Blue, who still used two hands to aim the small semiautomatic at him. "Regardless of what you now claim, Georgia, we really did have a deal."

He turned and walked through the door into the foyer. Standing near the stairs was Otherguy Overby, the Sauer semiautomatic he had borrowed from Artie Wu in his right hand.

When Broach saw Overby, he tried to bring the Uzi up. He was still trying when Overby shot him three times without hesitation. Once Broach lay sprawled on the parquet floor, Overby went over, stared down at him curiously, nudged him with the toe of a shoe, then looked up as Durant came through the door, holding one of Colleen Cullen's revolvers. He was followed a moment later by Georgia Blue, whose small five-shot weapon dangled at her side, seemingly forgotten.

Overby looked back down at the dead man, then up at Georgia Blue. "Jack Broach?"

She nodded.

"What about the tapes?"

"There aren't any tapes," she said.

"None they could use anyway," Durant said.

Overby frowned, then looked around. "What about Colleen?"

"Broach didn't want any witnesses," Blue said.

"Except you," Durant said.

"He didn't want me as a witness. He wanted me as a conspirator." She paused. "But then he and I had a deal, didn't we?"

"The guy had an Uzi," Overby said. "A fucking Uzi. How come you two are still walking around?"

"It's all Georgia's fault," Durant said.

Forty-three

After Booth Stallings hung up the telephone on the blond secretary's desk in Mott's hotel suite office, he turned to Ione Gamble, who was still slumped in the room's only easy chair. "More bad news?" she asked.

"Jack Broach is dead," Stallings said. "Somebody shot him. He was the one blackmailing you—the one we called Oil Drum."

The shock twisted Ione Gamble's face and made her eyes bulge until she said, "Jack's dead?"

Stallings nodded.

"He was blackmailing me?"

"Broach always was a no-good son of a bitch," Rick Cleveland said from his seat behind the brunette secretary's desk. He lifted his glass of Scotch, said, "To old Jack," drank it and poured himself another from the bottle that was now one-third empty.

The shock had gone away from Gamble's face, replaced by an odd serenity that seemed to erase all other emotions. "You knew Jack?" she asked Cleveland, as though inquiring about some mutual acquaintance neither had seen in years.

"Knew him when he was first starting out," Cleveland said.

"I was one of his first clients. When he got too big or I got too small, he dumped me."

She nodded politely, looked at Stallings again and asked, "Why would Jack blackmail me? Did he need money? I would've lent him money."

"You don't have any to lend," Stallings said. "He stole it all. Maybe embezzled's a better word."

"I have no money?"

"Not much."

"And you say Jack stole it?"

Stallings only nodded.

"Then how do I pay Howie Mott?"

"You don't have to worry about paying Howie," Stallings said, took the small .25-caliber semiautomatic from a pocket, placed it on the desktop and seemed to forget it.

"He won't defend me for nothing," she said. "I can't expect him to."

"There's not going to be any trial," Stallings said. "Not for you anyway."

"What the hell's going on, Booth?" she said, her serene look suddenly replaced by anger. "Spell it out. Use babytalk if you have to."

"We're going down to the sheriff's office in Malibu," Stallings said. "Or maybe it's called the substation."

"The three of us?" she said.

"Just Rick and me," Stallings said, picking up the small pistol. "And Rick's going to tell 'em you didn't shoot Billy Rice, but that he did."

"You're not trying to be funny, are you?" she said. "No. Of course you're not."

"Know how much it costs a day to rent a car like yours, Ione?" Stallings said.

"What the hell're you getting at now?"

"Four hundred a day plus fifty cents a mile. That's how much. Plus a five-thousand-dollar deposit—cash or credit card, providing your credit card can stand it. Rick here rented a car just like yours last New Year's Eve, didn't you, Rick?"

"Don't think so."

"Sure you did. Then you drove into Billy Rice's driveway that same night around eleven or eleven-thirty, parked it, got out and rang the doorbell. You told whoever answered the door, maybe Rice himself, that you wanted to patch things up—make amends. Something like that. Once you're both in the living room, you shoot Rice two times, then leave the gun on that little elm table in the hall beneath the Hockney where whoever comes in will be sure to see it and maybe even pick it up. Which is just what Ione did." Stallings looked at her. "Rick even left the front door open so you or someone else could go right in. The gun Rick used is kind of important because it was stolen off a movie set at Paramount where they were filming a pilot. Rick was a member of the cast—right, Rick?"

Cleveland ignored Stallings, finished his whisky, then poured himself another one.

Ione kept staring at Cleveland, who refused to look at her. "Why would you do it?" she said. "Kill Billy?"

Rick Cleveland downed his new drink, made a face, finally looked at Gamble and said, "Because the fucker spoiled my view, that's why."

"Your view?"

"You've got a view, don't you?" Cleveland said. "Sure you do. Suppose some asshole comes along and builds an eight- or nine-story building right in front of it. Wouldn't that piss you off?"

"Not enough to kill him," she said.

"What if your view was all you had left in the world?" Rick Cleveland said.

*   *   *

At just past 2 A.M. the sheriff's substation in Malibu locked Rick Cleveland in the same cell from which it had just released Artie Wu. By then Cleveland had freely admitted killing William A. C. Rice IV and even announced that, given the same circumstances, he would do it all over again.

At 3:16 A.M. the state Highway Patrol, acting on an anonymous tip, discovered the bodies of Colleen Cullen and Jack Broach in the Topanga Canyon bed-and-breakfast inn. Otherguy Overby, the anonymous tipster, had called the Highway Patrol because he remembered Cullen telling him she was paying off certain deputy sheriffs to let her keep the lie-low establishment in business.

At 3:38 A.M. Overby, carrying a blue canvas bag, rang the door chimes at Ione Gamble's house on Adelaide Drive in Santa Monica. After demanding that he identify himself, a fully dressed Gamble opened the door.

"Let's go up to your office, Ione," Overby said.

"I can't handle any more shit tonight."

"You'll like this kind," he said.

*　　*　　*

Seated in her office behind the Memphis cotton broker's desk, an extremely wary Ione Gamble watched Overby place the blue zip-up bag in front of her. "What's that?" she said.

"Open it."

"Why?"

"Because it's a nice surprise."

Gamble rose and zipped open the bag that was still stuffed with bound hundred-dollar bills. "Jesus," she said. "Whose is it?"

"Yours. Three hundred thousand—almost. It's part of what Jack Broach stole from you. I stole it back. Not all by myself, of course. I had a little help from Georgia and that fucking Durant."

"This is the mythical million, then, right?" she said. "The million that was supposed to buy back the tapes—except there wasn't any million and there weren't any tapes."

"That's about right," Overby said.

"What do I do with it?"

"You got a safe-deposit box, don't you? Put it in there. When you need some, take some out." Overby rose. "I've gotta go—but it's been awfully nice seeing you again, Ione."

"What'll you do now?"

Overby smiled contentedly. "Probably not much right away."

"Sit down, Otherguy."

He sat down. There was a long silence as she studied him before speaking again. "You want to be my agent?"

Forty-four

When Quincy Durant, seated at the old refectory table in the late William Rice's dining room, got off the telephone with Enno Glimm in London it was 2:05 P.M. there and 6:05 A.M. in Malibu. Durant turned to Otherguy Overby and said, "Mr. Glimm is very appreciative of our efforts. It may not be exact, but he said something like: You guys did a pretty fucking fair job."

"What about the money?" Overby said.

"Jenny Arliss is making the wire transfer. Glimm says Westminster Bank will handle it. It should be here by nine when our bank opens."

"All of it?" Overby asked.

"All of it."

"And our shares are still going to be what Artie said?"

"Nobody's going to stiff you, Otherguy."

"If you don't ask, they don't tell you."

There was a pause before Durant said, "How is she?"

"Who?"

Durant only stared at him.

"Oh. You mean Ione. Ione's fine. Sort of tired. Sort of mystified. But the money cheered her up a little. Not a hell of a lot, but some." He paused and decided to lie. "She asked about you."

"Asked what?"

"You know. If you were all right and what your plans were. Stuff like that." Overby paused. "She also asked me to be her agent."

Once again Durant's mouth clamped itself into its unforgiving line. His eyes drilled into Overby as the mouth opened just enough to ask, "And you said what? It sure as hell wasn't no."

Overby showed Durant his hard, white and, this time, strangely merry smile. "I said, Ione, that's the worst fucking idea you ever had in your life."

Durant slumped back in the dining room chair as if exhausted. "I don't understand you anymore, Otherguy."

Overby nodded thoughtfully. "Not many people do."

*   *   *

After they had walked approximately a hundred yards up the beach, Artie Wu and Howard Mott turned and started back to the Rice house. They walked in silence for several moments until Mott said, "I assume you heard about the war?"

"About it being over? One of the deputies told me. Perhaps it was a preoccupation with my own problems, but I had a very curious 'So what?' reaction. I think we must be living in strange times."

"The war'll be useful to them in the election," Mott said.

"You think so? That's what—twenty-two months off? If there's a bad slump, nobody'll remember it. Well, virtually nobody."

"You still vote?" Mott asked.

"Religiously."

"Against or for?"

"Against," Wu said. "I don't think anyone votes *for* anyone anymore."

They walked on in silence until Wu looked down at Mott and said, "Okay, Howie. How *did* you spring me?"

"Favors."

Wu nodded several times, the nods indicating his understanding, and also his curiosity. "I like details," he said.

"I called a senior partner in the law firm I'm associated with in the Gamble case. Or what was the Gamble case. He owed me a favor—a considerable one. I told him quite candidly that I would be in his debt if he could think of some way to quash the whole thing. I also mentioned that, if necessary, I could round up a dozen or so street people who'd swear you and Durant were passing out dollar bills on Ocean Avenue at precisely the time Miss Rosa Alicia Chavez thinks she saw *el chino grande*. I also hinted at other witnesses."

"He believe you?"

"No, but it gave him ammunition. So he called someone who owed him a favor and that someone called someone else and it went on up the line until they reached the somebody who could pick up the phone and make the call that set you free."

"I'm in your debt," Artie Wu said.

"You are indeed," Mott said. They walked on in silence for a few more paces until Mott asked, "Why'd you sit still for it?"

"Because they needed to arrest somebody," Wu said. "There were all those rental car receipts and credit card trails and too many people who knew we were in town. We had to give the cops somebody. It couldn't be Georgia since she was the most vulnerable because of her passport, which isn't quite kosher. Otherguy was a possibility. He could have tap-danced his way through it, but he had contacts we needed and, besides, we'd have to hear about his noble sacrifice until the end of time. Then there was Booth. But he, thank God, was off riding his own hobbyhorse—the Rick Cleveland connection—and he was also looking after the money and keeping us fed, if not very well. That left Durant or me. But I wanted to keep the Blue-Durant experiment going so that left only me. And as I thought about it, I had to admit I didn't have anything more constructive to do." He smiled down at Mott. "Satisfied?"

"Interesting," Mott said.

"Stay for breakfast?"

"What're you having?"

"I think Booth's about due back with some Egg McMuffins."

"Maybe I'll call Ione instead and see if she'd like an early lunch at—what d'you think—the Bel-Air?"

"Perfect," Wu said.

*   *   *

The passing out of the five certified checks and five envelopes, each containing $5,000 in cash, was done without ceremony at 10:19 A.M. by Booth Stallings. Durant then excused himself and went to his bedroom phone to call Ione Gamble and ask her to lunch.

"I can't make lunch," she said, "but I'm free for dinner."

"I'm leaving."

"Back to London?"

"For a while."

"Will you be coming back?"

"In about a month."

"Call me," she said, "and we'll have dinner here."

"I'll do that," said Durant and ended the call with the realization that if he did come back to Los Angeles next month, next year or even next week, he wouldn't call her and she knew that he wouldn't.

As Durant passed Georgia Blue's open bedroom door, he noticed her standing at the window, looking at the ocean. The envelope containing the check and the $5,000 in cash was on the bed, as if tossed there.

"You okay?" he asked.

She turned. "I'm fine."

"I was wrong, wasn't I?"

"Were you?"

"I think so. Thank you."

"Goodbye, Quincy," she said and turned back to the ocean.

*   *   *

Durant and Wu left to catch a plane to New York, where they hoped to fly the Concorde on to London. After Otherguy Overby packed, he phoned the Gemstar limousine service in Malibu and asked to be delivered to the Bridges Hotel, where he had booked a small suite for a week. If nothing interesting turned up at the Bridges, he'd try San Francisco. After that, there was always Hong Kong—at least until 1997.

After he saw Overby off, Booth Stallings walked into Georgia Blue's bedroom as she packed her clothes into a small carry-on bag. He sat on a chair and watched her fold the gray dress she had bought at Neiman's. After it was folded and packed away, he said, "How bad was it—at the inn?"

"I got to choose between Durant and Jack Broach and I chose Durant. But Broach knew I would, or seemed to, and just walked away. Or tried. He might have made it if it hadn't been for Otherguy."

"What did Durant say?"

"Thank you. What else was there to say?"

She looked around the room, saw nothing else that needed packing and closed the carry-on bag's zipper. She picked up the envelope from the bed and stuffed it into her Coach purse. She then knelt beside the bed, reached beneath the mattress and brought out the small .25-caliber semiautomatic that she had used to shoot Jack Broach high in the left arm, almost in the shoulder. "Here," Blue said and tossed the gun to Stallings, who made a one-handed catch.

"It's what I shot Broach with," she said.

"Looks like an ankle gun."

"It is."

"Where'd you get it?"

"That day I went shopping at the Gap?"

He nodded.

"I stopped by a bar afterwards and asked the bartender if he knew where a lady might acquire some protection. He happened to have a friend who delivered."

"Want me to dump it for you?" Stallings said.

She nodded.

"Still want to run off with me and live in fancy hotels and drink champagne till the money runs out?" he said.

She smiled. "Do you?"

Stallings knew she would go with him if he said yes and he also knew it would end badly. So he said yes silently, but aloud he said, "Not really."

"I'll be in New York," she said. "If you need anything—or change your mind. Howie will have my number."

He nodded and turned to go but turned back when she said, "Booth."

"What?"

"I'm still sort of stuck on you," said Georgia Blue.

*　　*　　*

By the time Stallings threw the .25-caliber semiautomatic out into the ocean and returned the Rice house keys to Phil Quill, the actor-real estate man, it was 2:47 P.M. He got in the Mercedes 500SL and drove to the Budget office in Beverly Hills, where he handed the car keys over to Gloria Ransome of the perpetually sunny disposition.

She greeted him with her usual warmth and together they went out to make sure the $100,000 car didn't have a crumpled fender or a broken window. On the way back to the office, she asked him how his movie deal was progressing.

"We've got a picture," said Stallings, who vaguely remembered somebody quoting somebody else as saying that.

After she said "wow" and "terrific" and "that's wonderful," as if it were happening to her instead of to him, Stallings said, "You work tomorrow?"

"I get weekends off."

"Want to go to Tahoe?"

"You kidding?"

He shook his head. "What time d'you get off?"

"Six?" She made it a question as if fearful it might be too late.

"I'll pick you up then. Maybe we'll charter a plane and fly up tonight."

"Oh-my-God!"

"See you at six, Gloria," Stallings said, smiled and left. Outside, he' crossed the street and walked down the north side of Santa Monica Boulevard until he came to a park bench, where he sat down next to a man in his late sixties or early seventies who said he was a retired film cutter. Eventually, they talked about the government and the economy and compared the just-ended gulf war with Korea and Vietnam and World War Two. The retired film cutter seemed very well informed and not at all optimistic.

When the man rose to go, he looked down at Stallings and said, "You're not retired yet, are you?"

"Not just yet," Booth Stallings said.